"An utterly spellbinding journey full of unexpected turns and nuanced characters, *In Berlin* reflects a triumph of the human spirit in the face of unexpected catastrophe. Silberstein has given us a gift: a deeply moving opportunity to look at tragedy with new eyes, and in doing so, to find hope and beauty in the most surprising of places."

—VIVEK MURTHY, MD, MBA, 19TH AND 21ST SURGEON GENERAL OF THE UNITED STATES

"Silberstein's portrayal of life with a spinal cord injury is about as intimate as one can get without actually having experienced SCI on a personal level. The reader enters the protagonists' lives and travels their difficult and complex journey, from devastation and anger to acceptance and, finally, empowerment and hope. His novel is for the universe, and all readers will find bits of themselves in places they might not have realized."

—HEATHER KRILL, AUTHOR OF THE NOVEL *TRUE NORTH* AND WRITER FOR THE CHRISTOPHER AND DANA REEVE FOUNDATION

"This is a page-turner of a novel rich in ideas. The story is packed with moments I recognize and yet it is wholly original, with characters who will surprise you again and again. They remind us what it's like to be alive now, in a tumultuous era of dazzling possibilities and tremendous challenges. An important book."

—STANLEY SAGOV, MD, FORMER CHAIR, DEPARTMENT OF MEDICINE, MOUNT AUBURN HOSPITAL

"Batul's encounters in Aleppo and abroad mirror many Syrians' experiences of starting anew multiple times. The detailed portrayal of her struggles and triumphs is a poignant reminder of the strength and resilience within us all. This story is both deeply personal and widely relatable, offering a profound exploration of agency and self-belief. Batul's journey is a testament to the human spirit, and it has left an indelible mark on my heart."

—ALI ALJASEM, PHD, SCHOLAR IN CONFLICT STUDIES AT UTRECHT UNIVERSITY

"*In Berlin* is a poignant and timely story about resilience, identity, and the quiet courage it takes to rebuild a life after profound change. Silberstein masterfully intertwines Anna's journey of adapting to life after sudden paralysis with Batul's pursuit of a new beginning in a foreign country. Both women navigate different forms of displacement—one physical, the other cultural—yet their stories are bound by a shared search for independence, belonging, and purpose.

"With a sharp eye for detail and a deep understanding of human connection, the novel captures the complexities of adapting to new realities—whether learning a new language or redefining personal strength. It's a narrative that speaks to our times, reminding us that even in isolation, we're shaped by the bonds we form and the kindness of strangers. *In Berlin* is an inspiring and thought-provoking exploration of perseverance and the ties that ground us, no matter where we are."

—ASHLEY LYN OLSON, FOUNDER OF
WHEELCHAIRTRAVELING.COM

"This beautifully crafted story resonated deeply with me, capturing the challenges and triumphs of love, faith, and resilience in an authentic way. Truly moving."

—HEND ELSHEMY, EGYPTIAN PARAPLEGIC
ENGLISH TEACHER

"The author masterfully captures the local details of Syria with precision and authenticity through the character of Batul and her family. The narrative delves deeply and systematically into the structure of the Syrian family as shaped by war, raising questions about the social transformations that have reshaped it in its aftermath. Moreover, the text sheds light on the afflictions that have plagued this family in the realm of exile and displacement, portraying the struggles it has had to endure—not from a broad, detached perspective, but through an intimate exploration of Batul's psyche."

—AHMAD BARGHASH, AUTHOR OF THE NOVEL
THALATH SHAMAT YAHRASNA AL-MADINA
(THREE BEAUTY MARKS GUARD THE CITY)

"Through a captivating story, *In Berlin* conveys the psychosocial aspects of a life-changing neurological injury that are often overshadowed by the injury alone. The novel is a reminder both of what is possible after a spinal cord injury, and that advocacy for oneself is paramount in the recovery process."

—ERIKA DIXON, PT, DOCTOR OF PHYSICAL THERAPY, NEUROLOGIC CLINICAL SPECIALIST

"A captivating and thought-provoking page-turner. Through intricate storytelling, carefully researched details, and exceptional insights into human behavior, the novel presents a tale of resilience. The story is particularly significant in our current climate where cultural biases often overshadow empathy and understanding. Silberstein takes us on a journey that lets us see beyond surface-level differences and appreciate the deeper connections that bind us together."

—ZEBA HYDER, PATIENT ADVOCATE

"*In Berlin* is a beautiful novel about one young woman's determination to rebuild her life after paralysis. I'm still thinking about Anna, Batul, and their families, about how the choices we make and the people we encounter, even in the most casual circumstances, can change our lives in huge and unexpected ways. Written with sensitivity and attention to detail, it depicts paralysis and rehabilitation in ways that will feel authentic to anyone who has experienced a spinal cord injury and educate those who thankfully have not."

—DEBRA POLI, UNITED SPINAL ASSOCIATION CHAPTER LEADER

IN BERLIN

A NOVEL

ERIC SILBERSTEIN

L B G

This is a work of fiction. Names, characters, places, and incidents either are the product of the author's imagination or are used fictitiously. Any resemblance to actual events, places, or persons living or dead is purely coincidental.

First Edition

Copyright © 2025 by Eric Silberstein

All rights reserved.

ISBN 978-1-7373519-7-9 (hardcover)

ISBN 978-1-7373519-9-3 (trade paperback)

ISBN 978-1-7373519-8-6 (eBook)

ISBN 978-1-7373519-6-2 (Kindle eBook)

Library of Congress Control Number: 2025906728

LBG / Boston

Cover design by Victor Mingovits

Also available as an audiobook

To Anthea Krings. Thank you for your friendship.

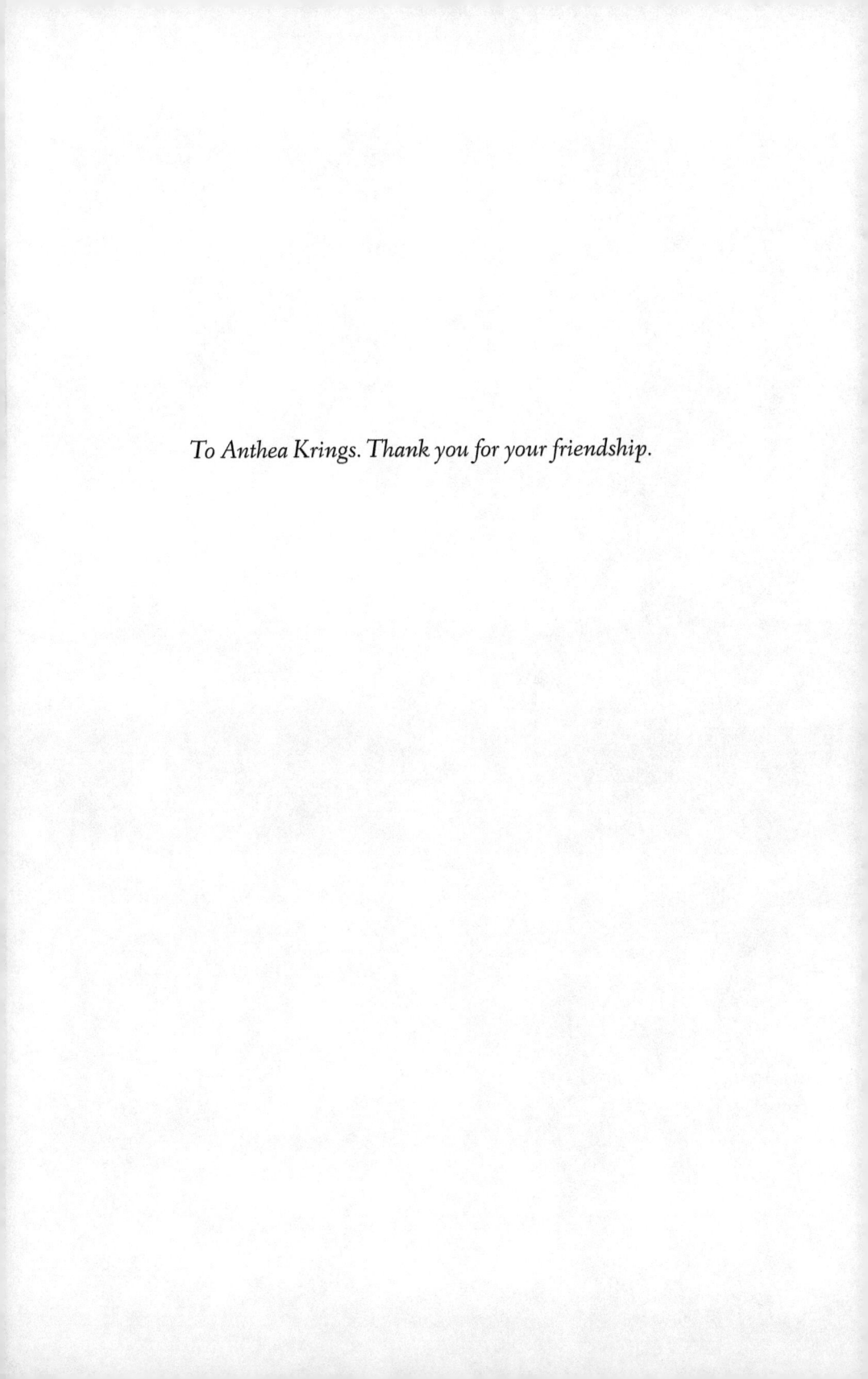

PART 1
SUMMER 2014

ONE

Unlike everyone else in the extended al-Jaberi family, Batul believed in being on time. "How can you be my daughter?" Baba had teased more than once when, as a kid, Batul stood by the door with her backpack on, impatiently waiting for Rami to finish his breakfast.

Well, now they were in Germany, and she was no longer in the minority. Things mostly ran on time here, but it wasn't guaranteed, and she didn't know her way around Mitte. So she'd left extra early for her coffee with Tasneem. Inevitably the U-Bahn came right away, there were no delays, and she had had no trouble orienting herself after she emerged from the station onto the wide, tram-track-lined street.

She passed the statue of Robert Koch—in Turkey she'd read a book about him and Pasteur—and spotted "Café Frau Schneider" printed on the flap of a red awning across the street. As she waited at the corner for the jaunty green traffic-light man to beckon her across, her phone buzzed. *Tied up with a patient. Will be 30 mins late.* A sense of lightness: the meeting was going to happen; Tasneem wouldn't need to cancel this time.

Inside, leather armchairs with brass frames filled the floor, positioned amid small round tables and long-limbed potted plants. Most of the seats were occupied—by people chatting, looking at their phones, or on their laptops. None of the other women had their heads covered. *I would like a cup of tea, please. I would like a cup of tea, please.* "Guten Tag," she said to the man at the counter, who wore rimless glasses and a black t-shirt. "I would like a cup of tea, please." She was confident she'd said the right German words. She was less confident they were intelligible.

He smiled and she had the feeling he was welcoming her to the country. "Sehr gerne. Mit Milch und Zucker?"

She understood. "No, thank you, no milk or sugar." She reached into her pocket for a two-euro coin.

"Black tea, no milk, no sugar," he said, placing a glass mug on the counter and then making eye contact. "I'll remember for next time."

She found a table, took out her laptop, and reviewed the long list of words she'd looked up this morning while very, very slowly making her way through an article from *Spiegel*. If she'd known they would end up here she would have started earlier. English was easy and German was hard, which she was beginning to worry had more to do with her age than anything else. With English, there was that time in sixth grade when she'd stayed up all night reading Harry Potter without a dictionary, and realized she'd crossed a threshold. She didn't know if she could do that again with this new language through which everything was foggy.

Studying, not thinking about studying, or inventing excuses, or resting on your laurels because you'd ordered tea. She had forty minutes—enough time to do the thing she'd been avoiding: a practice essay. She read the prompt: "Man kann in der Musik leichter und freier denken, als in der Sprache. —Alfred Döblin."

Man was "one" or maybe "you," *kann in der Musik* was "can in the music," *leichter und freier* was "lighter and freer,"—it was helpful that there were a lot of cognates between German and English. *Denken* was "think," but what was *Sprache*? "Speaking," no, not speaking, "language." Put it together: "One can think more lightly and freely in music than in language."

Not her. Listening to music could induce a state in which thoughts flowed, yes, she'd experienced that, but the thoughts themselves came in the form of words and sentences. Suppose she wanted to think about the situation back home. In Arabic her thoughts would be fully formed, rich, nuanced. Or she could think in English with almost the same fluency and speed. Even in her halting, childish German she could express ideas.

But music? To craft a melody representing a thought without allowing words to form first? For her, impossible ... although ... she *could* see a connection between language and how she thought. A freedom to how she thought, more specifically. When she spoke in English, and even when she thought in English, she exercised less self-censorship. In Arabic, for example, she never swore, even in her mind, but her brain didn't have those same antibodies when it came to cursing in English.

If thought defined a person, and language influenced thought, then she was a different person when her mind operated in English. No—that was taking it too far. Yet she probably did take on a different personality—one that was, going back to the quote, lighter and freer. So, for someone who *could* form thoughts in music, it could be that those thoughts would be less self-conscious, less bound by the conventions encoded in word choice in that person's native language, although—

She glanced at the time. Start writing! The goal wasn't to think. It was to use her scraps of German to write something coherent, even if it had only a tenuous connection to the prompt. Three hundred grammatically correct words. She could do that before Tasneem got here.

She started typing: Musik ist ...

When she reached the word count, she pulled up an English-to-German dictionary and began revising. It was in the midst of figuring out the right way to say *compose* in German that she saw Tasneem enter the cafe. The woman was taller than Batul had expected, still in her white coat, her head covered, her eyes puffy. She had a no-nonsense presence as she scanned the room, settled her sights on Batul, waved, and strode over.

"So you completed two semesters in medicine?" Tasneem asked after getting a coffee and rejoining Batul at the little table.

"Yes. What about you?"

"Five full years." At Damascus University, Batul knew, an institution better known internationally than hers, although back home both were considered excellent.

"You don't have a university degree from Syria, but you're too old to repeat secondary school here and apply as a local student," Tasneem quickly got down to business. "What you want is going to be difficult, maybe impossible. It took me two years to be accepted, then I had to pass the boards that are administered after the second year, and was able to start in year three, getting essentially no credit for my clinical experience. Are you prepared for a long and uncertain journey?"

"Yes."

"Do you speak German yet?"

Batul shook her head.

Tasneem took a sip from her mug. "The medical education here is among the best you can get anywhere, believe me. Between the facilities and the professors, the training is on a whole different level. During my rotation yesterday there was this obese patient—morbidly obese, over 180 kilos, BMI over 55—and the attending was explaining the special precautions we should take. Later I looked up the professor. He's published like twelve articles on the clinical management of obese patients in a hospital setting, all highly cited. In other words, it turns out he's one of the top experts—not only in Germany, but in the world."

Tasneem stopped, shifted. "Anyway, my point is, people know this. You'll need to compete for the handful of spots reserved for foreigners. Your competition is coming from China, from India, from

..." Batul was now only half listening. Her thoughts had been snagged by what Tasneem had said about the professors. Yes, she would need to get in, but the promise of mentors who were close to the latest techniques ... Up to now, she hadn't let herself think that far ahead. To imagine standing next to a hospital bed, being questioned by a professor who had personally conducted and published research on the disease being treated ...

"You need to study. You need to learn German and then you need to perfect it. You'll need C1 to apply, but you'll need an even stronger command of the language to not get lost in lectures. I assume your English is good?"

Batul nodded.

"That will help." Tasneem put her cup down. "Avoid distraction. Don't count on support from your family. If they're anything like mine, they won't understand how hard we need to work. And another thing ..." Tasneem looked directly at her. "You can't let yourself get distracted by men. You'll see, the situation is different here, families are more eager to see us married—"

More eager? Tasneem read her expression.

"Yes. We're in this new environment, and they worry about local influences. There's a lot of uncertainty. They're skeptical we'll be able to get a degree and work as professionals—and for good reason, most never manage—so they worry about supporting us. What's that word you use in Aleppo? To cover up. Security through marriage. And you—someone with your looks—"

Batul smiled.

"I'm not flattering you. This is not a good thing. Suitors will appear. Maybe not so many, but some. Before, back home, my parents were the first to say, 'Finish your degree first.' Now, here, each time they're approached, they're always telling me, 'Why don't you give him a chance?'

"You must get your parents to agree that they will not entertain any proposals until you've gotten into a medical program here. Then, when you, inshallah, get in, you tell them you'll consider suitors only after you complete your studies. They won't be happy about any of this, but trust me, every one of my former classmates who got married ended up giving up on finding her way back to medicine. Same with my friends in Sweden. Marriage can come later."

Batul wasn't overly worried about Baba not being supportive. She wasn't worried about working hard. She was only worried that even with hard work she wouldn't be good enough to compete here, or that she would get thrown off course again by something she couldn't anticipate—like the move from home, then the move from Turkey. She wrapped her hands around her mug, stared at them, then looked up at Tasneem. "I'm so grateful for your advice. You can't imagine how much this means to me."

"It's my pleasure to help a sister." Tasneem reached across the table, touched the back of her hand. "Have you thought about working part-time?"

"I don't think it will be necessary. My father hasn't found anything yet, but my brother is close to securing a software engineering job. That and the government benefits should be enough. I think. In truth, my father is secretive about our financial situation."

"I suggest you get a job."

"Won't that take away from studying?"

"Yes. But it will also help you—to get practice speaking German, to understand how things work around here, to have your own money, to give you a bit of independence from your family. You'll need this to stick to the path. Find a job that will expose you to medicine. I worked in housekeeping at a hospital. It's a job that's easy to get—you could probably find something similar."

TWO

Normally Anna would have been home an hour ago. But as she was wrapping up for the day, she'd started chatting with Rajeev, who told her about a bug he was chasing down. The customer, a Danish operator of offshore wind farms, had updated a machine learning model for detecting failing turbines, but when they went to deploy, they got an error, and worse, they were also getting errors when they tried to revert back to the old model. Support, stumped, had escalated. Anna got sucked into the puzzle and pulled up a chair next to Rajeev. Now two hours in, they were tantalizingly close.

"Add a log message here, too," she suggested, pointing at the screen.

He moved his mouse. Clicked. Started typing. Usually when they pair programmed, they did it the other way around, with her at the keyboard. The problem with this arrangement was that her mind kept wandering.

While running this morning, she'd seen an ad for the aquarium on the side of a bus stop: a photo of a bright-eyed axolotl, an amphibian she'd never heard of until a few months ago, when her niece talked about the one in her kindergarten classroom, and suddenly they were everywhere. The axolotl's smile made her think of the noodle-eating, chopstick-holding panda painted on her favorite Chinese food truck. Sitting next to Rajeev, watching him edit the file, the two came together. She imagined a sea creature floating in the Berlin sky. An octopus with billions of tentacles—and suctioned to the end of each, a chopstick. This being, with its supremely coordinated limbs, tapped out the tempo for every human.

Anna's tempo was fast. Tap, tap, tap, tap. Type fast, run fast, eat fast, think fast. Rajeev's was slow. That's not to say he was a bad engineer—far from it. They'd joined DDB at the same time, and she liked working with him because they both cared about—obsessed over—getting the details right. They just had different approaches. In a ten-minute span she tried three things; he spent the whole time thinking. Deliberation was good. But come on, man, type faster!

Rajeev paused, lifted his hands from the keyboard, turned to her. "Should we log the queries?"

"Let's run it first."

Last week she'd met with Tomás for her annual review. Going in, in the back of her mind she'd hoped to be promoted. Over the past year she'd built DDB's first model drift detection feature, a labor of love that had begun with combing through the academic literature for a feasible approach. "Nice job with that feature, Anna." She'd received a four percent raise, but he didn't say anything about a promotion, or even whether she would be in consideration next cycle. "Set up another meeting," Julia told her. "You need to confront him. How could he promote Rajeev but not you? It's bullshit and you know it."

The thing was that Rajeev had one more year of experience; he'd been at another company before DDB. His command of the underlying math was also likely stronger than her own—although in practice that hadn't mattered. And regardless, he deserved the promotion.

"Your problem," Julia said, "is that you hold yourself to one standard and give everyone else the benefit of the doubt." Tomás had accepted her calendar invite, and they would be meeting first thing tomorrow. She was going to let him know she was disappointed, which she hadn't said during the review meeting, and then find a way to explain her role in—

"Look." Rajeev pointed at two lines near the bottom of the screen.

She leaned in, laughed. The whole time the functions were being called in the wrong order. Probably coded wrong in the first place, undetected and inconsequential until now because no customer had hit this case before. "It's always the last place you look."

"Always!" Rajeev stood and stretched. "I'll get this cleaned up, test it ..."

She saw he was reluctant to ask. "Do you want me to review the PR later?"

"Yeah. Support promised we would get the fix out tonight."

"No prob, happy to," Anna said, packing up her laptop, noticing that her shoulder, which had been bothering her slightly all day, was still sore. "I'll look when I get home."

After exiting through the revolving door and walking along the elevated plaza, Anna turned and craned her head back to follow the exterior of her building up to its top, where the still-bright sun gleamed off its steel and glass facade. The structure was over thirty stories. She calculated—at three meters a story, roughly a hundred meters high. Possibly the tallest building in the city, and yet turbine blades stretched even longer. She visualized a blade the length of the building rotating around an axis, pushed by whipping wind. Something that massive breaking up and falling into the sea ... no wonder it was so urgent for their customer to get the monitoring back in place.

A woman approached. As Anna's gaze dropped from the sky back to ground level, she took in her white, frizzy hair, a missing front tooth, and a few too many layers for the warm weather. "I used to work here too, before they tore the old factory down."

Anna couldn't tell if the woman was all there. "What did you do?"

"I assembled low-voltage circuit breakers."

Maybe she was. "What factory was it?"

"Young lady," the woman ignored her question, "I only wanted to tell you not to look up. Keep your head down. There are cameras everywhere."

Or maybe she wasn't.

Anna nodded and moved away, continuing along the plaza to where she would descend to street level and cross to the S-Bahn station. *Keep your head down.* Words from her youth. Not meant literally back then, but still. She'd tried to convince her parents that things had changed, but her parents couldn't change. Now she accepted it. They'd spent their first thirty years in a country where everyone was suspicious of everyone else. "No good deed goes unpunished," her mother liked to say.

She had to admit that their attitude, though infuriating to her thirteen-year-old self, hadn't paralyzed them. When her parents were younger than she is now, they found each other (standing in line to buy jeans!), found housing, were assigned jobs they liked, and had Stefan. Eight years later the wall came down. Three months after that, she arrived. And then they had to adjust to a whole new system. When she was little, they were optimistic about it. Saved enough to buy a house. But later they felt things were rigged.

Not her. For reasons she didn't fully understand—perhaps innate, or perhaps the particular training cycles of failure and success that had wired up her brain—she'd always had faith in the people around her, and people generally. She believed that effort would take her to interesting places. "Sure, absolutely," her father had said.

She crossed the street. Bicycles of all makes and degrees of wear and tear were parked in scattered rows outside the station. Posters were plastered to every surface: the low wall surrounding the entrance to the underpass, the streetlight poles, the columns supporting the glass awning over the stairs. The few stretches without posters were scrawled with graffiti, mostly in German, some in English, some drawings. God she loved this city—the energy, the chaos, the scale.

When she was in ninth grade and Stefan was already here doing his work-study program, she'd taken the train in by herself, ostensibly to visit him. Mostly, though, she'd spent her days exploring on his bike while he trained to be a future manager at Obi. He and Christina were already living together, and talked endlessly about one day moving home; they still did, but Anna didn't see it happening, not with the better career prospects here.

Anna had also been homesick, she reminded herself: the first weeks of university. But after that, she hadn't thought once about moving back. Mom and Dad hoped she would eventually return, but this distance felt right—it let her step out from under the weight of their sense of what was and wasn't possible, as well as their tendency to rely on her. But it wasn't abandonment.

Now on the platform, waiting with a small crowd, she scanned the horizon of the city's landscape: the metal lattice of a crane, the tops of trees and, soaring above them, her building. In her imagination, suddenly, she saw not a blade turning but the entire office tower, all of the people, chairs and desks pushed to the walls at ninety degrees, falling to the ceiling at one-eighty, then sliding and banging to the other side at two-seventy.

Anna was lucky to find a seat on the crowded train. She texted Julia, asked how the trip was going, told her she would be meeting with Tomás tomorrow. At the next stop, two from where she would switch to the tram, an elderly man boarded, swaying slightly as he looked for a place to hold on. She caught his eye, gripped a strap of her backpack, reached for the pole on her left, and began to pull herself up—fuck! Intense, burning pain in her shoulder. She let go of the pole and let her arm fall to her side.

As she started to stand a second time, this time using her legs alone, the man motioned with his wrinkled hand: stay put. She swallowed, nodded at him, and sank back into the prickly upholstery. *Get home.* She'd been planning to see if Karoline wanted to meet for a drink. Now all she wanted was to wash her face and lie down.

"Landsberger Allee." The train slowed. She made to stand, careful to keep her left arm limp. The pain had spread to her right shoulder now, and her backpack, as it plunged from the seat to a hanging position at her side, felt like it was going to pull her arm out of its socket. She turned slightly, hoisted the bag back onto the seat, squatted to get her shoulders roughly even with the top of the bag, and slipped her arms through the straps. As the doors opened, she stood again and lunged, last minute, past the elderly man into fresh air.

She was at one end of the platform, her exit at the other. One tender step. A second. At this pace she would miss the tram and it would be another fifteen minutes for the next one to arrive, another half-hour at least before she could lie down. She forced herself to pick up her pace. At the stairs, which she normally flew down, she watched the other commuters descending and pictured losing her balance. Instead of trying even the first step, she turned right, in search of an elevator.

The doors slid open at ground level and she saw her yellow M6 pulling up to the tram stop. She began to sprint; within two steps she had slowed to a crawl. In the middle of that obstacle course last summer, she'd lost her footing scrambling up an angled wall and banged hard into the wooden slats. Her adrenaline was up and she didn't want her friends worrying about her, so she kept going. When it hurt to take deep breaths the next day, Julia had ordered her to the doctor, and Anna learned she'd broken a rib. Now, a little shoulder pain and she wasn't sure she could make it to the exit.

A few meters ahead she spotted a bench. She reached it, lowered herself down. It was hot out but she'd had plenty to drink today. Had she pulled a muscle? Overdone the running this morning? Okay, get up, she thought, you just need to get yourself out there by the next tram. She put her palms on the edge of the bench and pushed—no. This was more than a little pain.

If Julia were in town— if Melanie hadn't just had a baby— if her parents lived closer— *shoot*. She hated being dramatic. Making a big deal about small things. Julia thought her resistance to asking for help was absurd. But Anna didn't want to burden people. She wouldn't tell Julia this, but she cringed sometimes hearing her ask for favors— pushy, blithe, unconcerned about saving herself time and energy by demanding the same or more of someone else. Now, though, it didn't feel like a choice. She dialed 1-1-2.

There were at least two dozen people already waiting. An older man in the opposite row of chairs was holding his jaw and moaning. Behind her she could hear a toddler crying. "Shh, shh, I know it hurts," whispered his mother. Anna managed to get her fingers around her phone and flex them to pull it out of her pocket. A missed call from her mother and a text. *Call when you get home. Want to ask you something.*

She texted back. Her fingers kept tapping letters adjacent to those she was aiming for. *Will call later. Having some pain in my shoulders.*

Send.

Came to the ER to get it checked out.

Send.

Just to be safe. In waiting room. Busy here.

Send.

Her phone rang. It hurt to hold it up to her ear. "Don't come," she found herself insisting. She didn't want her mother driving two hours; didn't want the fear that was edging out her bafflement to be justified by such an effort. "I'm just being careful, so I don't worry about it all night. Remember my broken rib?" Mom saw the sense in that, eased up. "I promise I'll text after I see the doctor. Don't stay up."

An hour. Another hour. Maybe she should just go home. But it wasn't like she felt better. Instead, needles were digging into her shoulders, and no matter how she positioned her arms, she couldn't get comfortable. She pushed herself up and paced back and forth behind a row of chairs. Her legs felt light.

If they called her soon, and gave her medicine—a muscle relaxant? maybe it was just a pinched nerve—then she would get home by midnight. She could still get a decent night's sleep before her meeting. *I was disappointed.* What would he say? Better to start, as Julia would tell her, with an open-ended question. *I want to understand.* She kept pacing, holding the backs of empty chairs, sliding her too-light legs along the floor.

Now, abruptly, there was a sensation in her belly. Or more like the lack of sensation; a minute before, she now realized, she'd felt the waistband of her jeans against her skin; now she didn't. She brought her hand to her stomach, first over her shirt. Something was wrong. She moved her hand under her shirt, flesh to flesh. But she couldn't feel her palm on her stomach—or rather, she could only feel it one way, hand touching skin. Her stomach, meanwhile, barely registered the hand, it was numb, like how her jaw had felt under her probing fingertips after she'd had her wisdom teeth pulled four years earlier.

She should tell someone. But she felt so weak. *Go up to reception.* She let go of the back of a chair and slowly, struggling to walk properly, took three small steps toward the front of the waiting room. "Do you need help?" asked the mother of the now-sleeping toddler. "Yes, please." The woman guided her to an empty chair, then went herself to the reception desk, "Hallo? Hallo!" The favors were racking up.

Ten minutes later, Anna was on a stretcher being wheeled into a glass-walled room behind reception. "Someone will come soon to get you." There was only one other person back here: a man about her father's age, also on a stretcher, though sitting at a steeper angle than her forty-five-degree slant, and muttering about someone, possibly his wife or daughter.

She wondered again if she wouldn't be better off back home, logging a decent night's sleep. It's what the two paramedics who responded to her 112 call had suggested. After taking her temperature and asking what happened, they told her to raise her arms. "Can you stand?" She could, on wobbly legs.

"Please, is it possible to take me to the ER?"

They looked at her skeptically. She understood. She was twenty-four, appeared even younger, not coughing, not feverish, not bleeding, speaking coherently. "This isn't some pattern. I don't call ambulances every day." She was justifying things as much to herself as to them.

"Frau Werner, with this heat, we're very busy," said the taller of the two men, black grease stains visible on his red and neon yellow uniform pants. "Your vitals are normal. I suggest you go home and rest. We can't give lifts when there isn't a medical need." She was silent, contemplating. He saw she wasn't moving, and added, "If you want to go to the ER, you'll need to take a taxi."

"They've forgotten about us," the man on the other stretcher loudly declared, pulling her back to the present. Later, she'll curse herself for not taking out her phone and googling her symptoms, for not screaming to be seen, for stoically reclining here, willing herself to rest, nodding sympathetically at her temporary roommate, who had gone back to mumbling.

That would come. Here and now, after what felt like hours, a man in scrubs opened the door. "Frau Werner, how are you feeling? The exam room is free."

She gripped the side of the stretcher, moved her legs, began to pivot her body—

"Stay," the man said. "I'll wheel you."

She heard the crackle of walkie talkies. Two paramedics raced past, pushing a stretcher with a large body strapped down and an oxygen mask covering the mouth and nose. A reminder of what the hospital was dealing with and why she'd been made to wait so long. The man wheeling her turned a corner and pulled into an empty room.

"Where's the doctor?"

"He'll be here soon. It's busy tonight."

The doctor. Young. Disheveled, almost in a comforting way. Less so the way he swiveled the chair so his back was to her when he asked her questions, as if reading from a script on his screen. She described her symptoms, managing to keep any quiver out of her voice. She was precise about when the pain in her shoulders started and explained in detail when and how it spread to her upper arms, and how this nearly coincided with her first difficulty walking. Click, click, click. His eyes remained on the computer.

"Have you been under stress recently?"

A production issue she caused. Deciding if she should talk with Tomás. "Not really. A little."

"How much sleep did you get last night?"

That was easier. Eight hours normally, but she'd stayed up late in case Julia wanted to talk during her layover in Chicago, filling the time working, then watching brainless stuff on YouTube.

"Six, seven hours."

"And to confirm, your vision is normal?"

"Yes."

He finally stood and came close. He had her touch his finger and then her nose. He had her push against his hands. "I'd like you to stand and walk to the other side of the room."

"I don't think I can."

A rubber-tipped hammer struck her knee. After examining her for a few minutes, he sat, and swiveled away again. Click, click, click. "What you're describing sounds neurologic."

It took a moment for the implications of his phrasing to register. *What you're describing.* The condescension—as if she were making it up—as if, in a situation like this, she would be anything other than precise. Unlike the body being rushed through the hall, she'd been told to sit on a bench seat in the back of the ambulance and, upon arriving at the hospital, had walked into the waiting room. What had the paramedics said when they registered her? Why had she been moved to that room with the mumbler? Suddenly she questioned whether anyone had believed her. Was this doctor saying it was all in her head? Like she was hallucinating the pain? She could be slightly delusional from time to time. But crazy? Hysterical? Absolutely not.

"I'm not sure what you're suggesting," she finally responded.

"I'm suggesting that you rest a few hours here. We don't have a neurologist in the hospital this late. If you don't start feeling better, we'll page the service."

Maybe it was desperation, maybe the way her ears had warmed at *what you're describing*. "No. Please page them now. I've been resting for hours, and it's only gotten worse."

He turned and looked at her squarely for the first time. "Have you had similar symptoms in the past?"

Was she a moron? If anything remotely like this had ever happened, wouldn't she have opened with that? "No. Never."

His eyes narrowed, like he was calculating something. "Frau Werner, if this is in fact neurological, you'll need an MRI. There are only two hospitals in Berlin that conduct MRIs in the middle of the night. I'm going to transfer you. They'll have you seen by a neurologist there if necessary."

THREE

An hour waiting on the gurney in the hallway outside the exam room; a nauseating ambulance ride strapped to a stretcher, able to see only the vehicle's roof; answering questions from the triage nurse at this new hospital; two hours waiting to be seen by the doctor; the doctor, while reading her chart and examining her, interrupted again and again by nurses asking about other patients; the doctor deciding to order an MRI but seemingly not concerned despite the fact that she could barely move her left leg; and now he'd left the room, and she was again waiting.

With care, she took her phone out of her pocket. It was 3:08. It took her six tries to slide her finger properly and unlock it. A text from Mom: *Are you home yet? What did they say?*

Slowly, she texted, telling her she was now at BKM.

What? The response was immediate; Mom was still awake. *I'm heading there now.*

The last thing she needed was for her mother to get in the car at three in the morning. If Dad drove, that would be safer, but then he'd have to drop Mom off and race back through morning traffic or he'd be late for work. Neither of her parents were great drivers. She was in fifth grade when the family got their first car, and on trips it was always Stefan, and later her, who took the wheel.

I'll be fine. The doctor doesn't seem concerned. They're going to do an MRI. I'll call in the morning.

She thought about calling Julia. Two, one, twelve, eleven, ten, nine, eight. She'd still be awake, possibly still at dinner, or getting drinks with one of her contacts, getting information about where she stood versus the competition, or pointers on who cared about what. Anna didn't want to throw her off her game. She'd wait until she knew what was going on.

3:26. She closed her eyes. When she opened them again it was 4:22. They'd forgotten about her. Her left leg was still refusing to move. She tried to climb off the gurney; she couldn't.

"Please!" she shouted. Nobody came.

"Please! I need help!" Even louder.

A nurse came into the exam room.

"Please," Anna said, "I was supposed to be taken for an MRI an hour ago."

"Let me check for you."

They asked her a million questions. "Do you have a pacemaker, defibrillator, or implanted heart valve?" No. "Have you ever had any type of surgery?" No. "Have you ever been exposed to metal fragments that could be lodged in your eyes or body?" No. "Is it possible that you are pregnant?" No!

They transferred her to a table. A nurse put soft earplugs in her ears and a pair of large headphones over them.

"Can you hear me?" A male voice through the headphones.

"Yes."

"We're going to get started. It's important that you stay absolutely still."

A whining sound started up as she began sliding into the machine. She closed her eyes and breathed in and out slowly, determined to not move despite the urge to roll out the pain in her shoulders. Classical music played through the headphones and beyond the violin and piano, she heard clicks and bangs and knocks in a random rhythm. Then, the music alone.

Strange, she suddenly thought, how she felt no urge to pee; she'd last used the bathroom hours and hours ago, before she'd pulled her chair over to Rajeev's desk. Oh, shit. She'd promised to look at his PR; he was going to think she'd flaked—

The technician through the headphones: "You're doing great. Now we're going to start a hundred-and-twenty second sequence. Hold still." She sensed the table sliding, then heard knocks and fast-paced clicks again.

Out of the machine, back in the room she'd been left in before, she found she was out of breath. Odd, since all she'd been doing was lying down. She tested her left leg again. Still no movement. What the hell? She told her right knee to flex. No movement! What? She tried again, *flex right knee*—

Rapid footsteps. She rotated her head. Two men. "Frau Werner. I'm Dr. Huber. I'm in charge of the intensive care unit tonight. Your MRI shows damage to your spinal cord. We need to bring you into the ICU immediately."

"Why—" she started to ask, but they were already pushing her bed out of the room and down the hall at breakneck speed. In a new room at the far end of the corridor, past what seemed an interminable series of doors, a crowd of pastel green-cloaked people surrounded her. They began sticking probes on her skin, inserting IVs. A machine started beeping and a readout flashed across its screen. They put a mask over her face and she heard the hiss of a gas of some sort begin to flow. "To help you breathe," a nurse said.

"I'll be inserting a catheter into your bladder," a different nurse informed her. "Do you have allergies to latex or iodine?" "I don't think so." She watched the nurse tear open a package and lift her gown. She tensed up. Was this really necessary? "This won't hurt. I'm cleaning ... now breathe in and out slowly." The nurse was right about it not hurting. "Did you insert it?" Her own voice sounded strange through the oxygen mask. "Yes." Now, tilting her head forward, she could see the same nurse snake a tube over her leg. But it was like watching it happen to someone else. Had they injected an anesthetic? Why didn't she feel that tube on her leg; how could she not have felt *a catheter?*

"Frau Werner." It was the doctor again. This time, he was speaking slowly, seemed strangely still after the chaos of the last five minutes. "You appear to have had a stroke in your spinal cord and it caused severe damage high up. This is causing paralysis, the extent of which we cannot determine solely from the MRI exam." He paused. "Do you understand what I'm telling you?"

A stroke? Old men, slurred words. In her spine? It had been an utterly normal day at the office. She didn't do anything to her back. But her strange, distant legs—and her numb stomach. *Causing paralysis.*

She breathed in and out. Incident management 101. Do not panic. There was always a solution. Get the details. Ask questions. She nodded. "Yes, I'm following." Her voice was muffled by the oxygen. She felt like she wasn't articulating, like everything was blurry.

"This type of stroke is rare. My colleague from neurology reviewed your MRI and will be here soon to examine you. We believe the paralysis is extensive. We are concerned it could soon affect your breathing, which is why we've brought you to the ICU. Here we'll be able to monitor you and—"

"I could lose the ability to breathe?" Her voice still sounded strange through the mask.

"We—"

"Doctor ..." She forgot his name. She didn't want him sugar-coating things. "Doctor—I want to understand."

"We don't know. We're giving you oxygen so your lungs don't need to work as hard. If you stop breathing on your own, we will put you on a ventilator."

She suddenly felt she was already gasping for air. Deep breath. Another. "How long will it take to recover?"

"I ... We'll see what neurology says. Try to rest. That's what you need. We're monitoring you. You're safe here."

Mama. She needed her mother. She felt around with her right hand. Where was her phone? It'd been in her jeans. Now she was in a hospital gown. Where were her clothes? "Doctor—my mother—"

"Your mother called. She knows you're in the ICU. Your parents are on their way."

Just as quickly as everyone had appeared, they were gone, and when the doctor stepped away, she was alone. Moaning rose from the bed next to her; she rotated her head and saw it was coming from a man lying there. She closed her eyes, listened to beeps from near and far. Oxygen flowed into her mask. She was so tired ...

An alarm woke her. She drifted off again. Another alarm, and after a few seconds, back to sleep.

Now, after what seemed like hours, she opened her eyes and kept them open. She turned her head. Mom was there. Sitting next to the bed, her hand on Anna's.

"Honey." Mom stood, pressed her lips to her forehead, and slipped her fingers into Anna's hair, briefly cradling her head. Last night she'd kept it together. Now, with her mother here—she wanted to be hugged, wanted her to make this all go away, to tell her she'd get better soon.

"I'm scared."

"I know, sweetie. I know."

She was afraid to test herself, afraid that her legs were still frozen. Left leg. No movement. Right leg. No movement. Left arm. Nothing! My god. Right arm. It moved. Okay. Her right arm was okay. Now she tried to make a fist with her right hand. No. She couldn't move her fingers. Last night she could. And breathing, even with the oxygen mask, was harder too.

"It's getting worse."

"I'll get the doctor."

"Mama. Don't let me fall back asleep."

FOUR

After three days, clearance came to leave the ICU. She watched the ceiling tiles pass overhead, her parents at her side: hallway, elevator, hallway, turn, hallway, now into a room. She was lifted and placed in the bed close to the window. The other bed, closer to the door, looked occupied but was presently empty; the room was sunny, the quiet noticeable after days of beeps, alarms, and moaning.

Two women entered the open door, one all in white but for the thick, stylish black frames of her glasses. "Frau Werner, I'm Dr. Eckert, this is Nurse Ullrich." Dr. Eckert set her hand on Anna's right shoulder and squeezed gently. "I'm chair of the Treatment Center for Spinal Cord Injuries. Most of the patients we see here were in accidents. Spinal strokes are rare. I've looked through the medical literature and found only a handful of reports on patients with paralysis as extensive as yours. This means you and I are in relatively new territory, together. Do you understand?"

Finally someone who saw that her brain was working and who was taking the time to explain things.

"Yes."

"Good. My colleagues tell me you're sharp."

Anna smiled.

"But we're not on totally unfamiliar ground. Even though most hospitals have never seen a case like yours, your symptoms are similar to those of patients who have had accidents that resulted in physical injuries high in the spine. We'll treat you using the same methods and approaches that we use with them. This means that you'll undergo therapy to strengthen what you can control—your right arm at the shoulder, elbow, and wrist."

She nodded. This made sense, she guessed. "Slowly," Dr. Eckert continued, "you'll learn how to adapt to your new body. Part of that is learning how to do things differently, but part of it is about treating yourself with a level of care that you might be unused to. Keeping healthy will require constant vigilance for the rest of your life."

The rest of her life? What was she talking about? What about healing? Dr. Huber hadn't suggested this was in any way *permanent*.

She looked at her mother for confirmation that there'd been some misunderstanding, but she was staring at the floor. Dad, too. She noticed he was squeezing the pair of glasses he held in his hands. She glared at this doctor. "But I'm *not* someone with a broken spine. I can heal. I'll do the therapy, I'll take whatever medicine. You're acting as if I'll never have control over my body again."

"Frau Werner." Dr. Eckert paused. "May I call you Anna?"

"Yes."

"Anna, I'm always going to be straight with you. Every patient is different, and every injury is different. I'm not saying it's permanent, only that you need to be prepared for it to be. The improvement you'll see will be incremental. You stabilized your first day in the ICU. Since then, despite a reduction in inflammation, there has been no sign of any function returning. And with every passing day it becomes less and less likely that something dramatic will occur."

"I'm not saying some miracle recovery—"

"You will undergo physical therapy, yes, but I promised I would be straight with you. This physical therapy will be mainly about strengthening the muscles you can control and learning to live within your new physical constraints. That said, our facility and our therapists are the best in Germany. You don't believe this now, but you'll be amazed at what you can learn to do within those constraints. You will be able to lead a full life, you will adapt. You are still you."

This doctor had no idea. She was young, fit. She was going to heal. And besides, nothing had actually happened to her! You can't be whole one minute and the next—nothing, for the rest of your life your brain can't control your limbs. Absolutely not. This whole thing was absurd.

Dr. Eckert looked at her with soft eyes, but let silence fill the room. Finally, she asked: "May I examine you?" With a glance at Anna's parents, she added, "Would you be more comfortable without your parents here?"

A week ago, yes. But privacy had gone out the window in the windowless ICU. Anna shrugged with her shoulder that could still shrug. Dad walked out, Mom stayed, and Dr. Eckert moved to the other side of the bed, from which she opened the back ties on Anna's gown and began a close inspection of every centimeter of Anna's body. Anna heard the sound of a camera snapshot.

"I want to show you something." Dr. Eckert came back around to where Anna could see her, holding a phone. "See this red area?"

A photo of her back came into focus, showing a slightly reddish splotch the size of a coin. Anna shifted her eyes, saw Dr. Eckert looking at her with concern, sympathy. Like she was about to break the news that she would require a skin graft, or—who knew at this point?—that aliens were writing coded messages on her back. But Anna refused to accept that the sky was falling on their heads. Dr. Eckert didn't know her. She was overreacting. "I'm shocked," Anna began. "I'm shocked and disappointed that you have bed bugs in this hotel."

Dr. Eckert didn't react for a moment, then smiled briefly. "It's from the skin covering your tailbone. It's a bedsore. It might seem like a small thing, but it's not. It could develop into an infection, even into an open wound. With your paralysis you're prone to get these types of ulcers because you can't shift your position and your body can't warn you when one is developing. You were in the ICU for a few days and already one has appeared. This is not good."

Anna saw Mom's grip tighten on the railing at the side of the bed.

"Don't worry," Dr. Eckert saw it too. "Our staff will keep an eye on the sore, rotate you at the correct frequency, make sure you're lying in the right ways, make sure sheets aren't crumpled up under you, make sure your skin and the bedding stay dry. And with that, it should go away."

A tiny spot could not be such a big deal.

"This is what I mean about vigilance, Anna. You can't trust your body to protect you. You'll need to use your brain and your eyes. You'll need to make sure you never remain in one position for too long. You'll need to examine yourself. You'll need to get others to examine you. If you bang a shin, or drop something on a toe, or any little thing, you'll need to make a mental note to get it checked out. The system you've relied on your whole life—where your body alerts you to problems using pain or discomfort—that won't work anymore."

Could she be that vigilant? Exercise aside, she'd never been all that careful about her body—wasn't one to always put on sunscreen or check for ticks after a hike. She wasn't a meticulous planner or list maker (actually, she was decent at making lists, just not at following them). On the other hand, she was disciplined about certain things—like reviewing every line of changed code before making a commit.

But what was she thinking? She was going to get better. And if she needed to be extra careful and guard her body before then, sure, she could do that. A few weeks from now this would just be a crazy story. She would take it easy for a little while after that—skip her morning runs, miss out on the obstacle course this year, no big deal.

Dr. Eckert was again leaving space for silence. Anna wouldn't fight this fight for now. "Okay," she said.

"Do you have any more questions?"

She shook her head. Dr. Eckert smiled at her, shook her mother's hand again, and left with the nurse.

Anna could see her mother deliberating. She finally turned to the corner of the room. "I charged your phone. You have texts and missed calls from Julia."

She asked her mother to copy Julia's number onto a piece of paper and tape it to the railing. Her parents kissed her goodbye, told her they would be back first thing in the morning, and she found herself saying to each of them, "I'm going to be okay." It felt good to say it, at least.

As soon as the door closed she figured out how to use the voice-controlled speakerphone mounted above the bed. She tilted her head up. "Place call. 0-1-7-1-3-9 …" And then: "Cancel."

Julia would not want to hear this. In the middle of her business trip. The customer she'd been chasing since the middle of last year. She wouldn't understand. Anna couldn't even understand.

"Place call."

"Julia Keller."

"Julia, it's me."

"What the fuck, Anna? I'm out of the country for like four days and you ghost me? Jesus Christ! What number is this?"

"I'm in the hospital."

"What? What happened?" Julia's tone shifted instantaneously. "Are you okay?"

"No. I mean, not really—"

"What happened?"

She told her.

"How long is the recovery? How long until they'll let you go home?"

"They …" Her voice trailed off. "They can't say. They don't know. A week or two? That's what I'm hoping."

"I can … let me see … I should be able to get a flight back today …"

She could hear the hesitation. Julia would be pissed if she lost the deal.

"No, finish your meetings, I'll be okay."

"Are you sure?"

"Yeah. My parents drove up. They've been taking turns keeping me company. They're staying at my place."

"Okay, well, tonight I'm taking the VP out. Tomorrow's the big demo. I'll skip New York and book a new flight for tomorrow night. I should be back on Saturday."

"Really, you don't even need to do that." No harm buying a little more time.

"I know you. You'll have your laptop out and be coding away from that hospital bed by the time I arrive. Relax. Don't do any work. You'll get better soon. I love you."

FIVE

The day had started poorly. She'd woken before dawn, unsure how much time had passed since her last rotation, hungry, thirsty, thinking of Julia somewhere over the Atlantic, or maybe already in Frankfurt, drinking a latte at a coffee bar, waiting for her flight, looking at her phone or chatting with the person next to her. She, meanwhile, had waited for the door beyond her roommate's sleeping body to crack open, bringing breakfast.

When breakfast did come, the aide didn't introduce herself, pulled the straw and drink away before Anna was done, played with her phone with one hand while shoving marmalade-smeared bread into Anna's mouth with the other, not noticing that each bite, chewed lying down, left her winded. "I'm still hungry," she'd said, still trying to catch her breath, when the woman stood. "And I'd like more juice, please." Instead of complying, the aide peeled off her latex gloves and threw them in the trash receptacle in the wall. "I'll leave the tray for now."

And now, hours later, it was still there, a jagged piece of bread and an unopened container of yoghurt. Leave the tray, sure. So Julia could feed her when she got here? Julia could make a propeller sound and loop-the-loop the room-temperature yoghurt past her lips.

She'd sworn she would stay positive, but how, when at the mercy of hospital workers who didn't give a shit? Plus the whole setup. She was used to living by herself—even at university she'd had her own (tiny) bedroom in a shared apartment. Now she was lying two meters from a semi-catatonic, deeply unfriendly senior citizen who refused to turn off the TV. "Hello, Ingrid," she'd said two days ago. "I'm Anna." No response. An hour later, "Ingrid, I'm going to turn off the TV." And then to the voice-controlled box above her head, "TV off."

"TV on," Ingrid immediately called out, the first words Anna had heard her speak.

When Julia got here, Anna wanted her to stroke her head, to climb into bed, to lie down next to her, put her cheek on the same pillow, and tell her she'd get better soon. But she couldn't see it—not here, but maybe not anywhere. There was that time with her swollen rib cage, and the time Julia was hit with the flu, but for the most part, they'd never needed to care for one another.

She closed her eyes, squeezed them shut, then forced them open. Even lying here she should be working on her recovery, starting with the right-hand exercises from the therapist who'd come yesterday. *Curl index finger. Uncurl index finger. Curl middle finger. Uncurl middle finger. Curl ring finger. Uncurl ring finger. Curl pinky. Uncurl pinky. Curl thumb. Straighten out thumb.* Back to the index finger. She sent instructions and she visualized her fingers responding exactly as they had all her life until five days ago. Nothing, no movement, and yet, somehow, she felt a little better, knew that this motionless exercise would cause her fingers to wake up. *Curl. Uncurl. Curl. Uncurl.*

"Incoming call. Incoming call." It was the stiff, synthesized voice from the device mounted above the bed.

"Answer," Anna instructed.

"Hi, honey. How are you feeling?"

"Okay."

"Just landed. I'm coming right over."

"I'll be here."

Over the phone she sounded like her usual self. It was only when you saw her that you could tell. Should she have done more to prepare Julia? Mentioned the catheter? Mentioned she would be lying on her side, her head on the pillow, unable to turn? She'd said she couldn't move her legs, but she hadn't spelled it out, hadn't made her understand.

She rotated her head into the pillow, breathed out. Could she get a nurse to come now? They had their routine and their order and she hated asking for special treatment. But—this didn't seem unreasonable. "Request nurse," she said to the voice-activated box.

"I was wondering," she asked when the nurse, a tall man with a closely shaven head, arrived, "could you brush my teeth?"

"Sorry. It's busy this morning. The aide will be here to help you within the hour."

"It's just that my ... girlfriend is visiting. I'd really appreciate it." Her mind, watching the conversation, was hating that she was asking for an exception, especially for something frivolous, but even more hating that she needed to ask—that she was begging someone to brush her teeth.

The nurse smiled. "In that case." He went into the bathroom and came back with a toothbrush, a cup, and a plastic container. She watched him put gloves on. Then he was next to her and she could smell the hospital on his uniform. He reached into her mouth with the brush and gently scrubbed her top teeth and gums. "Spit," he said. He brushed her bottom teeth. She drank through the straw, swished the water around, spat it out, then repeated.

"May I clean your glasses? They have a lot of spots."

"Yes, please, thank you."

He removed her glasses, which she'd asked the nurse who'd rotated her earlier to put on her so she could look out the window. She heard the faucet running, then he came back with a warm washcloth and wiped the bits of toothpaste from the edges of her mouth and rinsed her face. He put her glasses back on. The tree, the pane of glass, the wall, his uniform became crisp.

"You have such beautiful eyes."

"Thanks." She swallowed.

How long would it take her to get here? Forty-five minutes if she took a taxi. An hour at least by train. Of course she would take a taxi. Julia never took public transportation, especially not when she could expense it. So, soon. She wished she had a private room.

She watched a red squirrel chase another on the branch of the oak tree, its back legs propelling it forward with powerful thrusts. The first time she'd noticed Julia was at an all-hands, in the atrium, three rows down, laughing and chatting—flirting?—with one of the sales guys before the meeting started. Mesmerizing, confident, outgoing, tall, straight. Her opposite. Later, she looked through the org chart under the head of sales until she found her photo. Julia Keller. Account Executive, Enterprise Customers. Then at LinkedIn: with DDB for nine years, did the dual education program, started as Sales Trainee.

The first time they talked was at a company party in June last year. It was a weekday night, the company rented out the entire club, and a woman from the quality assurance department was DJing. The whole thing was a little awkward. Who wanted to dance in front of their coworkers? Not her. She was holding her beer bottle and half bopping, her feet glued to the floor, when she felt a hand on the small of her back.

"You're Anna, right? From machine learning?"

Julia knew her name. What she did. She felt Julia's hand still touching her back through her t-shirt, looked up from her beer, swallowed. "Yes!"

Click. "Anna. Honey."

She heard the wheels of Julia's rollaboard. Then Julia was standing next to her. She was wearing her suit—must have gone straight to the airport from the meeting yesterday.

"My god." Julia leaned over and kissed her on the temple. Her skin, her perfume, even the airplane on her clothes. The week was like a year and tears came to Anna's eyes.

Later, Julia's hand was in hers. "Are you trying to close your fingers?"

"Yes."

"You're really trying? Squeeze my hand. Tell your hand to squeeze mine."

"I am."

"And the doctor thinks it will get better in a couple of weeks?"

She looked at Julia in her suit, a loose strand of hair over her ear, her luggage in the corner. Anna swallowed and made a small up and down motion with her head.

The slice of orange was sweet and cool. Julia's bare fingers had none of that latex taste of the aides', and being fed by her had become, in the course of a week, less strange.

"Honey," Julia said, "do you want another one?"

"Yes, please. One more."

She chewed. Eating on her side was slow.

This was Julia's third visit. The guests had poured in this week: her parents daily, her brother, Grandma, Tomás, the CEO of the whole company, Rajeev, Melanie and two other friends from university, three friends from school, her landlady—who found out when she asked her mom why she and her dad were staying in Anna's apartment.

"I'll pray for a miracle every day until you're better," promised her friend Natalie, who'd dropped out of university, converted to Russian Orthodoxy, changed her name, and fallen off the map. It meant more to her than she'd expected.

Stefan had come alone, and then again with Christina and Mia. Mia had at first kept her distance. "It's okay, little mouse, climb into bed."

"Are you sure?" Stefan asked.

She nodded and Stefan lifted Mia onto the bed. Mia hesitated, then hugged her. "Aunty Anna, can we still do the race?"

She'd told Mia that after she finished teaching her how to ride they would race, Anna on foot, Mia on her bike. "Yes, mouse, I promise."

Anna swallowed the orange slice. Julia bent over and put her mouth close to her ear. She could feel Julia's breath. For a second she thought she was going to kiss her. Instead, she whispered, "Does Ingrid watch TV all the time?"

She nodded, the side of her head rubbing against the pillow.

Still whispering, "You must hate it."

She nodded again. She was sure Julia wanted them to be able to talk privately. "As soon as I can stay upright for longer I bet we can go for a walk outside."

"That would be great," Julia said. It sounded forced. "Do you want water?"

She looked down the bed at the bag clipped to the side. She shook her head. "What's going on with Caterpillar?"

"Work? Sure you care?"

"Yeah." She did care. And they'd already talked about everything new with her in the hospital. She didn't know how to bring up the things she really wanted to ask. Would Julia wait? What if she didn't get completely better? Once, when she was replacing the trim around the bedroom door in Julia's apartment, standing on the tips of her toes, Julia sitting on the bed, watching her, joking but serious: "You look hot with that hammer." Without the physical—

"There's not much to tell. Haven't heard anything new. They asked for three more references. They want them all to be heavy equipment manufacturers. Yesterday I sent two and asked for clarification on the third, but they didn't get back to me, not yet anyway."

"Are you worried?"

"A little. It hasn't been too long. You know how these big companies move. And people hold their cards close."

SIX

Pushing her mop along the hallway floor, Batul looked up at the sign marking the departments in this wing: *Orthopädie Handchirurgie* and *Rückenmarkverletzte Unfallchirurgie*. Last week, her first, she'd been assigned to the B wing. It bothered her how few of the signs she understood. Even though memorizing exam vocabulary was more urgent, she wanted to learn it all. She took guesses, used her commute to look up the words she didn't know, and by Thursday had it all down. Now, in this new wing there were new signs, a new challenge.

The first department was easy—*Orthopädie Handchirurgie*—orthopedic hand surgery—similar to English, from the Latin, she supposed, except with that German habit of smashing words together. The second department wasn't so easy. Ooh, *Unfall*, she did know that word—accident—so *Unfallchirurgie* was accident surgery, perhaps trauma surgery, but what was *Rückenmarkverletzte*?

She wanted to take out her phone and snap a quick photo, but they had emphasized at orientation last week that taking photos was prohibited—verboten—to protect patient privacy. Back home, the regime was killing doctors. Functioning required a split brain.

Rückenmarkverletzte.   Something-injury.   Rückenmark, Rückenmark—

She lifted her mop from the floor, plunged it into the bucket and whirled it around, then shifted it, dripping, to the wringer, and pressed the lever hard to squeeze out the water. A young couple carrying flowers had entered the hall and was walking toward her, murmuring about, she thought, a car accident. A female doctor in a white coat, white pants, and black glasses and a younger man, also in white—a doctor in training?—walked briskly past Batul, the woman giving instructions about *dekubitus*—another word to look up—before both turned left into an office.

It was busy here. Patients, visitors, doctors, and nurses, but also nurse aides, technicians, food service workers, translators—even staff whose only role, as far as she could tell, was watering the plants. Suits, scrubs, lab coats. Medical equipment, computers, carts, monitoring stations, alarms. She loved watching, listening in, deciphering how this hygienic, miniature city operated.

Of course she wanted to learn how to practice medicine, not mop floors, scrub toilets, and empty trash bins, but even with this job, she liked being a part of the place. She didn't exactly enjoy the physical labor, but she didn't hate it either, and if she was going to work, she wanted to do it well. Plus it was a break from studying, and she could drill vocabulary and grammar just as well cleaning these corridors as sitting in the tiny apartment she shared with Rami and her parents.

"In Deutschland werden Nüsse vor allem zur Weihnachtszeit gegessen"—in Germany, nuts are mainly eaten at Christmastime. From this morning's practice exam. Why would Germans (or anyone) save nuts *mainly* for one time of year? Those bulging burlap sacks of pine nuts in Grandpa's shop. The raw pistachios of late summer, their hulls blushed maroon and pink. The smell of roasting almonds.

There was a smudge of grease on the molding where she'd just mopped. She bent down and went at it with a soapy brush. There! The spot faded to gray, then disappeared completely. She dropped the brush back in her cart, stood, and stretched her back.

SEVEN

Confident steps. White pants. White jacket. Black glasses. Dr. Eckert came into the room, positioned herself in Anna's field of vision, and grasped her shoulder briefly. "How are you feeling today?"

"Good. The pain in my shoulders isn't too bad. I think I could try being upright for more hours. And I like the new exercises in physical therapy."

It would be easy to complain. About the lazy food service worker. About the nurses being so overwhelmed in the mornings that twice, by the time she got to the gym, her appointment was already over. It would be easy to go negative. That she couldn't fall asleep. That when she did, it never seemed like more than a few minutes before the nurses woke her for another rotation. That Ingrid refused to turn off the TV. That the pain in her shoulders never went completely away. That Julia had visited only once this week. But she would not go negative.

"I'm glad to hear it. Peter tells me you're the most determined patient he's ever had. And he's worked with two national-level athletes, so that's saying something."

Her main physical therapist. She smiled.

"Anna, I'm sure you realize, you've been here for a month now, and you haven't regained control of any muscles. I know you've been hoping for more, and so have I, but at this point we need to assume there won't be drastic improvement."

Why did Dr. Eckert have so little faith? What had happened to her was so rare—Dr. Eckert herself had said as much—how could she be so confident? And what counted as drastic or not drastic?

"The reason I say this is that I want to talk about the physical therapy, about the program Peter and I are putting together for you. We're going to keep strengthening your right arm, but I also want to start taping your fingers at night. There's a technique where we can train your fingers to close and open when you bend your wrist. You'll be amazed at how much you'll be able to do."

She would bend her wrist, and her fingers would flop closed? She would open her wrist and her fingers would flop open? It sounded like trying to pick up a toy with that claw machine in the arcade. And yet—if she could close her fingers over a piece of bread—she would train and train and train. So yes, just until she got her fingers back.

"Why didn't we start taping earlier?"

"Well, if you were to regain a little control over your fingers, this trained motion could work against that. When you bend your wrist it might fight the instructions your brain is sending your fingers."

No. She wasn't giving up. Her fingers were coming back, and until then she would continue to use her hand loop. "In that case, no."

In the dark of night she woke, anxious about going against Dr. Eckert's advice. She felt dread—but a strange form of it. She used to feel it in her gut—an incapacitating, fearful, pessimistic knot. What she was feeling now was instead embodied in a stiffness in her neck and shoulders. Since she couldn't sense her stomach, this made sense, she supposed, but why should that matter, since dread was mental? To the extent that her brain was projecting the knot into some part of her body, shouldn't it still be her disconnected stomach? Maybe not.

Maybe all nausea, even nausea caused by anxiety rather than, say, eating old potato salad, was in fact a physical sensation, what they meant by psychosomatic, and her brain had rerouted the dread.

Before, when she had this feeling, she'd tell herself to get out of bed—just do that one thing. And then, out of bed, she'd tell herself to get dressed. And once dressed, to go outside, no matter how dark or cold. Outside, she would force herself to take a step, then another, not to worry beyond that, and then those steps would turn into running, and whatever had been worrying her would shrink into perspective; the knot would melt.

Could she do this without the standing up, the fresh air, the pounding of pavement? She wasn't expecting visitors today. Mom had needed to go back to work. Nobody was counting on her for anything. There were no emails demanding a response. No PRs waiting for her review. No tickets to complete this sprint. No brother and sister-in-law pissed at her for keeping Mia out late. She didn't need to buy groceries. She didn't need to do chores. People longed for this. To have no responsibility.

A release from nothing, then. That's what she needed. She'd always been good at daydreaming. She could transport herself from a boring meeting to any number of more interesting scenes sealed in her memory—the time she'd tried windsurfing on the Wannsee and wound up swimming for two hours to get her board back to the beach; on Julia's bed, the two of them lying on their stomachs, propped up on their elbows, glowing laptop in front of them, cracking up at a bad stand-up routine that a friend of a friend had thought wise to upload—Julia's hair in her eyes, snot coming out of Anna's nose; her right hand on the gear shift of her car, her left foot on the clutch, downshifting at 120, accelerating; in the crowds near Brandenburger Tor cheering on her friends running the marathon, drinking with them afterward.

Now it wasn't working. She could picture the scenes but they brought no escape. Not when she was stuck here, unable to move, the seconds ticking by like minutes. It would be better if she could sleep.

Would they give her medicine? A sleeping pill? Let her mind dissociate, let time pass until—

No. She listened to herself and heard self-pity. That wasn't her. She was an optimist. Stehaufmännchen, her friends called her: the roly-poly toy—you pushed it down and it always righted itself.

Curl right index finger. Uncurl right index finger. Wiggle right toes. She went through every paralyzed muscle. She did it again. The first rays of dawn filtered through the glass.

Maybe she was being too deliberate. Instead of exercising one muscle at a time, she should just *do* and let her subconscious worry about instructing her limbs. She would go through her usual morning routine in her mind, visualizing every detail, and theoretically her muscles would contract on their own and her heart would race.

Anna closed her eyes and imagined herself in her kitchen. Be specific. Let's make it winter. On this early mid-January morning, still dark outside, she would need to turn on the lights. She would reach for the dial controlling the under-cabinet Ikea fixtures she'd installed herself, turn it, bringing them to a glow, just barely illuminating the counter—she didn't want to ruin her night vision. She was in the sweats and t-shirt she slept in, and moved slowly, still sluggish from sleep.

She filled the cezve with water from the tap and set it to boil on the stove. She unfolded the creased-over top of the bag with coffee beans, breathed in the aroma, poured the beans into the bin of the burr grinder that Stefan had given her for Christmas. She lifted her arm, put her hand around the grinder, pressed her thumb to the settings wheel with its little plastic ridges and pushed against it, confirming it was turned all the way to the finest setting. She pressed the on button with her index finger and listened to the rumble of the motor. The beans were sucked in and milled—to the *consistency of flour*—those were the instructions from the barista at Cafe Izmir who'd sold her the coffee and cezve.

When the water came to a boil, she removed the cezve from the heat, poured in the ground coffee and cardamom, swirled it around, and put the pot back on the burner. As soon as the liquid foamed she lifted the pot from the stove, let the foam subside, and put it back on the burner. When the coffee was ready, she wrapped her hand around the cezve's wooden handle, pivoted her wrist, and poured the thick liquid into her cup.

She pulled out one chair at her kitchen table, sat down and raised her legs to rest on the other chair. She could feel the padding on the backs of her bare heels. She scrolled through her phone and sipped the coffee—much stronger than the watery hospital stuff. She was so immersed that she could smell the caffeine and the cardamom. Was this a sign of losing her connection to reality? With such a paucity of sensory input from her limbs, her brain was now hallucinating smells?

Now the caffeine was pulsing behind her eyes. She moved back to her bedroom, pulled on her running tights, sports bra, long-sleeve base layer, jacket, gloves, beanie, and GPS watch. Outside, she pivoted her foot clockwise and counterclockwise on the pavement, testing whether it was icy. Nope. Cold and dry. She loved these conditions.

She ran two kilometers at a moderate pace. Left leg. Right leg. Left leg. Right leg. Arms pumping. She approached and then passed the weirdly red building at the intersection. Now the yellow stucco apartments with the barbershop at ground level, the one whose sign had a photo of a man with a hideously large mustache and slicked-back quiff. She passed from behind the two tall women who she always passed—they walked together every morning around this time; one wore earmuffs.

She glanced at her watch. Now she pumped her legs, pushing as hard as she could. She wouldn't let up until she hit kilometer four. She was at three, now running along the canal. She blew by a man also out for an early run. Now 3.4. Half a kilometer more. Push. The next bridge would be four. Faster. If she wasn't uncomfortable it meant she wasn't achieving anything. Von nichts kommt nichts— from nothing comes nothing.

The bridge. She looked at her watch again. Exactly 4.0. She let her legs slow. In her imagination, her heart was racing and she was sweating under her winter running jacket. She turned and started back along the canal at a slower but still brisk pace. She thought about the egg she'd crack and throw in the pan when she got home, her second cup of coffee, the toast. She saw those two women again and nodded—

Click. She opened her eyes. Her mind switched from the crisp, dark morning next to the canal to her hospital-room window glowing pink as the September sun rose over Marzahn-Hellersdorf. She heard the quiet brush of the door sweep against the floor. Facing the window, she couldn't see who was entering. It wasn't a doctor, nurse, or food service worker: They always did a quick knock, never waited for a response, and announced themselves immediately, naming the task they were there to do. *Frau Werner / Anna / Frau Tillmann (never Ingrid!), it's so and so, I'm here to dress you / feed you / bathe you / rotate you / cut your nails ...*

It wasn't Mom or Dad or Julia, or any of her regular visitors, either. They'd learned that it frustrated her to not know who was coming in, and always said hello right away, letting her ID them by their voices.

So this was someone else. A janitor, she suspected. Yes. A moment later she heard the wheels of a cart, the squeak of that metal door, and the sound of the garbage bag being lifted from the bin inside the wall. Now she could hear a new bag being fit into the bin.

She heard steps, then saw a brief reflection in the mirror as the janitor passed the foot of the bed. Now she was standing next to her, square in her field of view. Her head was covered. She looked young, at most the same age as Anna herself.

"Frau Werner, may I?" she asked, pointing.

She pivoted her head and looked. Her container of yogurt.

"Thank you, yes. And please call me Anna."

The janitor lifted the container, catching the dollop that dripped from the lid.

"Thanks," said Anna. "What's your name?"
"Batul. Batul al-Jaberi."
Batul. Al-Jaberi. It was harder to memorize the foreign names.
"Have you been working here for long?"
"*Nein.* For a few weeks." With this longer utterance an accent was more apparent.

"Ah, so you arrived around the same time as me, but they didn't give you a bed! Life isn't fair. Well, anyway, you're not missing out on much. The beds aren't so comfortable and the food's nothing to write home about. The rooms, though, are spotless, which I attribute to the excellent janitorial services."

No reaction for a few seconds, like she was processing or translating. Then a restrained chuckle.

"Do you like working here?"

"Yes, I do. This place is huge, like a university."

"It is?" She'd been in this hall, the one below it where her PT took place, and when she first got here, the ER, the room with the MRI, and the ICU, but she had no sense for the size of the hospital, the layout of the floors, the number of patients.

"Yes. It is a ... campus with many buildings. People are walking all the time here to there. There is a long ... how do you say ... river, no, hallway, with glass windows and ... glass ceilings ... with arts ... drawn by the patients ... are hanging. There are rooms for research, and this is ... what is this called ... a learning hospital, no, teaching hospital, for students of medicine. You can see the ... zeal to taking care for the patients."

It took her a long time to say all of that. Funny that Anna was now slow at everything except speaking, where she was just as fast as before. This girl was so enthusiastic. It was refreshing—and more of a conversation than she'd had with most of the staff here, at least one that didn't focus on her bladder, or rotating her in bed, or her bowel routine.

"I didn't know all that. How long have you been speaking German?"

"I started studying in March."

March ... Six months. "Wow! You speak so well." She had colleagues who'd been living here for years and still relied on English most of the time. One of the engineering leads on her team, an American, had been in Berlin for a decade and still couldn't order a coffee in German—well, maybe that, but not much more. "How'd you learn so quickly?"

She raised her hand, palm out. "It's not good. I'm working hard to improve. A lot of words are similar to English."

"You speak English?" Anna switched. It felt good. It was the language she spoke more than half the time at work but hadn't used once since the stroke.

"Yes," she said, now in English, too. "English is easy for me. Can I ask you ..." Her voice dropped off.

"It's okay, ask me anything."

"You have tetraplegia, yes? You've only been here a few weeks, but your back is not in a brace. How could this be? I would expect you to still be recovering from spine repair surgery as I've seen with other patients."

How did she know the word *tetraplegia* in English? Anna looked at her. With Julia, with friends, with colleagues she hadn't been able to bring herself to say it, and with her parents the doctors had done the explaining. She took a deep breath. "I do have tetraplegia." It felt right. "I can use my right arm and wrist but haven't regained control over my other muscles yet. It's not from a physical accident. I had a stroke in my spine; it's something very unusual. But as you can tell, or at least I hope you can, it didn't touch my brain." She had the urge to go on, to tell her that she was a software engineer, that she'd had a normal day at the office, about what happened on the train, about how long it took to figure it out. It was the first time she wanted—really wanted—to tell someone.

"Thank you for explaining." Pointing at the door, "I need to keep cleaning."

She was imposing. Still, should she ask? It wasn't her job, but who knew how long before the nurse came.

"Buh ..."

"Batul."

"Sorry, Batul, could you help me with one thing?"

She nodded.

"There is a spot below my left eye that's been itching. I've been waiting for the nurse, but maybe you could ..."

She came closer. There was the swish of the baggy uniform pants. She took off her nitrile gloves. Now her body was close and Anna could smell actual cardamom—unless she was still hallucinating it, and roses, and, less pleasant, bleach. Batul touched her face below her eye. The pad of her finger was soft and warm. "Here?"

"A little below."

Batul made a small, gentle circular motion which only exacerbated the itch.

"Sorry. Can you use your nail?"

Now she felt Batul's fingernail scrape back and forth over the right spot.

"Ahh! Thank you."

Batul backed away and put her gloves back on. Anna noticed her glance at the urine drainage bag clipped to the side of the bed, and felt shame warm her cheeks. Then Batul dropped out of her field of view, her reflection appeared in the mirror for a second, and she was on the other side of the bed, on her way out.

"Good to meet you, Anna."

She liked how Batul said her name, elongating the first syllable and pronouncing it with a mild intonation: *Ah-nah*. She heard the janitorial cart wheels turning, and then the brush of the door, then the click.

EIGHT

That night, Batul's one cousin still in Aleppo called. She'd ask him to get official copies of her school records, all of which would require certified translation into German. She was far from being ready to apply—a year in the most optimistic case, but more likely two—but Tasneem had warned her it might not be so easy to get her documents, and the longer she waited, the harder it would get.

There was a war on. The city was divided. There were checkpoints. Streets were split into civilian and military lanes. Water and electricity were cut off. Markets and hospitals were being bombed. Her cousin had much, much bigger problems. She had waited until what seemed like the return of calm before asking him to risk the trip.

"Finally, finally, the administrator was there this time."

Alhamdulillah.

"But he refused to give me your transcript."

No.

"He said I need the proxy form signed by you and to pay a fee. I'm positive the form doesn't matter. Only the fee. Fifteen thousand lira."

"Are you serious?" What was wrong with people? They knew

there was a connection to someone abroad and their first thought was how to extract money.

"I didn't have anything close to that on me," her cousin said. "I'll get the cash from Grandpa and go back next week if I can."

"Thank you, Cousin."

Now Uncle was sure to learn of this favor she'd asked. This was the uncle who'd told her to forget about studying and get married. He would be angry, he'd call Baba. What she wanted—achieving it meant being selfish, she knew that. Looking back to high school, when all she needed to do was score well on the baccalauréat, it was hard to believe that that had once been her biggest worry.

She forced Uncle's voice to the back of her mind and returned to studying German conjugation. Male nouns needed male pronouns and masculine conjugation of adjectives, female needed feminine, and neuter required neuter. This was one thing about German that was more like Arabic than English. She sped through online flashcards. *Löffel*—spoon—masculine. Correct. *Gabel*—fork—masculine. Wrong. Feminine. Why was *spoon* masculine, *fork* feminine, and *knife* neuter?

She did a hundred words and got seventy-two right. She did another hundred cards. Eighty right. Another hundred. *Der Saft*—the juice (masculine). *Das Wasser*—the water (neuter). *Die Milch*—the milk (feminine). Anna. Struck by an unthinkable, unpredictable, unimaginable catastrophe. She'd googled it on her commute home. Spinal strokes resulting in tetraplegia were not only rare, there was nearly no chance of one occurring in someone Anna's age—which she estimated to be about the same as her own: early twenties, twenty-five at most.

Say there were half a billion women in the world in their twenties; say that five out of a hundred thousand suffered a stroke each year; say that one in two hundred strokes were spinal; say that one percent of spinal strokes resulted in tetraplegia. Anna could be the only woman her age on the entire planet to whom this happened this year. A horrible, life-altering, forever disaster. And yet she'd asked Batul about herself, their brief exchange invigorating.

Here she was, occasionally down, questioning if she was fooling herself that she could pass all these tests. Feeling sorry for herself for being forced to drop out of university and leave Syria. Believing the uncle who had told her she was naive to waste suitcase space on heavy textbooks. "How will those help you? You think there's still a chance you'll become a doctor?" Anna was weeks—*weeks*—into losing the ability to move her arms and her legs, and instead of anger or depression or denial or self-absorption there was a lightness and a smile Batul hadn't seen on anyone since moving here. Not the Germans, who were often cold, and not the Syrians, who were always anxious.

Anna was the only patient who'd asked her her name. Lying there, her head on the pillow, looking at her sideways, her urine draining into a bag. A sharp mind evident in a crisp voice both in German and in English. She couldn't move her body. She couldn't scratch an itch on her face. What could she do when there was no one to talk to? Lie there and think.

Batul took out her phone and found the accessibility settings. She turned on voice control, put the phone on her desk, and rested her hands on her lap. She practiced until she was able to unlock, send a text message, make a call, and get online. If she could manage with her broken, accented German, Anna could certainly do it.

But seeing the screen—that was another thing. Batul pictured the hospital bed, the pillow, Anna talking with her. Anna could rotate her neck but not her shoulders. Batul lay down on her own bed. Laying the phone flat on the sheet was no good. Propping it up vertically didn't work either—too much of the screen was occluded by the pillow.

What she needed was a way to suspend the phone in the air, the correct distance from Anna's eyes, positioned such that she could look at it or look away with small rotations of her neck. She searched online. Yes—a holder with a long, flexible arm was what she wanted, one with a clamp on the other side that could connect to the frame of the hospital bed.

She found one that looked promising for nine euros, plus delivery; a quarter of what the school administrator was demanding for her transcripts; about what she earned in two hours. Good she was working. Back home neither she nor anyone else in the family would have thought twice about spending that kind of money. Here, though, it wouldn't have felt right if she wasn't contributing.

She got Rami to go with her to buy an Amazon gift card from the Späti down the block. When the package arrived, she took the holder from the box and squeezed the alligator clip. Ugh. It felt like those cheap plastic accessories you could buy back home for nothing. She connected it to the side of her bed, twisted the gooseneck arm until the holder was positioned over her head, and snapped in her phone.

In the middle of the night the whole contraption fell on her face. What if—she tasted bile in her throat. What if she were paralyzed, and the phone, the plastic holder, the cable had crashed into her head; she imagined pushing with her tongue, turning her neck left and right to get the charger cable out of her mouth, trying to shake the holder off.

She returned it and ordered one many times more expensive. She bought the gift card on her own and didn't tell anyone that she was spending what she made in two full shifts. The package came. This time it passed her overnight test. She simulated jostling and knocking the holder in the ways she could imagine happening with hospital staff moving around the bed. The clamp stayed connected, the phone stayed in place, the flexible arm held its shape. Il-ghaali tamanuh feeh. What Grandpa taught her about buying ingredients for the shop: Quality is worth the price.

The next day, after her shift, she made her way to Anna's room. If the phone holder was a good idea—it was certainly an obvious one—why didn't the hospital provide one? Or her father, or a friend? It could be against hospital policy. It could hinder recovery —if she got too used to voice control or spent too much time online.

Or safety, like if the charging cable got tangled up with medical equipment.

She opened the door. Her other hand, gripping the holder, was sweating. She'd had one image in her mind at home. Here, in the bright lights of the hospital, Anna in bed—it didn't seem appropriate how much money and planning she'd put into this. They'd spoken once. There was no reason for her to be bringing a gift. She might not want a phone holder. She might not trust her. She might feel that she was imposing, and then feel obligated to keep it attached.

She wiped her palms on her jeans and stepped across the threshold. She looked at the slim form of Anna's body under the sheets, lying there, facing the window. "Frau Werner? Anna?"

"Batul?"

"Yes," Batul switched to English. "Do you have a little time? Is it okay if I come in?"

"Yes, of course, come in."

She walked around to the other side of the bed, keeping the phone holder by her side. "How do you feel today?"

"I'm good." Then a pause. "Well ... to be honest ... not so great. I didn't sleep well, and things were disorganized this morning, and I was delayed for breakfast and therapy, and it all reminded me again how dependent I am on others. I don't get to decide when to leave the room, when to get out of bed, or even when to be washed up. The whole day was like that, and, I don't know, I guess it makes me sad."

"You missed your physical therapy?"

"Most of it. Yes. It's not intentional. It's not because they don't like me. They're overwhelmed. Nurses are out sick. Everything gets behind. Things that are so normal for everyone else—when you can't sleep, you can look at your phone, or stand up, or do whatever you want ... but when I can't sleep, well, I know I will lie in the bed waiting until someone comes and gets me, but at least I know they'll come and give me breakfast, put me in the chair, take me downstairs. When they don't show up, it's so disappointing. I asked them, please, tomorrow, can you make sure I'm on time for my PT appointment, but that's all I can do."

She'd been thinking about her this whole past week; she hadn't understood. "I'm sorry."

"Don't say that. It has nothing to do with you. I'm sorry. I don't mean to burden you with my problems. It's just that—this tiny bit of physical exercise, the therapist pulls on my arm and I pull back, it's so important to me. I used to play sports. I used to run. I can't just lie in bed. Also, each day I skip therapy hurts my chance for recovery." Anna paused, looked at her own body under the covers. "My doctor doesn't believe I'll regain much function, and maybe that's another reason they don't prioritize me in the mornings, they think there's more hope for other patients."

Now she was even less certain about the phone holder. Anna had to focus on her recovery. Yet having access to her phone would restore a modicum of control, and she could research—

"What's that?" Anna was looking at the holder in her hand.

"I ... uhh ... got this for you. I'm not sure you're allowed to have it, or if you would want it. It's a phone holder with a flexible arm and I checked: the bracket on the other side can be mounted to the bed. If you want to try, I can connect it, then you'll be able to see your phone from the pillow, at an angle that should be comfortable for you." She was speaking quickly now, too nervous to stop. "Have you tried voice control yet? I practiced on my phone. I can show you."

Anna looked at the phone holder, then up at her, then swallowed, then began to cry. Batul froze. Anna squeezed her eyes closed. "Thank you," she said. "I wish I could hug you. I'm so grateful. Being able to use my phone ..."

Batul saw light glint off the railing; the whole room felt bright suddenly, sparkling. If this holder wasn't good enough she'd find a better one. She connected the bracket.

"Did you buy it?" Anna asked as Batul tightened the thumbscrew. "I'll pay you back when my parents come with my wallet."

Batul adjusted the arm so the holder was a comfortable distance from Anna's eyes and off to the side. She double and triple checked that it was firm. "Please, allow it to be a gift."

It took Anna five minutes to memorize all the voice commands.

"Do you want me to leave your phone in there? Should I connect the charger?"

"Wait one second." Anna gave instructions. *Open photos. Scroll up. Scroll up. Scroll up. Show grid. Tap 7.* "Take a look."

Batul pivoted the holder so she could see. Anna was on the left. Her arm was around the shoulders of an Indian-looking man, whose other arm was around a tall woman, whose arm was around another man on the far right. All four were smiling, wearing identical purple t-shirts with DDB in big white letters. Behind them a building with the inscription: Dem Wahren, Schönen, Guten. The—or to the?—true, the beautiful, the good.

Batul looked again at Anna in the photo. Her blonde hair was pulled back, her arms toned, and sweat glistened on her forehead; she smiled hugely and looked directly into the lens with bright blue eyes: confident, strong, happy. Batul turned the phone holder around. "Thanks for showing me. I hope tomorrow everything is on schedule."

Later, falling asleep, she couldn't get the image of Anna and her friends out of her mind. Anna was the shortest, but she stood the tallest. The humor and the warmth in her eyes were familiar, and it made Batul feel like anything was possible.

NINE

"C'mon. It'll be fun. You never want to go out."
Half true. Anna likes going out. Just not when it's already after midnight.

"Okay, let's go."

The place is small. Two floors. They're in the basement. Julia's friend is friends with the woman DJing down here and Julia knows everyone. Anna feels like she does too.

The thumping rumbles her stomach. She feels the vibrating floor in her feet. Julia's friend's friend is good. She stops stressing about work. Her self-review—yeah, she'll get it done. People are staring at Julia in her slinky shirt. Her Julia. It doesn't bother her. Julia keeps sweeping her hair back; smiling with a reckless, mischievous exuberance. She watches the DJ, pulsing, headphones over one ear, dark bangs covering her forehead, hands out and upturned, obviously loving this. Anna swivels her head, takes in the LEDs blinking in their trippy pattern. Her hips and feet are moving—it's easy, natural, fun, uninhibited. In the back of her mind—she knows she shouldn't be able to move, and there is joy that she can.

Julia moves closer, wraps her arms around her, puts her hands in the back pockets of Anna's jeans, stares at her. Anna looks back into her green eyes, stops hearing the music, and then looks away. Julia pushes her against the wall. Now her mouth is on hers, and they're making out. She puts her hands on Julia's hips. She loves her. She loves everyone. It feels good. She likes being surrounded by all these living, breathing humans. Smelling the cigarettes, the weed, the alcohol, the sweat, the deodorant, Julia's skin. She pushes her tongue into Julia's mouth, relaxing, letting herself get absorbed in the sensation of Julia's pelvis pressing against her, the music pounding, lights flashing, bodies around them.

Julia's arm is on her shoulder, shaking her, out of rhythm. No. Let's keep dancing. Shake. Shake.

"Anna. Anna."

This kept happening. The sensation of her limbs responding to her brain was still with her. She could feel her legs moving. She could feel Julia's soft skin and the texture of her denim jeans on the tips of her fingers.

That was July. They were out all night. It took her two days to get back into her routine. She told Julia, and swore to herself, no staying out all night again. God. If she'd known then what would happen, she wouldn't have worried about sleep. She would have taken time off from work. She would have spent hours sprinting with Karoline, feeling the explosive power of her calves; she and Melanie would have biked the entire 160-kilometer Berliner Mauerweg, like they'd always talked about; she would have taken the two minutes to follow the advice she'd paid no attention to during orientation, and signed up for the supplemental health insurance—for, like, ten euros a month—so she would now have a private room. She would have climbed out onto their roof and helped Dad replace the broken clay tiles; over and over she would have wrapped herself around naked Julia and felt her convulse; for as long and as often as Mia wanted she would have crawled on all fours, with Mia on her back, then tickled, wiggled, squirmed, and rolled together on the carpeting; she would have pressed her palm to the ceramic in her warm shower and aimed the wand; she would have jogged solo kilometer after kilometer after kilometer.

"Anna."

What time was it?

"We need to empty your bladder."

"Okay."

The nurse lifted the duvet. A few days ago they'd removed the indwelling catheter. She was thrilled, happy to trade the longer interruptions in the night for not having a tube and a bag.

The nurse put her on her back, then opened the package, cleaned her, inserted the catheter, and drained her urine. She never felt the urge to pee, but the tension in her neck and shoulders increased when her bladder was full, and there was relief that it was now empty. The nurse changed gloves, rotated her onto her side, and put pillows behind her back.

Now she was lying on her left side. This was the last rotation of the night, right? She tried to remember how many times she'd been woken up. Yes. This was the last, and facing the door meant she wouldn't be able to see out the window when the sun came up in the morning. She needed to remember to ask to be started on this side tomorrow night—this side, that side, this side.

The nurse pulled the covers back over her. "Are you comfortable?"

"Yes." It was all relative.

She closed her eyes. Another three hours to go until morning. Julia. The dream seemed real. She couldn't stop feeling her hands on Julia's hips, her fingers squeezed between her waist and the denim. Julia's fingers touching the base of her spine under her shirt. That her mind was even going there was a sign of something—a type of psychological recovery. An ache for physical touch.

When Julia visited on Sunday, Anna had been in her wheelchair. Julia leaned forward. Anna tried to kiss her on the lips, but Julia's mouth went to her forehead instead. Anna had reached forward and put her hand on Julia's arm. Julia pulled back, for just a fraction of a second, then let the hand rest. If she could only move her fingers—she knew—without that, it must feel impersonal, like a paintbrush, or maybe more rigid, one of those plastic beach-toy rakes. She wanted to put her hand on Julia's hip. She wanted to feel her skin. She wanted to go back to Saturday mornings when she stayed over at Julia's, when she would get up to go running and Julia would pull her back down, "No, stay in bed, you're making me feel guilty."

Stop! Sleep! Eins, zwei, drei ... Counting sheep wasn't doing it. Something else. Counting the neon tetras in Stefan's aquarium? An impossible task with so many swimming in all directions. Did counting animals, imaginary or otherwise, ever help anyone anywhere fall asleep? Hard to believe. A desperate invention of some shepherd in the Middle Ages, annoyed with his son, waiting to get things on with Frau Schäfer on the straw floor of their single-room house, bleating from the attached pen.

"I can't fall asleep."

"Count sheep, my lad."

She needed something that would truly occupy her brain. A math problem. Multiplying matrices. Let's say a two-by-three matrix with one, two, three in the first row and—

Back in calculus, in twelfth grade, she was study partners with Mirko, the best math student. They were trying to calculate the derivative of an equation and there were a lot of steps—the chain rule needed to be applied twice, the quotient rule, something like that. He was sitting there working it through in his head. She was taking the common-sense approach of writing the steps out with pencil and paper, being careful, avoiding sloppy errors. They got different answers. They checked. He was wrong. She was right.

"Why are you so stubborn?" she'd asked him. "You get wrong answers. I can't see your work. What are you proving? It's pointless."

Now she was in the one situation where it wasn't pointless. She didn't feel old, but was she too old to get good at mental math? All these things she was so fast at—typing, texting, googling, programming—they were out of reach. Voice was a layer of molasses between her and the digital world.

There was that physicist. What was his name? The one from England. Perfect example. If she could google, she'd type *paralyzed british physicist* and know in a second. Her phone was on the window side, plus, she wouldn't talk to her phone at this hour—it might wake Ingrid. (If only Ingrid showed her the same consideration. If only she would talk with her at all.) The scientist—he did physics in his mind. Was he born paralyzed? Or did he, also as an adult, need to figure out how to think without paper?

She'd been taught that the way to think was to write. She would have an idea, say at work. It would be squishy, fuzzy. Maybe good. Maybe bad. Then she would start typing it out—what problem was she solving? How would the idea solve it? What else had she considered?—and only then would the idea crystalize, or fall apart—that was okay too. Thinking was writing, writing was typing, typing was fingers. Thinking without typing was like navigating a corn maze without legs, not impossible, but—

Please, brain, stop! She needed to sleep. Her body needed the rest.

What was a body? Some strange form that evolved over four billion years. Disgusting if you thought about it. Hairy, smelly, FRAGILE, needy—shelter, food, clothing. Evolution's least bad option for collecting energy for the brain, for giving the brain—the self—a way to reproduce.

Messy organic stuff. No matter how often she thought about it, it still astonished her, filled her with awe, that neural networks could now recognize images. She'd watched Mia learn her first words, point to objects, and thought it the exclusive domain of the human mind to spot something in the grass and label it: a box turtle, or a mud turtle, or a toppled-over soup bowl, or an umbrella. If sixty million numbers in a bunch of matrices multiplied together could be as good as the brain at image recognition, what would be possible with six hundred million numbers, or six billion?

You could tell yourself you were a machine, that the brain was the thing, but you'd never believe it. You couldn't not care about the body. It was wired in. Julia's smile. The way she pushed her hair back. The way she moved. Her fingers. It shouldn't matter. In her present condition, conversation needed to suffice. Humor. Moments when ideas crashed into each other. But her mind always came back to the physical. Feeling Julia's arms around her, their lips pressed together, her scent.

Focus on matrix math. Settle your mind. A two-by-three matrix. One times two, plus two times three, plus three times four, twenty, goes in top left, then ...

She opened her eyes. The far wall was bright. Gray limbs swayed on the white bedding covering Ingrid. *Please let everything happen on time this morning.*

When the food service worker came, she downed the nutella-smeared bread and drank her milk in double time.

The wall grew brighter. No nurse. She clenched her jaw. Twenty minutes. Come on. Shit. Another day short of staff? Or where "unforeseen difficulties" with other patients put her needs last? Another five minutes. She could *request nurse,* but hesitated. Last time the woman who picked up had said immediately that they hadn't forgotten about her, told her to be patient, clearly annoyed. Another five minutes. Come on! Steps. Click. The door was opening. Batul.

"Good morning."

"Good morning," Anna replied, disappointed. She took a deep breath and, more friendly, "Isn't this early for you?"

"A little. I came by to say hello and ... I was thinking about what you said about getting to physical therapy on time ... and I wanted to check. You should be in your chair by now, no?"

Exhausted from the restless night, powerless, ignored. Except by this one person. Quieter now, "You're right. I should be in my chair. I don't know where the nurse is. I'm going to miss PT again."

Batul turned around, looked out the door. "I'll go check for you."

She returned. "Two nurses called in sick, so they're running behind. They said it may be a while still."

Come on. This was basic capacity planning. At DDB, when they had an outage, even a blip of fifteen seconds, they owed reports to the boss, had to get to the root cause and make sure it couldn't happen again. Was the head of the hospital aware that a patient in his facility had missed PT on two of the last eleven days? Was he losing sleep over it? Of course not. She looked at Batul. She breathed in, breathed out. "I appreciate you checking." Batul frowned. "It's not your fault."

"Would you like me to wait with you? Until my shift starts?"

Anna nodded, feeling strange about taking this near-stranger's free time with such desperate gratitude. Batul lowered herself into the chair, gracefully, the opposite of how Anna used to plop herself down. They stayed in silence for a moment, Anna's pulse still heightened but slowing. She noticed the shape of Batul's fingers on the armrest, saw that a blister was forming on the side of her middle finger.

"Where are you from?—" she asked at the same moment that Batul began, "How did the stroke—" They both laughed, and Batul gestured for Anna to try again.

"Where are you from? How'd you end up in Berlin? And working here? I'm not trying to pry. Only if you're comfortable talking about it."

"I'm from Syria."

Syria. Violence, civil war, the refugee crisis, ISIS, chemical weapons. It'd been in the news for years, she thought, one of those subjects she felt she should know more about, but it never stuck with her the way technical stuff did. Like she remembered her shock, in the fall of 2012, when a convolutional neural network won the ImageNet competition, but she couldn't say for sure if the trouble in Syria started while she was still at school or later, during university.

"From Aleppo."

She'd heard of it, but wasn't sure if it was a state or a city—maybe it was the region that ISIS took over, which felt like something she should know. Had Batul fled from ISIS? At one point in seventh grade she could label all the countries of the Middle East on a map, but now she was a little fuzzy. Damascus was the capital, and Syria would have been part of the Ottoman empire—

"It's our largest city. In the northwest, near Turkey, and famous since ancient times. It's nearly the oldest continuously inhabited city in the world, settled thousands of years before Rome. We can trace my family back for six generations there. My grandfather—"

A nurse came in. "Good morning, Frau Werner. Let's get you into your chair."

Batul rose quickly, moved her chair back to the corner, and stood against the wall. The nurse looked at her closely, then tilted her head toward the door. "May I stay," Batul asked Anna, in English, "to watch how the transfer is done?"

Anna was still in her sleeping gown, so the nurse would need to undress her. She didn't want Batul to see her naked, or see how her limbs were manipulated like dead weights.

The nurse, who had evidently understood the English, answered for her. "No. It's not appropriate for housekeeping staff to be present."

Why did the nurse get to decide? "It's okay with me," Anna interjected. "I'd like you to stay."

TEN

Door, window, door, window ... Last night, she'd asked the nurse to start her on her left side. She'd slept well. Now, after breakfast, she watched a blurry squirrel scurry along the trunk, then jump, the thin branch oscillating up and down from the sudden weight. This little guy was fearless. Innate? Some squirrels were born risk-takers? All squirrels? Or it was more like he'd taken big leaps in the past, missed, figured out he could land on his feet, gotten more and more daring—

"Good morning, Anna."

Batul! Batul walked around the bed. She was wearing a purple hijab today.

"I like your—" Maybe hijab wasn't the right term. "Your scarf. That's a pretty shade."

Batul placed her hand over her heart.

"Has your shift started?"

"Soon. Did the nurse come yet? I thought, if not, I could ... I mean only if you're comfortable with this ... I could help you transfer to your chair and bring you down to physical therapy so you won't be late."

"I ..."

Out of the corner of her eye she saw the squirrel, the effortless, coordinated movement of its four limbs. In this place, where people were well-meaning but overwhelmed, where even the nurses and therapists who she knew cared could forget about her in their sea of other patients, here was Batul. She felt a lump in her throat.

But would she know what to do? Anna needed to protect her body. She needed to be paranoid. *Ever vigilant.* A wrinkle in a sheet pressing into her, a crease in her gown under her weight in the wheelchair, friction on her skin—she couldn't take anything for granted. Mia had dropped a tray on her foot and Dr. Eckert insisted on an x-ray to confirm no bones were fractured. The staff here were trained in this stuff.

"I'm grateful that you're thinking about me. It means so much more to me than you can imagine. Only ... I don't know if it's such a good idea. I have to be transferred to the chair in a very careful way. If you don't do it correctly it could hurt me, and with the way my body works I wouldn't know, and also, could you get in trouble with the hospital? We're real rule followers in Germany—there might be some insurance-related prohibition against non-medical staff doing medical work ..."

Batul's face dropped. "I didn't think about that. I watched carefully yesterday. After, when you left the room, I wrote the procedure down."

The *procedure?* "What did you write?"

She read from her phone. "One: Wheel the chair next to the bed leaving a quarter meter of space. Two: Remove blanket and pillows. Three ..."

Listening, looking up from her pillow, Anna began to smile. Batul had paid attention to every detail, even ones Anna herself had never noticed or couldn't notice. "You're like—I forget the name—a scientist famous for making careful observations, who figured out that germs cause disease—"

Dimples appeared. "Robert Koch."

"Yes. Koch!" He was someone they learned about in Syria? Screw hospital rules. She was an adult. She could decide.

"Okay, let's do it this way. If a nurse comes, I'll say that we're friends and you're helping me out before your shift. I'm worried that if you're moving a patient you'll get reported."

Batul's dimples disappeared, replaced with a nervous expression.

"Maybe better to wait for the nurse," Anna quickly retreated.

But Batul bit her lower lip. "No, I want you to make it to PT on time."

Batul went into the bathroom. The faucet turned on and off. She came back and rolled the wheelchair to next to the bed and locked the wheels. She removed the pillows, exactly as the nurses did, until Anna was lying flat on her back. Then—

"That's not allowed," Ingrid, in German. "It's only for the nurses."

This she noticed? She was going to make a fuss? Her obliviousness had been an act. She looked at Batul. "Don't worry about her."

"Are you sure?"

She nodded. Batul put one hand under Anna's left knee, and the other hand on her left foot, and slid her foot back along the bed until the knee bent up. She did the same thing with the right leg and now both of Anna's knees were peaked like small mountains on the bed, held by the friction of her feet against the sheet.

Next, Batul lifted her right arm and laid it on her stomach, and positioned her left arm along her side, at the edge of the mattress. She reached forward and rolled her onto her left side, letting her legs dangle off the edge of the bed. Now she put one hand on her hip, and the other behind her shoulder, and pulled her up into a sitting position, and, supporting her, sat herself down on the bed so they were next to each other, their heads almost touching. They stayed like that until Anna caught her breath.

Batul, still sitting, lifted both of Anna's legs and put them over her own right leg. She wrapped her arms around Anna's chest, held her tight, and with Anna's full weight on her right thigh, pivoted her right foot on the floor—toe-heel-toe-heel—until Anna was positioned over the seat of the chair. Very, very gently, Batul lowered her down. Anna inhaled. Exhaled. Steadied herself.

The oak tree was vertical. The window was vertical. Batul, across from her, sitting on the bed, was vertical. She could speak with her while looking at her the normal way people looked at each other. Such a simple thing made all the difference. Made her feel human. Made Batul seem like a friend. And she saw now, looking straight at Batul, that she was exceptionally, breathtakingly beautiful. She worried she was staring and shifted her gaze to the window, then back to Batul. Dark eyes; a long, elegant nose; an intelligent, oval-shaped face; high, prominent cheekbones.

"Yesterday you started to say something about your grandfather in ..." The city that was older than Rome. "In Syria."

"Yes, my grandfather owns a famous sweets shop in the middle of Aleppo. You ask anyone from there and they will know it: Nawwar Halab. Even now, in the war, it's still operating."

Plate glass windows decorated with lollipops, bright lights, shelves lined with chocolates, plastic bins full of gummy bears. Hard to picture that coexisting with fighting. "Sweets like candy?"

"No, I didn't mean candy. Arabic sweets. More like pastries, I suppose. Like baklawa."

"Is that the same as baklava?"

"Yes. Similar. A different flavor and texture than the Greek type. And mabroumeh. You know what that is?"

She shook her head.

Batul formed a circle with her thumb and forefinger. "Pistachios wrapped in shredded phyllo dough, fried, soaked in syrup, sliced into round disks. Also, this is to die for," Batul reached across the short distance between them and clasped her upper arm, "knafeh with cheese—"

She felt her skin flush. Panic in Batul's eyes. "Are you having trouble breathing? Did I put you in the chair wrong? I'll get a nurse!"

"No, no." Her annoyingly pale skin. She could feel the color draining already. "I'm fine. I want to hear more."

"Let me get a nurse." Batul got up.

"Batul! I'm fine. Really. Tell me about your grandfather's shop. Is it safe for him, with the war?"

Batul sat back down on the edge of the bed and looked at her. Anna smiled. Batul seemed reassured, then, not answering her question, "My father also worked in the business. My uncle too. He started a second shop. My brother and me, though, we are more academic, and—"

"Is he here too?"

"Yes. Rami. He was studying computer engineering, in his third year. And I was in the first year of my studies, first of six, to become a doctor ..."

A doctor. Then a thread of doubt. She'd begun to think that they had a connection that transcended her paralysis, that Batul was the first person she'd met post-stroke who saw her as something other than a patient. But a doctor, or future doctor. Anna wasn't a specimen.

"... You know about the Arab Spring?"

She nodded. "Yes. But not in much detail."

"That's when we left. In 2011. To Turkey for almost three years and then to here."

"What happened in 2011?" She had so many questions.

"I'll take you downstairs and then I need to start my shift."

The next morning, Batul came early again. Anna was facing the door this time and noticed, as Batul crossed the room, that she had an almost gliding gait, like she was floating, the opposite of her own more frenetic, harried way of moving through space.

"Did you continue with medical school in Turkey?"

"In Turkey—no." Batul looked down. "I tried a hundred different ways. I lost so much time. I need to start over. First I need to learn German, take tests, achieve the C1 level, then I'll apply."

"Sollen wir Deutsch sprechen? Würde dir das helfen?"

"*Ja,*" Batul answered, and continued in her halting German, "That will be very helpful to me."

"Which exams exactly?" This was something she could do. Where she could be of genuine assistance. That went beyond herself and her rehabilitation. Her mind was racing. She'd look up practice tests on her phone and learn the material. She'd ask Melanie for tips for Batul—she'd had a job at a test prep center during uni.

"Are you married?" Batul asked her the next morning. Now they were speaking German, with English words where necessary.

"No," Anna said. Of all her close school and uni friends, only Melanie was already married. Not to mention that, for her, it would technically be a registered life partnership—a level of commitment she wasn't ready for and had never discussed with Julia. "I'm glad. I'd want my partner to choose this ... situation."

Batul gave a slight, slow-motion shake of her head.

"I mean, someone should decide if they want to be with someone in my situation. Not have it forced on them, you know, because they took a vow, to be loyal in good times and in bad—in guten wie in schlechten Zeiten."

She was talking a good game. But with Julia—she hadn't been able to bring herself to say the words she'd rehearsed in her mind. *I don't want to be a burden. I don't want you to feel obligated to stay with me. My paralysis is showing no signs of going away. Do you want to move on? I'll understand if you do.*

"I see," Batul said.

"And what about you?" People got married younger there, right? She looked at Batul's hand. No ring. How universal a custom were wedding rings, even?

"Oh, no, no, I'm not, although by my age it's not uncommon ..."

Her age—if university started there around eighteen, and in the spring of 2011 she was finishing her first year, she would be around

2011, 2012, 2013, 2014—nineteen, twenty, twenty-one, twenty-two—so two years younger.

"... My parents were approached by another family on behalf of their son while we were living in Turkey. They were also from Aleppo. I told my parents I needed to focus on my studies. They didn't put on any pressure, and it didn't go any further, thank goodness."

"How did you two know each other?"

"I didn't know him! He saw me in Gaziantep, in the neighborhood there where we were staying. He knew, of course, of my grandfather's shop, and it turned out our families had distant friends in common. I knew only that he was involved in some business, something with renting cars."

"So this wasn't even like an arranged marriage where the parents organize a suitable match? This guy saw you, found you attractive, went home, and told his parents: go talk to her parents and propose marriage?"

"Yes. It was his mother who came—maybe not exactly to propose marriage. Only to say that he was interested. Then, if we agreed, he and I would have gone for coffee or tea and talked, with a third person there, too. We would do this a few times, then see how we both felt. My family would never force me. That would be old-fashioned."

Another morning, two weeks later, Batul was accompanying her down to PT. "I looked at your company's website ..."

Anna doubted Batul would be able to make any more sense of all the marketing jargon than she herself had back when she was prepping for her interview.

"... I don't understand what it means by *signals* or why you send them to a *platform*."

This was Anna's second day using the electric wheelchair. Her wrist rested in a U-shaped throttle on the right and she drove by moving her arm. Now, instead of trying to talk with someone pushing her from behind, she could have a conversation, side by side. She stopped and turned her head. "You're actually interested?"

"Yes."

A willing audience. She nudged her throttle forward and dove in. "Let me ... let's try this: You know how there are all these devices in the hospital to monitor patients? Heart rate, let's say."

Batul nodded.

"Suppose you wanted to, every single second, take a patient's heart rate, and record it in a central place. And now imagine doing this not only for one patient but for every patient, and not only for pulse but for temperature, blood oxygen, whatever information you can get."

She paused and looked over. Batul was slowly nodding. "You could trigger an alarm when a patient's heartbeat gets too low."

"Exactly. And do what's called machine learning—"

"Machine learning?"

"Automatically finding patterns in data. That's the part I work on. I'll come back to it."

They got into the elevator and Batul pushed zero.

"Okay, so our company's software, it's a central system—a *platform*—and our customers send all their information—the *signals*—to it. Not for medical. For industrial equipment, commercial vehicles, wind farms, water treatment facilities, things like that." She thought about Julia's demo prep for Caterpillar. "Like, take a modern tractor. It's got all these parts—an engine, hydraulics—and those parts have parts. Let's say you monitor all this stuff—the sound of the engine, its temperature, rotations of the crankshaft, and a gazillion other things you and I would never think of. Unless you also happen to be an expert on tractors?" Batul did seem to collect a lot of random knowledge.

"Tractors?" Batul shook her head as they got out of the elevator, and was now walking so slowly that Anna was having a hard time moving the throttle gently enough to not pull ahead of her.

"So you take all this information, across the entire global fleet of tractors your company manufactures, and send it all to our platform, and now you can see everything centrally, and catch that an engine is failing months before the tractor breaks down."

They were almost at the gym. "What about the machine learning?"

Once, in tenth or eleventh grade, a friend's older brother who was home visiting his family for the weekend had mentioned coding. She'd peppered him with a million questions. Batul reminded her of herself. "That's the fun part."

Anna could talk about ML and AI all day. Her favorite course at uni was on random forests. Where to start? "First, in case I'm confusing things, I want to clarify: the *machine* in machine learning is the computer, not like the tractor. Second, so this makes sense, let's go back in time. A decade ago, when DDB was founded, our customers created rules by hand. Like you make a rule that if the heart rate drops below fifty beats per minute, sound the alarm. Simple, but not so easy to set the right threshold—I learned that in the ICU when I kept getting woken up by false alarms.

"Now getting way more complicated, let's talk about how to create a rule that would give an early warning that a tractor's engine is going to fail. Forgetting about the computer for a second, could a human tell?"

They were at the gym. Batul closed her eyes. "I'm imagining I'm on my tractor. There's an unusual vibration. I remember from the last time my engine failed, many years ago, it was preceded by a similar vibration. I rule out other factors because I'm not doing anything out of the ordinary like picking up a heavy load." She opened her eyes. "It's like a doctor making a diagnosis, a combination of intuition and logic and process of elimination."

"Exactly! Now take the human out of it. How are you supposed to write a rule for all that? There's a strange vibration. Okay. What constitutes strange? Maybe it's strange if the strength of the shaking is two standard deviations from the mean, if it persists for ten seconds, and the tractor isn't moving or lifting a load. Play that out across a few signals, not to mention hundreds or thousands, and you'll see it's impossible to, by hand, write a rule that codifies the intuition of your human driver. Either the system would fail to detect problems, or it would be crying wolf all the time. Enter machine learning. We give the computer lots and lots of historical data, and tell it when engines failed in the past, and it figures it out. At least that's the promise."

"That's what you do?"

"Yes. I mean, a small piece of it. The system my team works on lets our customers run their machine learning models."

Batul was staring in the direction of the aerotrim machine on the other side of the gym. It looked like something used to train astronauts. "It's so interesting."

"What?"

"I was just thinking that machine learning could have caught your stroke before you became paralyzed."

"Believe me, I've had that thought many times."

ELEVEN

Four years earlier, Aleppo

The bell on the door chimed. Batul looked up from the tray of mabroumeh, the light reflecting off the glistening pistachios, and watched an older man with a cane step inside and approach the counter. "Abu Ali," the man said to Grandpa, "as-salamu 'alaikum."

Grandpa leaned across the counter and pressed his right cheek to the man's, then his left. "Wa 'alaikum as-salam."

"I see you've brought your granddaughter into the business," the man said, glancing briefly at her.

Grandpa chortled. "I wish! The daughter of my son is studying medicine at the university. She's today helping out only because I wanted to see her."

She'd been thrilled when Grandpa asked her to help. It got her out of going to Uncle's, where she would've been trapped with Mama, her two aunties, her two cousins, and her other cousin's wife, talking in circles, with no way to avoid being pulled into the conversation, and, because Mama had been so upset last time, she wouldn't have been able to disappear upstairs and read. Here she'd spent the morning in the back making mabroumeh and baklawa, and now, standing behind the counter, the chatter from the packed tables blending into white noise, she could think.

"Medicine! So you'll have a doctor in the family?"

"Yes. We knew it since she was nine years old ..."

Please, Grandpa, do not tell this story.

"It was an unusually warm day in October ..."

She didn't remember what the weather was like that day and she was sure Grandpa didn't either. He was always changing the details anyway.

"The little one was in her classroom. Their teacher, Mrs. Halawi—she is a long-time customer, like you, my friend—was writing on the chalkboard and had her back to the students. Like a car crash, from a desk on the other side of the classroom, a boy, Abu Farid's grandson—What is his name again?"

"Majid," she said.

"Yes. This poor little boy—well, these days of course there's nothing little about him, have you seen him? Like a bull—the boy fell out of his chair and started convulsing. All the kids froze. Except for my granddaughter—she jumped up, ran over, crouched down next to him, put her palm under his head, and called out to Mrs. Halawi. Mrs. Halawi turned from the chalkboard and shouted for someone to run and get the principal."

"And what happened?" the old man, now excited, asked Grandpa.

She answered for him. "He was fine. The seizure was brief. He was back in his chair and Mrs. Halawi kept going with the lesson before the principal even got there."

"Yes!" Grandpa said. "But then, after class, Mrs. Halawi asked how she knew what to do. She figured that someone in our family had seizures. No, Batul told her, she didn't know anything about seizures. She was acting on instinct, protecting the boy's head because it was banging on the floor. 'You should be a doctor,' Mrs. Halawi told her."

Yes, that she remembered.

Grandpa held his hand out at chest level, a reference, she assumed, to Mrs. Halawi's short stature. "That day Mrs. Halawi made a special trip to the shop to tell me, 'Your granddaughter is so smart. So caring. She's destined to be a doctor.' She still brings it up. Last time she was here she told me how proud she was when she heard Batul was accepted to study medicine."

The story was more or less accurate, at least she thought, considering it happened when she was in fourth grade and had been repeated so many times since. To her it illustrated these things that she knew about herself: she was calm under pressure and she was competent. However, she wasn't any more or less caring than anyone else, she certainly didn't consider herself to be an especially warm person (although later, in Germany, everyone would say that even the coldest Syrian was warmer than the warmest German), and her interest in medicine had nothing to do with Mrs. Halawi.

Medicine was because she liked science. Chemistry had been her favorite subject in high school. She loved reading books—mostly in English—by doctors and scientists. She was proud of how much modern medicine was influenced by the work of Muslim physicians who lived a thousand years ago, people like al-Zahrawi whose encyclopedia had been the world's most important surgical text for half a millennium. And, while she hid it, she was competitive. Medicine required the highest score. She'd managed a 238 on the baccalauréat, high enough to study in Damascus, but Baba had insisted she stay in Aleppo.

"Can I also get a slice of knafeh?" the old man asked. Batul put it on a plate for him, followed him as he shuffled with his cane over to an empty table, pulled a chair out for him, set the plate down, and poured the syrup. Just as she slipped back behind the counter, the door opened again.

Yaman. She'd noticed him earlier, smoking shisha with a bunch of guys at the cafe across the street. His height made him easy to spot. When they were little, she, Rami, and Yaman used to play together.

Now he was, like Rami, two years ahead of her at university, doing computer engineering.

"Batul," he said. Grandpa, helping another customer, looked over.

"Yaman."

He touched the counter. "How are your classes going? Medicine, right?"

She was surprised he knew. "Good. Busy."

Grandpa looked over again. Yaman nodded at him, then studied the trays on the counter. "This is what the hajjah asked me to pick up …"

He smiled, and she assumed by *the hajjah* he was talking about his mother.

"… Mabroumeh—half a kilo. And a kilo of the baklawa. And asabe—half a kilo."

She used a metal spatula and her fingers to transfer the sweets to the scale and then into a box. She folded over the lid and knotted a length of red and white twine over the top.

"Are you thinking about surgery?"

She laughed, to be polite. Grandpa turned his head and stared.

Yaman took the box from the counter. "Please say hello to your parents. They are well? We miss them. Tell them to visit."

Three months later she and her classmate Sarah exited the Faculty of Medicine's main building, blinking, into the sun. Sarah was saying something about Tahrir Square and Mubarak, and Batul was hearing the words, but her mind was still on abdominal walls and subcutaneous tissue.

"Batul." The subcutis consisted mostly of adipose connective tissue. "Batul!"

She looked up. Yaman was leaning against a column.

"Yaman. What are you doing here?"

"Waiting for someone."

"Ah." She introduced Sarah.

"Can you believe what happened in Tunisia?" Sarah asked Yaman. "It's impossible. Is it real?"

Yaman shook his head and Batul half listened to him and Sarah talking about how Ben Ali had fled to Saudi Arabia, and then about the demonstrations in Egypt.

"Well," Batul said, when Yaman's friend still hadn't shown up, "it was good running into you. Please give my best to your parents."

"Are you in a rush? Can we talk for another minute?"

"Uhh, sure."

"I need to get home," Sarah said, and kissed her on both cheeks.

Yaman wrapped his hand around the back of his neck, looked like he was collecting his thoughts. A hand was, say, one percent of the body's total surface area, so over a hundred million cells in the epidermis of that one hand alone, except a hand was less fatty than— "With Tunisia, with what's happening in Egypt, who knows what could happen here. I'm thinking we should exchange numbers, you know, in case we need to get in touch, in case I need to make sure you're safe, or you need to reach me."

It was a nice gesture. Good of him to worry about her. But if she put him in her phone, or if he called her, Rami would definitely notice. "I'm not—"

"You're worried about Rami, right?"

She nodded. "Who is this?" Rami was always asking.

"A classmate."

Since the start of the first semester, she'd been adding everyone to her phone to coordinate study groups. When it was a female name the questioning stopped there. For male names it turned into, "What's his family name? Is he religious? Where did he go to high school? Why were you talking to him?"

Oddly, Yaman smiled, as if he wanted them to have this secret. "I understand. Put me in with a different name."

What was that smile? Romantic interest? She supposed he would make a good match—religious, educated, handsome. It couldn't be that though. He was Rami's friend and the families, though not exactly close, were acquainted. He would know that she intended to finish her degree first and that would be another five years. Plus, if he were interested, he wouldn't play games, he would ask his mother to talk to Mama.

No, she didn't need to worry that he would interpret exchanging numbers as anything other than what he said—a precaution. Because maybe he was right, just in case, in an emergency, they might need to contact each other. She would add him as Yasmin. She pulled her phone out of her pocket, unlocked it, and looked up, waiting.

In April, she and Rami were studying at the dining table when his phone rang. She looked at the display. Omar. Rami answered.

"Come with me to University Square," she could hear Omar's loud voice.

"Why?" Rami asked.

"There's going to be a wedding. Wear a scarf."

"What?"

She looked at Rami and shook her head. Then he got it.

"Everyone's gonna be there," Omar said.

She shook her head again. Rami looked past her at the wall, then at his watch. "I'll be outside your place in ten."

"Don't worry," Rami told her, "Aleppo isn't Daraa. I'll be careful. I'll keep my face covered."

She didn't argue because he wouldn't listen. And she felt the pull too. What had happened in Egypt could happen here. It would take numbers and conviction, and Aleppo had up to now been so quiet—which told the world *what*? That Syria's largest city supported the status quo? At any rate, he was right, Aleppo wasn't Daraa. "I'm coming with you."

There were a lot of people. Everyone was standing around. The tall man scanning the crowd—he could be secret police. A guy around her age had his phone lens pointed at her, and she turned away. She looked to see if she knew anyone—because if she could recognize them, they might be able to recognize her. Her whole face was wrapped so only her eyes showed, but still, she was exposed. She moved closer to Rami and Omar.

Nobody was demonstrating exactly. They were shuffling, like they weren't quite sure what they were doing here. Even Omar was acting timid. That photo she'd seen of a teenager in Tahrir Square with the animated face, pumping his arm—she didn't feel that at all. Her hands were by her sides, as were Rami's, as were Omar's. Everyone here had spent months watching protests on TV, they knew what to do, but to actually do it …

Ending corruption, introducing democracy, rule of law, free press. In the abstract she was for all of that. But did she want democracy more than she wanted to become a doctor? Did she want an end to corruption more than she wanted Grandpa's shop to keep thriving? Did she need there to be a free press when she already had the freedom to read books, to pray, to think? Everyone here was doing some version of that calculation. Things in Aleppo weren't—

"Freedom!" It was shouted, in a scratchy, straining voice by a man, his lined face uncovered, standing not far from her. Then others started shouting, "Freedom." They must have been thinking—if an old man has the courage, why not them? She thought *freedom* in her head, then she said it aloud, quietly, in a whisper. Goosebumps on her arms. Now she said it louder, in cadence with everyone else. "Freedom. Freedom. Freedom." Now she was screaming. Now they were marching. Now everyone was shouting. "Freedom. Freedom."

She'd never been so much part of a group. These were her sisters and brothers, her mothers and fathers. This was her country. These were her fellow citizens. "Freedom! Dignity! Allahu Akbar! Freedom! Dignity! Allahu Akbar!" She was one with the others. She moved without thought. She was not afraid. Her voice was strong. She was alive. She thrust her arm into the sky, pumping her fist, exactly like she'd seen on TV, shouting, insane, no consideration for consequence. "Freedom! Dignity! Allahu Akbar! Freedom—"

"The Shabbiha are coming." Word flew through the crowd. Her chest tightened, she lowered her fist. It started shaking. The chanting stopped. Everyone dispersed. She followed Rami and Omar. They walked out of the square, melted back into the streets, headed home. Judgment returned. What had she done? She'd been alive. She could have been arrested. She wanted to feel that way again. She'd never risk it.

One evening in May, close to the end of the second semester of her first year, she was at home reviewing material for the Clinical Anatomy final when Baba got a call from the father of one of Rami's friends. Rami had been demonstrating near the Faculty of Mechanical Engineering. He might have been beaten. He might have been arrested by security forces. He might have been forced onto a bus. Nothing was clear. Baba tried Rami's phone. He didn't answer.

"I'll go to campus and look for him," she told Baba. "He could be hurt."

"No. Absolutely not. Do not leave the house."

"La hawla wa la quwwata illa billah," Mama kept repeating under her breath, crying, praying: There is no power and no strength except with Allah.

Batul went back to her room. She didn't have Omar's number. She did have Yaman's, in her phone as Yasmin. She hesitated for only a second and then dialed. Ring. Ring. Ring. No answer. She waited two minutes and tried again. No answer.

Facebook. It had been unblocked in February and overnight everyone was on it. She looked at her feed. There was nothing about a demonstration near the Faculty of Mechanical Engineering. She went to Rami's profile and started scrolling through his timeline.

A photo of the old green, white, and black flag—liked. What was he thinking?

Bashar! Time to leave!—liked. Careless. Stupid!

A cartoon with six squares. In the top left there was a less-than-flattering drawing of Ben Ali standing behind a lectern with the Tunisian flag, his palms open in a conciliatory gesture, the words "I understood you ..." printed above his head. In the next square, Mubarak, standing behind a podium with the Egyptian flag: "Egypt is not Tunisia!" Then Gaddafi, then a mustachioed cartoon of the king of Bahrain, then Saleh—"Yemen is not Bahrain!"—and in the last square, Bashar, drawn with a rectangular head, a long neck, a wisp of a mustache, and the caption: "Syria is not Yemen!" Liked.

A post Rami himself wrote about how to get around firewalls.

Her finger shook on the trackpad. The posts were right there, under his real name. They would find his profile. It was evidence. Yes, lots of people were liking similar posts, but lots of people hadn't just been arrested.

She went to his room and looked on his desk, searching for a scrap of paper tucked away in a corner, opening drawers, feeling for anything taped under the desk. She raked through his shelves, flipped through the pages of books. She tried his birthday. A combination of his birthday and her birthday. Combinations of Manchester and United. Nothing worked, and then she got locked out.

Baba and Mama were in the kitchen, Baba on the phone with Grandpa.

"Did Rami ever say anything about hiding his passwords?" She couldn't imagine.

"Please, don't distract your father."

She tried Yaman again. No answer.

Rami wasn't the first person in this situation. She googled. Yes—this could work.

She reported his profile for abuse. Then she texted her classmates and everyone else she knew and asked them to report it to Facebook too, and asked them to ask their friends to do the same.

She kept refreshing. How many reports could it take? Refresh. She texted everyone again. After nine she took a break and did the ritual washing before prayer.

"Let's skip," Baba said to her, still on the phone with Grandpa.

"No, not now of all times."

He hung up.

She stood on her mat behind Baba, next to Mama, and they prayed Isha. After, she refreshed again. She fell asleep, head on her arms on the desk. Hours later she woke. She hit refresh. Gone.

There were lots of gifts. Grandpa talked to friends and friends of friends. He talked with a long-time customer who had connections. This was a misunderstanding. Rami was young. He didn't know what he was saying. She heard Baba and Mama whispering. In mere days they had drained all their savings and borrowed large sums from relatives. Baba was called to an office of the Amn Aldawla—state security—and lectured by an official. He was called to a different office. He gave more gifts. He explained over and over that it was a mistake. That they were loyal.

Six days after the arrest, they heard a knock on the door. Rami stood outside, his face blotched, one eye swollen, wearing the same clothes as the day he was taken.

"My son. My son." Mama held his face in her hand, kissed his forehead and cheeks over and over, hugged him, cried, stroked his arm.

"Baba, please pay the taxi driver."

Rami borrowed Baba's phone.

"Who are you calling?" Baba asked.

"Yaman. He was with me at the demonstration. I don't know if he was arrested."

She didn't tell Rami that she'd tried him or that he'd never called back.

"It just keeps ringing," Rami said. Rami called Yaman's father. Yes, Yaman was missing. Yaman's father had been talking to everyone, but so far no one knew where he was.

Rami collapsed on the bed. "We were chanting, but it was peaceful. Then out of nowhere these thugs appear. A big guy with a shaved head is next to me. He yells, 'Bashar rabbak,' knocks me to the ground, kicks my shin with his boot ..."

Mama put her hands over her eyes. She put her arm through Mama's and held her hand.

"Then a skinny soldier screams at me to get up. He puts a hood on me. I hear a diesel engine. The soldier grabs my arm, makes me walk, and then I'm stepping up into a bus. The soldiers on the bus are slapping me and punching me and then they push me down into a seat. 'Hold your wrists together under your legs.' Hands reach down through my thighs, click, click, click, they use a cable tie, so tight, I'm bent over, my head almost touching my knees ..."

Sitting on the bed, he showed them, putting his hands under his legs, bending forward. Mama walked out of the room. Rami kept talking. "As the bus starts moving, I hear the boots of soldiers in the aisle, and then them screaming and cursing over the accelerating engine. 'Bedkon hurryeh ma haiki? You want freedom? We will show you what freedom means, you sons of bitches!'"

"Did they tell you where you were going?" Batul asked. "Did they say why?"

A dry laugh from Rami. "No. Hatred. That's what I could hear. The soldiers sounded young, with coastal accents."

This was her country? They asked no questions? They beat people? Her brother? A student of computer engineering? These were not the Syrians she knew. Baba, who'd been pacing, sat down now next to Rami and put his arm around him.

"We're on this bus for I don't know how long. The whole time these soldiers are shouting and slapping and kicking. All I'm thinking is I want to survive, I want the bus to arrive, wherever it's going. Then we do stop. They cut the plastic ties. I'm outside. Then I'm going down metal stairs. They take off my hood and shove me into a room."

She put her hand on Rami's desk and lowered herself into his chair.

"It's dark and hot, smells like blood and old clothes. There must be a hundred people, some standing, some sleeping on the cement like sardines. Two times they take me, blindfolded, to be questioned, they shout, they threaten, but no more slaps, nothing like on that bus. The second time the officer even gives me ibuprofen and a cup of water to swallow the pill. 'You protest, but you see how well we are treating you?' he says."

This, she thought, was thanks to Grandpa and Baba's efforts, and the huge gifts. Rami had no clue.

"Then," Rami continued, "this morning they put me in a car and dropped me off near the stadium, and I took the taxi."

They sat in a triangle of silence. This is what happened to other people. Not to them. They weren't criminals, they weren't political, they were a normal family. It could have been worse. Rami was free. His injuries were not serious. Where was Yaman? Where were the other people who were arrested? Was it—

Baba looked at her and then back at Rami. "We're going to leave tomorrow. The four of us. The situation is going to get worse before it gets better and it's not safe, especially for you."

Her exams! She couldn't leave. She'd fall behind. Attendance was required. She'd face academic dismissal. Would they let her back in after they returned home? Plus, where would they go, and what money would they live on? Rami just needed to stop going to demonstrations. They would keep their heads down and be fine.

Rami looked less shocked. "Go where?" he asked.

"Turkey. Until the situation settles. Then we'll come back."

Weeks? A month?

"Baba," Rami said, "I'll stop demonstrating. I promise."

She looked at Baba. "If you go, I could live at Uncle's."

Baba raised his voice. "No. My decision is final. Mama won't survive another week like this. And history is missing lots of people who waited too long to leave."

TWELVE

In the two months leading up to her stroke, she wrote and reviewed lots of code, shipped the model drift detection feature, received kudos from the sales team after they used it to win a competitive contract with Bosch, participated in five stand-ups a week and more sitting meetings than she would have liked, introduced a bad bug into production and pulled an all-nighter to fix it, did her thirty daily sit-ups without fail, ran three hundred kilometers, went to Frankfurt with work friends to race in the Corporate Challenge, stayed over at Julia's a dozen times, flew with her to Lisbon for a weekend, visited home twice, and taught her niece how to ride a bike at Tempelhof Park.

Also in those two months: ten cans of tuna and one tube of mayo, a half-dozen Berliner Weisse, her share of three bottles of Vinho Verde, and two or three (oh god, *that* night) martinis; and she lost her temper twice, only one time regretting it.

In the two months after her stroke, the leaves changed color, the days grew shorter, and she lay in bed. Out of over fourteen hundred hours, she'd been upright for fewer than two hundred of them. She'd been on this floor, in her room on the floor above, and outdoors on the hospital grounds. At no time had she been further than a few hundred meters from where she was right now: in the gym.

Peter pulled on her right arm. Her job was to pull back, to resist his pull. He pulled again. She strained against him, feeling the tension in her bicep. This little exercise, something a normal person wouldn't even consider exercise, was intended to help her regain power in the one limb she could control—and was the most vigorous she undertook in therapy. Sweat dripped from her forehead. She liked it. She could feel her mind calming—not to the same extent as during a morning run, but in that direction.

"You're doing great. You're pulling back with more force than last week."

There were staff in the hospital who treated her like a fifty-kilo sack of grain to be transported from place to place. Others were encouraging, except she could tell it was due to them defaulting to positivity over honesty, and they expected little from her. Peter was neither. He believed in her, pushed her and demanded she do the exercises he assigned. For him, as much as for herself, she tried hard, and then even harder. In years to come, she would remember his behavior towards her here; it would give her a model to aspire to when she was trying to get the best from others.

"You should see some of the characters we've treated." Peter's patter was a comfort, part of the calming effect of these sessions. "There was this one guy. A former pimp, believe it or not. His claim —'former.' A bunch of us figured he was still running things from here. He'd been in a knife fight, that's how he got paralyzed, lower down than you. He was so manipulative—had the whole staff wrapped around his finger, managed to arrange the schedule so he could wake up late and see only his favorite therapist, at the inconvenience of other patients." She murmured in recognition.

"And of course we've seen a lot of athletes. You know Kerstin Ünal?"

The name sounded familiar. "Not sure."

"She's an Olympian. Competed in Beijing and London. BMX

racing. Was in a horrific crash a few months after London. When you go back down the hall, look on the right, there's a photo of her in a handcycle, wearing a yellow jersey. I've never seen anyone pick up physical skills faster."

She nodded, her energy still going into pulling back on his arm.

"You know that blue Audi parked outside?"

Another nod. She'd wondered who was allowed to park there.

"You know what it's for?"

She shook her head.

"For practicing transfers. For people injured lower down than you, who have full use of their arms, they can learn to slide themselves from their chair to the driver's seat, and then fold and lift the chair in behind them. It's a difficult skill. Many people never learn—and they don't need to, even if they want to drive, because they can use a van and come in through the back.

"Now picture the abdominal and arm strength you need to lift your chair, but not only that, think about the balance, the grace. Anyway, she learned how to do it in two sessions. By the third she could wheel up to the car, open the door, and a minute later be buckled in behind the wheel with her folded chair in the passenger seat. She's the only person I've ever seen learn the skill that fast. And to watch her do it—it was beautiful."

Among the blind, the one-eyed ... She was thinking how lucky these people were, with the use of their arms and abdomens. It was all relative. She, too, had things going for her that others did not. Her brain worked. A gruesome either/or she'd pondered during sleepless nights was tetraplegia or brain damage. She would choose tetraplegia.

"Have you worked with other patients like me?" she asked. "I mean, with paralysis caused by a spinal stroke? Did they get back any muscles?" Why not go whole-hog. "Will I ever be able to move my fingers? My left arm? Walk?" She knew Dr. Eckert's answer.

Peter didn't blink. "Every person is different. I've seen people accomplish things they never thought they'd be able to. My advice is never give up hope. Never stop telling your muscles to move. Never stop strengthening and training what you have. Never assume that your limitations today will be your limitations tomorrow."

He relaxed the tension, then pulled on her arm again. "But don't wait around for function to come back either. That's a dangerous trap. Adapt, learn, get ready to go back and resume your life. Another thing I've seen: You weren't a couch potato before, so you won't be one after. You'll go back out there, you'll get on with things, you'll find physical activities you enjoy. Not the same ones as before, naturally, but you'll find a new routine."

That night, in bed, she remembered her sit-ups, and focused on her new exercises. *Curl index finger. Uncurl index finger. Curl middle finger. Uncurl middle finger. Curl ring finger. Uncurl ring finger. Curl pinky. Uncurl pinky. Bend thumb. Straighten out thumb.* Back to the index finger. *Curl. Uncurl. Curl. Uncurl.* No movement.

Peter was right about adapting. The loop was becoming second nature. It went over her hand and connected to a spoon or a fork. For three weeks now she'd been able to sit in her wheelchair and feed herself lunch and dinner. Funny how relearning a skill she'd first gotten the hang of when she was a baby could bring so much joy. Each spoonful transported to her mouth a little victory.

But no matter how good she got with the loop, and no matter what Dr. Eckert said, she wasn't giving up. *Curl. Uncurl.* Even after these two months it was a—well, the only appropriate word was mindfuck—to be looking at the hand you knew was your own, telling your fingers to close exactly the same way they had your whole life, and then watching as they lay there, no more sign of movement than in a spring roll on a plate.

Flex right thigh. Bend right knee. Wiggle right ankle. Go through each muscle. Her eyes kept closing. Stay awake. Complete the left leg. Then sleep. *Wiggle ankle. Bend ankle forward. Bend ankle back. Curl toes. Straighten toes.*

In the morning, lying on her right side, right arm positioned with a bend at the elbow so that her right hand lay in her field of vision, she heard a voice: *Curl pinky.* She tried. Push. Push. She imagined there was a heavy laptop pinning her finger to the bed. Push. Push harder. Movement? Movement! Caution. Could be a spasm. Try again. *Curl pinky*. Push up the laptop. Deep breath. Push. Push. Movement again! She watched her pinky rise a tiny, tiny distance, then settle again into the mattress.

Breathe out. Breath in. She felt like she'd just thrown her full body into sliding a washing machine along a cement floor. Breathe out. Breathe in. There was no question. From her brain, through her spinal cord, to her finger—a miracle. Proof that function could come back, *would* come back. Her fingers had been dead for two months; she'd mentally exercised them for two months; now her pinky had woken up. Her spinal cord could heal; her other fingers would be next. She would be able to grasp a piece of bread, brush her own teeth, touch Julia. For now, though, she'd call Mom and tell her—just as soon as Ingrid woke up.

THIRTEEN

Yesterday, at the recommendation of her occupational therapist, the guys from assistive technology had switched the throttle on her wheelchair from the U-shaped controller to a joystick. She was now using her reconfigured chair to drive herself to the lounge, and it was awkward and wonderful and human (primate-like she supposed) to close her fingers around the rubberized stick; it made her think of the first time she saw her niece, how the tiny thing had wrapped and unwrapped her miniature hand around Anna's pinky. That pinky that was first. Now, only days later, she could move all her fingers—without feeling winded—except the pinky and ring finger always moved as if taped together.

The new message tone on her phone beeped and she took her hand off the joystick. She carefully lifted the phone out of its position tucked between her waist and the velcro seat belt, and balanced it on her lap. A text from Julia, who was at a trade show in Florida: *Fucking lawyers. Change of plans. Flying to Peoria to try to get it over the line.*

With her index finger, slowly, she tapped out her response. *Good luck. Guess what? I'm typing with my finger.*

Julia: *Back on Sat.*

No comment on using her finger? Typical of Julia's tunnel vision. She could shine her light on you or look right through you; she could be the most perceptive listener in the world or, if the topic didn't interest her, fail to realize you were speaking.

Ok. Anna tucked her phone back in, closed her fingers around the joystick, rolled forward, and turned into the lounge. Sun streamed in through tall windows with low sills. At a table to the left, two men—one in his teens, the other who could be his father—were playing chess. A woman in her sixties was reading a book, her manual wheelchair nestled in the corner. A man around Anna's age, also in an electric, was staring out the window. She pulled up next to him, followed his gaze. Outside, a gardener was raking leaves.

"I'm Anna."

"Leo," the man said flatly, glancing at her without turning his head.

"How long have you been here?"

"August."

Same as her. She noticed the wedding band and, now that she looked more closely, the beginnings of vertical lines between his eyebrows.

"How'd you get injured?"

"Sand diving."

"Sand diving?"

"A joke."

He didn't say more, and they returned to gazing silently out the window. On her first date with Julia, which Anna at first didn't even realize was a date, they'd run along the Spree, then picked up coffees to go and sat on a bench watching city-tour boats navigating the river. Julia, stunning, older, sure of herself, had at one point set her cup to the side, reached for Anna's face, and kissed her—coffee, her vanilla lip balm, surprise.

As she watched the gardener, she could feel the rounded top of the wooden handle in the palm of her right hand, her left hand gripping the shaft. He reached forward, brought the tines down on top of a rumpled plane of red and brown, effortlessly stepped back and dragged the rake, lifted it, reached forward again—

"We were at Kleiner Müggelsee. There's a little beach there. My wife was sleeping and I was reading. I hear a scream. I look up. A boy is waving his arms. I run into the water, the boy is still screaming, the water is up to my shins, I dive forward. My head hits the sand. Game over. I fractured my spine at C3."

The back of her head tingled. She'd talked to a woman who was in a car accident, an old man who'd taken a nasty fall, an older woman who'd been thrown off her bike, but this story hit her harder. This guy was being a hero, and in his terse description she could see it like a movie: sprinting along the beach, the rush to get into the water, to get to the boy, to save him, a dive, not like from a diving board, but horizontally, which would seem safe, except a lake wasn't a pool, the slope was gradual, you could hit the lakebed.

"You ... after you hit, you, how did you keep your head above the water? And what about the boy?"

"The kid was fine. He was fooling around. My nose and mouth were submerged. I tried to use my arms to push myself back above the water, to get air. Immediately I understood. I couldn't hold my breath. I breathed in water. I thought for sure it was the end. But my wife—something woke her—the kid screaming, or me running—she pulled me out of the lake."

"Thank god."

"You think so?" He went silent again.

And then: "My first thought after I came out of surgery and saw the images of my spine was that I wish I had drowned. And I haven't changed my mind."

What was wrong with this guy. "No."

"Yes. If I had the guts, if my wife would cooperate, I would go to Switzerland."

"You don't mean that."

"Why wouldn't I mean it? Everyone thinks about it."

Had she thought about it? Yes, she admitted, she had. But only briefly. There was a certain cold logic to it. Mom and Dad wouldn't need to worry about her. In time, Mia would scarcely remember her. Julia would grieve and move on. Same with her friends. Her fingers had woken up and other muscles would be next. Yet even if she believed that her recovery was over, that this was it, even then ... no.

There was too much to do. Never once had she wished to not wake up the next day. If anything, no matter what happened during the day, no matter how sleepless the night, she looked forward to mornings: the anticipation of learning new skills in occupational therapy; to hearing the latest on Julia's attempts to get the Caterpillar and DDB lawyers to agree on license terms; to finding out things like what she'd been told yesterday by a former classmate who was now pursuing a PhD at Cambridge—that with these new word embeddings, the vector representing *king* minus the vector *man* plus the vector *woman* approximated the vector for *queen*. She'd initially thought it was his idea of a joke.

She looked forward to training with Peter in the gym; to chatting with Batul—this morning she'd told her about this unbelievable word vector stuff; to cracking often-failed jokes with the hospital staff; to rolling her eyes at Ingrid's antics. She looked forward, if nothing else, to seeing what that squirrel was up to.

"I honestly don't think about it."

"Why not?" Now he turned his head, looked at her directly. "Why do we exist?"

We as in paralyzed people? Or humans? He wanted to talk philosophy?

He didn't let her answer. "We exist to carry forward the species. Does the species need me? Does it need you? We are a burden. How old are you? Twenty-one? Twenty-two? Have you calculated the lifetime cost of caring for you? How many starving kids in South Sudan could be fed?" Seemed he was keeping up with the news. "Think about all the things our so-called loved ones, now burdened with us, will never get to do. What life is this? Being moved over a toilet and waiting there for the shit to fall out? Then needing someone to wipe our asses?"

How quickly could she roll away without seeming rude?

"I'll never be able to support my parents, my wife. We could still have kids, Dr. Eckert said—I will not. At another time, in another society, I would be left to die, or be killed ..."

Was he really going there? She, too, had thought about this country's past and shuddered. If this was 1939 ...

"But our society is rich, and it values so-called life, and there is quote-unquote modern medicine—so instead I will be kept alive pointlessly for decades. Listening to these fucking occupational therapists telling me I just need to learn how to use my new—read, damaged—body, tying a spoon to my hand, celebrating when I transfer a french fry to my mouth. What, honestly, is the point?"

Okay, no need to worry about manners after all—she should get out of here. But she'd been baited: "Apparently your mind is in good shape. Why don't you use it to earn a living so you won't have to feel bad about the state supporting you? What do you do?"

"I'm an economist."

She laughed. "Then you can earn a living now exactly as you did before, with your thoughts. You *can* support your wife. You *can* support your parents. You can accomplish things."

"There is nothing I want to accomplish."

"Right." She tried to imagine this man before his accident. He'd wanted to save someone's life once, if not his own now.

"The truth is I never gave a shit about my job. I wrote reports so our sales team could show so-called research to our clients. Did anyone care? No. Did those reports change anything? No. You know what I liked about my job?"

She shook her head.

"Guess."

"The pay."

"Yes. The money. So I could lie on the warm sand with my hot wife, and then drive our expensive car to an expensive restaurant, eat an expensive cut of steak, down an expensive bottle of wine, and then go home to our expensive house and fuck like rabbits. Sorry."

Bitter. Miserable. Not the potential friend she now realized she'd been imagining as she'd pulled up to that window. Or maybe he hadn't always been so cynical. It was a show. "Don't be sorry," she said, looking directly at him and keeping her expression neutral. "Anyway, rabbits are always talking about fucking like economists."

She saw a little bit of a smirk.

"What did you do?" He'd finally asked her something about herself. Why the past tense?

"I'm a software engineer. Working on machine learning. At DDB."

"Sounds tedious."

"It's not. Coding infects your brain. Once you start, it's all you can think about."

"Good for you. The ability to delude oneself is an underrated life skill. So you tricked yourself into enjoying your work. You tricked yourself into believing in all that ML and AI stuff. And now you've tricked yourself into thinking you have a future in your dead body. Good luck when your delusion collides with reality."

FOURTEEN

Day eight trapped in bed. Enough. She wanted to sit up, swing her legs over the side of the mattress, say, *Come on, joke's over, nice knowing you, stop this now, I'm going home.* The fever was still there, as was the pain in her shoulders. How fucking hard was it to figure out the right antibiotic? How had she gotten the UTI in the first place? That nurse—the careless one—probably hadn't followed the procedure. The nurse didn't care, just another paralyzed body to her, and now over a week of being stuck.

No exercise. No therapy. No sitting up. No Julia. Why be saddled with this? She was putrid, weak—and angry. Unlovable. She wouldn't want herself. Not in a million years. A partner in a wheelchair? No—she couldn't see that, couldn't imagine being attracted to someone who couldn't walk.

And the fucking TV. From seven in the morning to eleven at night, stupid people arguing about stupid things. *He slept with my best friend.* Yeah, stop complaining, bitch, be thrilled that you can sleep with someone, that your body works, that you can feel, that you can walk outside and reach your hands toward the sun. Get a divorce. Don't get a divorce. Who gives a fuck.

And the fucking nurses who made up the beds, made them look nice, like at a hotel. Didn't they get it? The bed wasn't some cozy place: collapse into the pillow, pull up the covers, fall asleep. The bed was a prison. She was at her most disabled here—trapped, horizontal, unable to do anything.

Eight days. Dr. Eckert pretending to care. "We'll figure this out. You'll be out of bed soon." Yeah, right. She didn't give a shit. She went home and lived her life and didn't give Anna a second thought until she was staring at her fevered body again the next day. You watered a houseplant, you repotted it, you moved it into the sun, you told yourself you were a good plant parent. Anna didn't buy her false sympathy for a second.

Fucking Julia. To have twenty-four more hours together where her body was whole. Make Julia remember what she'd be missing. They'd run along the Spree. She'd tuck Julia's hair behind her ear, press her nose to her, smell her sweat. They'd eat lunch at that sushi place near Helmholtzplatz, Julia would explain the company politics that passed Anna right by. In the afternoon they'd bike out to Teufelssee. At night, dancing, pressed in by other bodies, staring at each other, knowing they were together, that they had something special. Fuck her. *Fuck* her.

It had been two weeks ago, on Saturday. She'd wanted to be upright, but Julia changed her plans and decided to go home first rather than coming directly from the airport, and so she'd been back in bed, on her left, waiting. The door opened. Julia was wearing her soft, white V-neck tee half tucked into her jeans, the pair with the rip on the thigh.

"Hello, Ingrid," Julia said, walking past the foot of Ingrid's bed. Ingrid grunted something that might have been a greeting. Then Julia was beside Anna and kissed her—on the temple—and then sat on the edge of the chair, her posture tense, like when she was about to call a prospective customer to find out if she'd won or lost their business.

Anna opened and closed her fingers and Julia flashed her a tight-lipped smile. She slid her hand over the edge of the mattress to Julia's leg and pressed the denim with her thumb, then her index finger, her middle finger, and her ring finger and pinky together. Julia placed her hand over hers, on top of her leg. She could feel Julia's cool, moisturized fingers on the back of her hand. Somewhere she already knew it would be the last time. That it was not a return to normalcy, not a promise of how things would be when more muscles woke up.

"Any word?"

"They signed."

"Congrats!" She swallowed. "So they agreed? Or our lawyers gave in on the liability stuff?"

"They agreed. Finally."

"Seven million dollars?"

"Euros."

She calculated Julia's commission. This would be her best year yet. "Why aren't you more excited?" Though she knew.

"I'm supposed to get excited about winning a customer while you're still here? Your ... illness ... puts everything in perspective."

They were going to get into it. "Hey—life goes on. It's going to be really boring if we pretend the only thing worth talking about is me and, I don't know, that I was able to stay in my wheelchair for three hours. Which, by the way, I did yesterday."

"About life going on ..." Julia's leg was bouncing. She glanced over her shoulder at Ingrid who couldn't give them privacy even if she wanted to. "I've been thinking—"

Don't say it. Words became commitments. "Let's get the nurse to transfer me to my chair." And to the box above her head, "Request—"

"Anna," Julia cut her off. "What I've been thinking ... there's no great way to say this except to come right out ... we should go our separate ways. I'll ..."

No. The ceiling was coming down. Julia should see her trapped in bed, trapped in her body, and want to climb onto the mattress and hold her, not end things.

"... I'll be here for you. I can help you with, you know, with whatever you need."

"Julia. Not now. We need more time. My hand woke up. More muscles will come back. Let's wait. And then once I'm out of here ... see how things are?" She squeezed her eyes, tried to hold Julia's hand.

"I've been thinking a lot, every time I visit, I'm sorry ... I can't feel our connection ... I know I should. I try. I read blogs, I watched videos. Lots of happy couples—I know. But I don't feel it, and I can't see it. And I don't want to keep lying to you. Or to myself. We've always been honest with each other. If we were older, if we had lived more of our lives, it would be different. I can't see the next year, five years, ten years, fifty years taking care of you ... I'm sorry. I'll still be here for you ... whatever you need."

Julia. Cold as glass. But never trying, with her, to be anything but as transparent. Still, just for this moment, she wanted Julia to be different. She wanted her to wrap her arms around her, to pull her close, to *love* what she held. She couldn't breathe. She needed to go outside, sit against a wall, put her head between her knees, and weep. "I understand," she whispered.

Day seventeen. Leo's words: At another time, in another society, I would be left to die ... instead I will be kept alive pointlessly for decades. She'd been so confident he was wrong. Naive.

Excited she could move her fingers. Naive.

Thinking she could guard her body, protect it for when she got better. Naive.

If they said, take this pill, you won't wake up, she would take it. Her parents would grieve and then move on. Their lives would get easier.

No dread. No anger. No fight with the TV. No guilt about ignoring calls.

Knock. "Anna, I'm here to rotate you."

The nurse did her thing. "Honey, the fever will break soon."

She stared into space. The nurse left the room.

Shadows crawled across the wall. Sleep. Awake. Sleep. Awake. End this.

The door. Batul. Not again. With her *good morning*.

"Guten Morgen, Anna. How are you feeling?"

She stared at the wall.

"I want to show you this article I saw yesterday ..."

Batul came closer. "It's about AI."

She closed her eyes. Go practice your German with someone else.

"I'll come back after my shift."

Don't.

As Anna's mind moved from unconscious to awake, she felt sunlight warming her eyelids, her face. She felt strangely normal, like she had slept well for the first time in weeks. Better: she *had* slept well. She opened her eyes and saw the branches of the oak tree outside her window, the leaves a backlit blur of yellow and red. Her mind was clear. No fog. No fever. Tenuously—she took stock—there was desire, a tug, to get out of bed, to move her muscles, to be showered, to eat, to talk with someone.

Last Saturday, Mom, holding her hand, had assured her: "Dr. Eckert said this happens. You need time to fight the infection."

"This isn't living," she'd responded. "I can't keep going."

"Sweetie, don't say that."

She needed to call Mom, tell her that wasn't her, that she was back. She'd shut out Batul—she needed to explain. She would apologize to her nurses. Ask them to get her out of bed. What day was it—could Peter make time for her in the gym?

Fever aside, she'd let Leo get in her head. Never again. But he'd been right about one thing. She'd deceived herself. Until the infection, for—August, September, October—three months—she'd thought she was stronger than this thing. It was a more even match than first met the eye. Julia plus an infection, a fever plus being confined to bed, delirium plus no responsibility—her mind was not tougher than her broken body. Round one—her mind. Round two—her body.

She'd let the fever rewrite reality, erase the knowledge that it would eventually break. She'd let the pain sap not just her energy but her belief she'd have energy again. And she'd let how Julia saw her reshape how she saw herself. Excuses. She would be stronger. She wasn't going to be left here to rot. Time to get back on the horse. Exercise. Start now. Right leg first. *Stretch. Move thigh. Flex knee. Bend ankle forward. Bend ankle back. Curl toes.* The sheet above her foot shifted. Movement? Movement! She tried again—

The door. "Guten Morgen," Batul whispered.

"Look." She curled her toes.

Batul walked over and placed her hand on her foot over the sheets. She curled her toes again. She felt Batul's hand, not as resistance, more like a tickle or a tingling, as if she were tapping her sole.

Batul looked at her cautiously. Then she sat on the chair, wrapped both hands around her foot through the sheet, and bowed her head.

PART 2
WINTER 2014-2015

FIFTEEN

"The situation I want to be in is working," she repeated to Herr Bergmann for what felt like the fifth time, unintentionally raising her voice, and as a result struggling a little to breathe. "I want to live in my own place and commute to the office." It was two weeks after her fever broke. Her physical therapy was back on schedule and she was lying in bed, back from the morning session. Her parents were here, too, to meet Herr Bergmann and learn how this would work. It was the first time the insurance company had sent someone to the hospital. It was only last week that she'd found out she even had a case manager.

Herr Bergmann wrote something down on his clipboard, and then looked up, at Dad. "It is not possible now to say precisely what support your daughter will receive when her rehabilitation is complete. I can say that living on your own is not so common. She may be better off in a group home, something like an assisted living facility, with all the services to care for her." Her parents nodded. "There is also, of course, the possibility that you could learn the relevant nursing skills and she could live with you, and funds can likely be provided to cover the necessary adaptations to your house."

Dad and Mom nodded again. She was about to turn twenty-five. She hadn't lived at home since she was eighteen. For her sake and for theirs, she couldn't move back. Plus there were no tech companies in Dessau, certainly not ones doing work in machine learning. And an assisted living facility? Like a nursing home? Like where Grandpa was? She would commute to work from a nursing home?

Dad blinked, then after a few seconds, "When will you be able to determine what support you will have for Anna?"

"This all depends on her disability rating—her Grad der Behinderung. And her Pflegegrad—her need for nursing. These must be assessed around the time she is leaving the hospital. If the grades are higher, she will be entitled to more services."

"For the sake of argument," she spoke up, with more force than Dad. Herr Bergmann looked vaguely at her. "For the sake of argument, suppose I have the worst possible disability rating and my desire is to live in my own place and resume work, as a software engineer, which, again, is my profession, and one I am capable of doing within my current abilities. How would that be achieved?"

She listened to herself and heard the shaking in her voice. She hadn't touched a computer since the day of her stroke and didn't know what DDB had in mind. It would be hard to code until she could sit up for longer. She saw herself back in the office, people averting their eyes in the elevator, or doubting her contributions were worth the hassle. She squeezed her right hand and stared at Herr Bergmann. *Before every meeting I put my game face on,* Julia had once told her.

Herr Bergmann looked up and focused on a spot above her head. "You would need to find an accessible apartment. This is usually not possible so you would need to find a landlord who will allow renovations to make the bathroom large, a wheel-in shower, lower counters in the kitchen, and so on. If the disability rating is high, we can provide funds for this."

His eyes drifted back to Dad. "If, at that point, your daughter still requires around-the-clock care, then an agency can be engaged to assemble a private care team. There would be a head of the team, a registered nurse, with the appropriate medical training and experience, and under this person, two to three aides to cover all the shifts. At night, at work, for meals, and so on."

Yes. If, *if,* she still needed so much assistance when it was time to leave, she wanted this personal care team in her own place, not to move into a nursing home. She'd be able to decide when to go to bed, when to wake up, what to eat for breakfast, when to go out. She wouldn't be stuck until *they* got around to her. She could live like the adult that she sometimes forgot she was.

"Won't this all take a lot of time?" her dad asked. "Finding an apartment, renovating it, hiring a team. Shouldn't we get started on this now?"

"No!" Herr Bergmann said—the most emphatic he'd been this whole conversation. "We cannot. We cannot approve anything until we know her Grad der Behinderung."

"But," Mom spoke up for the first time, "you said this grade needs to be assessed at the time she is leaving the hospital."

"Yes. This is why what your daughter is asking for is not practical. I think it will be better to look for a bed in a home, or to consider if she can live with you. I've been doing this a long time. People think they want to go back to work. But actually most patients are happy if we can guarantee a monthly allowance, find a bed in a clean group home not so far from family, and fit them with an appropriate wheelchair. For your daughter, to live on her own, it's not such a practical thing."

Mom and Dad both gave a slow nod. Anna was stunned. Herr Bergmann looked at Dad again. "The good news is your daughter is still making improvements, so we are approving another three months here. This will give everyone time to make decisions about the future."

Downstairs at her physical therapy that afternoon, she cursed herself. She should have asked more questions. She shouldn't have let Dad take the lead. How was it possible to be assigned a disability rating only when leaving the hospital, but you couldn't know where you would be going without it? What was the exact process for determining if she could get her own care team? Who made the decision? What was she entitled to by law? By her insurance? How much money would there be to renovate? How far in advance would those funds be made available?

She should have asked the types of questions Julia used to talk about. The ones where just hearing her repeat what she'd said to a prospective customer made her cringe. "You never leave a sales meeting with vague pleasantries, 'It was great meeting you, let's talk soon.' You need to get information and pin them down, and you do that by asking pointed questions. 'When will you make a decision? If you had to make a decision right now, are we your first choice? Who makes the decision? If you were to go with a vendor other than us, what would the reason be? Who will sign the contract? Can you approve a purchase of this size?'"

"Don't you risk pissing them off?"

"Babe, not if you're confident. Ask the questions in the right way and you earn their respect, and then their business. Be passive, be scared to ask where you stand, fail to understand the decision-making process, and you lose."

SIXTEEN

On her break, Batul walked toward Anna's room carrying a plastic bag with her lunch—a container with rice, a second with okra stew, both leftovers from dinner yesterday that she'd reheated in the microwave.

She heard laughter—a voice she didn't recognize, mixed with Anna's higher pitched, higher cadence, quieter—and to her ear, forced—chuckle. A woman with shoulder-length wavy blonde hair, wearing a white blouse with gold buttons down the front, sat facing the door, across from Anna, who was in her wheelchair, back to the door. There was a styrofoam container in front of Anna, and the woman held another in her left hand. In her right the woman had two sticks, and now, Anna raised her hand, and Batul could see she too had them. Anna had been training her fingers and there'd been visible, week-over-week improvement in her fine motor control—Dr. Eckert had been shocked, Anna told her—but enough to use chopsticks?—incredible.

"Try the hamachi," the woman said, and used her chopsticks to move a roll from her container to Anna's.

Anna picked it up, dipped it in a sauce, and raised it to her mouth. "Ooh, that's good."

A week ago, Batul had been coming back from the basement meditation room, walking through her favorite hallway, the one that connected the main lobby to the J wing. Airy, long, and light, the high ceiling was made of glass and one wall was lined with paintings by patient-artists. The other side was all floor-to-ceiling windows, creating the sense that you were walking through the courtyard. She noticed a middle-aged woman, one hand on a painted steel column, body pitched forward a few degrees, staring out at a building across the campus. Now closer, Batul recognized Anna's mother.

"Frau Werner."

Anna's mother turned. Her eyes were red; her face was wet. "Batul. How are you?"

Batul reached into her pocket, felt for a tissue, handed it over.

Anna's mother blew her nose. "They grow up. They leave the house. You become a grandmother ... You slow down ... You don't expect ... I try to act positive, to never say ..." She tilted her head in the direction of Anna's floor, turned back to Batul.

Batul reached out, touched Frau Werner's arm just above the elbow, hesitated, took a tiny step forward, embraced her, rubbed her back. Batul felt Frau Werner's arms hugging her in, holding her. "Your daughter is strong."

"Do you mind coming back later?" By now Batul had been hovering in the doorway for a good fifteen seconds. Anna's friend must have noticed her the instant she appeared, but only now acknowledged her, perhaps confused because she was wearing a janitor's uniform but holding only the plastic bag, and making no move to clean.

"Certainly." Batul turned around.

"Batul?" Anna couldn't see her and wouldn't be able to unless she put down her chopsticks, grabbed the joystick, and pivoted her chair—or unless Batul ventured further into the room.

"Yes. Hi Anna. I'll stop by later."

"Okay."

"Janitors call you by your first name?" the woman asked Anna. She was out of earshot before she could hear Anna's response.

After her shift she popped into Anna's room again. She would say a quick goodbye. *Janitors call you by your first name.* She could come and go. Anna could not. This morning, like every morning, while cleaning rooms, she was also organizing thoughts to share, a little like she used to do before visiting Grandpa. Of course they didn't need to eat lunch together every day. Of course she had other things to do besides practice German with her. *Janitors call you by your first name.* Anna had lots of close friends.

"Bye, Anna. I'll see you next week."

"Do you have a minute? I saved you some sushi."

She walked over and Anna gestured toward the styrofoam container on the table.

"Try a roll. Take the chopsticks—"

"I saw you using them. I didn't know you could hold the sticks."

"Me neither. My friend—sorry she was rude to you, she didn't know—she brought them. I thought no way my fingers would be able to push the sticks together, but actually, they were better than a fork. I didn't have to be so careful to stay level …"

The first time they talked she couldn't scratch an itch on her face.

"… it came with salad. And guess what? I could manage that too. Finally: a way to eat lettuce again without touching it with my fingers and getting them covered in dressing." Anna laughed. "Can you imagine getting so excited about lifting a leaf to your mouth? People need to know about this. Disabled or not, chopsticks are better than forks for salads! I've got to email the Verein der Salatbars so they can publicize this."

The Association of Salad Bars? "Is there such an organization?"

"I hope so. You know how Germany is. How about, after I leave the hospital, you and I will go to a salad bar, place an official-looking stainless steel cup with chopsticks near the other utensils, do a little test, see if people use them …"

Leichter und freier. Her own thoughts were lighter and freer when Anna was in a good mood. And this idea! To go somewhere together outside the hospital, a salad bar, or anywhere else, just the two of them—

"... I need to keep training because I couldn't pick up the noodles. Too thin and slippery."

"Could you before?"

"What?"

"Pick up noodles."

"Yes, no question. Since I was a kid. Our parents used to take us to the local Vietnamese restaurant as a treat, and we always used chopsticks. Try a roll."

Considering that one of her favorite dishes was made of finely-ground raw lamb mixed with bulgur and mint, she wasn't sure why her stomach flinched at uncooked fish. Though where could the fish in German takeout sushi come from? The murky, feces-infested, foul-smelling waters of an aquafarm? Then sitting out on Anna's table all afternoon, bacteria growing exponentially—

Anna, as if reading her mind, "These are vegetarian. Take the chopsticks."

She ripped the paper and pulled apart the two wooden sticks. She started to put one between—

"Give me your hand. I'll show you."

She brought her hand close to Anna's. Anna placed one stick in the crook of the V between her index finger and thumb. Anna's fingers were dexterous, surprisingly strong. "Okay, push them together."

She tried. Anna laughed at her. "Not like that. It's more like this one stays still, and you move this one up and down." Anna's fingers were slim, the nails trimmed, her hand was warm. "Now you know how awkward it felt relearning to use a spoon! Try grabbing it."

She positioned one stick on one side of the seaweed-wrapped roll, and used her fingers to move the other stick to the other side, and then gripped, then lifted. The roll stayed in the container. She tried again. Anna's hand was on hers. "Apply pressure with this finger." No, she couldn't get a grip on the roll.

Anna took the chopsticks from her, and resting their tips in the container, slid the backs of the sticks into her own hand, and lifted the roll. "See." She brought her face forward and Anna put the roll in her mouth. It touched her tongue—

Pungent, sour, soapy, slimy; she wouldn't feed this to a cat. She kept her expression neutral, chewed, swallowed. The soapy flavor lingered.

"Strange, right?" Anna said, raising her eyebrows, already reaching down with the chopsticks for another roll. "Ume shiso maki, I wanted you to try it—pickled plum and shiso leaf. I love it, but it's an acquired taste."

Batul chewed and swallowed the second roll. On the train home she could still feel Anna's fingers guiding hers, still taste the salty pickled plum, now slightly pleasant. She imagined a little girl with blonde hair shoveling noodles into her mouth with chopsticks. Of course, it was easy to learn things as a kid. She'd rinsed the chopsticks and stuck them in her bag. She'd find a video and practice.

SEVENTEEN

"Did Dad talk to Herr Bergmann?" Anna asked Mom over the phone.

"Not yet."

He hated this type of thing. Ever since her parents messed up their house payment when she was sixteen, and she'd called the bank to straighten things out, it had been the other way around: they asked her for help with paperwork. "You'll definitely call this week?" she'd asked Dad on Sunday, after he'd been unable to reach Herr Bergmann the week before. "Yes," he'd promised.

"But next week won't they be closed?" she asked Mom.

"We think it's better to wait. Sweetie, you know nothing ever gets done this time of year. Speaking of ... on Wednesday, I'm going to cook in the morning, and we'll get there mid-afternoon. Your brother too. I'll reheat everything that needs it in that microwave in the lounge."

She took a deep breath. Of course Mom was right. Nothing happened around the holidays. It would be the first time she wouldn't be at home for Christmas, in the house they'd moved into just before she started first grade, Stefan going into seventh. Her family had spent weekends redoing the kitchen, painting, replacing the windows. Thinking back, at six, she must have been more nuisance than help, but Dad always found a job for her. When she was in fourth grade, when they fixed up the downstairs bathroom, Dad trusted her with his new toy: a wet saw. "Are you crazy?" Mom screamed at him. That was the end of her cutting tiles.

DDB would be closed through New Year's. There would be parties. Drinking. She didn't love mulled wine, but on a cold day with friends, her hands wrapped around the warm mug …

Then the train home, Dad waiting at the station. The smell of butter, baking, cinnamon, even before she opened the door. Waking up in her old bed on Christmas morning and creeping quietly out of the room she was sharing with Mia to go for an early run through the empty and, if she got lucky, snow-covered streets. Stopping on the no-longer-so-new pedestrian bridge, the one that looked like an egg slicer, and watching the water of the Mulde pass under her. Rituals.

This year of course would not be that, except for buying gifts, which she'd already done online, along with silver and gold gift bags. Only for Mia's Playmobil set—a veterinarian's operating room—had she asked a nurse for help wrapping.

"Will I still have PT?" she'd asked Peter.

He frowned, looked down, then back up at her. "I'll come in for you."

"Are you sure?"

"I live close by."

"Would your parents want to spend the night on the twenty-fourth?" Batul had asked her last week. "If the visitor room isn't already booked, I can ask to reserve it for them. Then they wouldn't have to drive home after your Christmas meal. It's two hours, right?"

There was a visitor room? And did Batul remember every single thing she'd ever mentioned?

"Are you working on the twenty-fourth?"

"Yes."

"Are you … will you be able to stay a little later after? Would you want to join my family for dinner? I would love for you to meet Stefan, and Mia, and Christina."

Dad pushed two of the tables in the lounge together. Mom spread a tablecloth and served all of them on the ceramic plates she'd brought. They sat around the table—her in her wheelchair, Mia next to her on one side, Mom on the other, across from them Stefan, Christina, Batul; Dad at the end. It was not so different from eating at home.

She reached forward with her right hand, put her spoon into her potato salad, and brought two potato pieces to her mouth. The little bits of parsley, the vinegary tanginess—how Mom always made it, except with slices of turkey bratwurst instead of pork. She looked over at Batul who was picking at the edges of her plate with her fork. Not her holiday. Not her family.

"So Batul," Stefan said, "Anna tells me that you were in the middle of med school when you left your country? And that you will continue here?"

Good of him. She looked at her brother, then over at Batul.

"Yes. That's my goal. To become a doctor here."

"What kind of doctor?" Stefan asked. Anna noticed Christina rolling her eyes.

"I'm not sure about the specialty, perhaps internal medicine. I would like to be a physician scientist. I mean … it's my hope … to do research and also take care of patients … to publish papers." Batul's German was still hesitant, but so much more fluent. They talked all the time, maybe that's why she hadn't noticed, but listening to her speaking with Stefan, you would never guess that nine months ago she didn't know a word of the language.

"It will be difficult for me to be accepted to study medicine here. I'm so grateful to Anna for helping me with my German, and helping me prepare for TestDaF."

"Will you need to start over?" Mom asked. "Couldn't you transfer credits from back home?"

Batul lifted a carrot slice to her mouth. "No. It's not possible. I am fortunate, though, that the Syrian education system is strict and Germany recognizes this, so my high school grades will directly transfer, except they remove the religion subject."

Conversation shifted to a neighbor who'd won a seat on the town council representing the new AfD party. He was outside city hall three weeks ago protesting a naturalization ceremony. "You remember him, right sweetie?" Mom asked. "The beige house with the garage in the front. What a creep."

During a lull, Batul put her fork down and glanced at the dark window. "I need to head home." She pushed back her chair and looked around the table. "I want to wish you a Frohe Weihnachten. Thank you for including me."

"Where do you live?" Stefan asked. "We'll drop you off after."

"No, thank you, I don't want you to rush on my account, and my parents are waiting for me."

"Well, at least eat more first," Mom said. "You barely had anything. Or let me pack it up for you. I made so much food. Maybe you'll bring some home for your parents?"

"Thank you so much, I'd love to take a little, but please eat first and leave any leftovers in the fridge." Batul turned from Mom to her, "Anna, I can get them out for us on Friday."

After Batul left, Christina said, "I don't know why you invited a headscarf girl for dinner on Heiligabend. She's not getting into med school, that's for sure."

What the fuck? But before she said anything, Mom snapped, "Batul cares about Anna more than anyone else in this hospital."

EIGHTEEN

She squeezed the ball.

"Relax for a minute," Peter said and pointed to the bathroom. "I'll be right back."

She rested her now throbbing hand in her lap.

Something had happened as she was waking up this morning. It was subtle, slight, almost subconscious, and she hadn't been able to make it happen again. She wanted to show him; it seemed so unlikely; if nothing happened they would decide it had been a hallucination of her half-awake brain. She was aware of a dangerous shift. In the two months following her stroke, deep, deep down, her mind didn't believe it couldn't control the dead muscles on her left; now it didn't believe it could.

"Okay," Peter said, "I'm going to push your shoulder back."

"Wait, I want to try something." She used her right hand to move her left arm from her lap to the armrest. "Watch."

She concentrated. *Move left arm.* Push. Push. Her heart was pumping. Push. Movement! Her arm slid forward half a centimeter.

"Anna! Try again."

Move left arm. No movement. She breathed in. She breathed out slowly. She counted to ten. She concentrated on sending instructions to her shoulder. She visualized her left hand up against a heavy punching bag hanging by a chain from the rafters. Push. Push. She *could* move it. She blinked the sweat from her eyes. Push. Her arm slid forward. Again by about half a centimeter. She breathed in and out. In and out. Looked at Peter, who was beaming. Took another breath. "What do you think?"

"What do I think? This is huge! The first time anything on the left has come back. This is so good for you. Now we can work on training it. You can't imagine all the things you'll be able to do. Use a manual wheelchair. You're going to love that. And we'll switch the throttle on this chair to the left side so your right hand can be freed up. It's a really, really big deal. I mean—let's take it a step at a time, we'll need to see how much control you regain, but that your brain is moving your arm, even this tiny amount, makes me optimistic." He held up his right fist. Still catching her breath, her forehead covered in sweat, she raised her right arm and gave him a fist bump.

Her right hand had woken up in October. The toes of her right foot in November. In December she got back the ability to bend, a little, her right knee. And now, a New Year's gift, her left arm. If her body kept healing, if she kept training, if everything woke up—she'd be able to walk, to run, to skip, to hug.

NINETEEN

Two months ago, Batul had seen a little bird through the window of a coffee shop hopping from table to table picking up crumbs. She mentioned it to Anna later that day. "What kind?" Anna asked.

"I'm not sure."

Later Batul had scrolled through photos on *Birds of Berlin* but still couldn't be sure. Possibly a sparrow.

The next weekend she'd been at the market at Hermannplatz where, when she touched the dates and oranges and listened to the vendors haggling in Arabic, she could almost imagine she was back home. Anna's voice was in her head, hungry for detail: *Haggling, like over the price of fruit, or do you mean not haggling exactly, but that the vendors were shouting things like 'five for a euro?'* The latter. *Do they have anything there you can't find in other markets?* Yes. Mana'eesh za'atar—made from a dough of flour, yeast, salt, and sugar, flattened into rounds, topped with a mixture of za'atar and olive oil, and baked. She bought a bag of four for Anna even though she could have made them herself.

Once, still early in the fall, she and Mama had seen two ponies grooming each other in Volkspark Hasenheide. The next day she told Anna.

"I know you're making that up." Anna poked her shoulder with her right hand. "You don't find ponies walking around parks in Berlin."

"Not walking around. There's like a little zoo in there for kids. They're in an enclosure."

She took out her phone and showed Anna. One was whitish gray with a black mane. The other had a brown coat with white spots, like a cow. They stood intertwined, nuzzling each other's backs.

She thumbed over to the next photo: her mother petting the brown-and-white pony's forehead.

"You look like your mom! You have the same nose, the same cheekbones."

"Yes. Everyone says we look alike." She swiped to the next photo.

"You've noticed the *Stolpersteine*," Anna said. "Good."

The photo was of one of the brass plaques embedded in the sidewalks all over the city, inscribed with short, chilling lists of facts. This one she'd seen in front of a building in Neukölln, for a woman murdered when she was two years younger than Batul is now: *HIER LEBTE / MARGOT PESE / JG. 1921 / DEPORTIERT 27.11.1941 / RIGA / MASSENERSCHIESSUNG / 30.11.1941 / RIGA-RUMBULA.*

"You know, when my parents were growing up in the DDR, they were told that all the people responsible were in the West. That wasn't true."

Now Batul sat on her train to work, hardly noticing the cool, damp, winter weather outside as she watched a video on her phone. She paused it, slid her other earbud under her hijab and into her ear to hear better, and dragged her finger left. Chancellor Merkel, wearing a rose-colored blazer and seated at a table, was delivering a speech. Ebola. Then Syria—this was the part she wanted to watch again.

"One consequence of these wars and crises is that worldwide

there are more refugees than we have seen since World War Two. Many have literally escaped death. It goes without saying that we will help them and take in people who seek refuge."

Batul pressed pause, closed her eyes. Her fellow citizens were being imprisoned, maimed, murdered by the regime. There'd never been news of Yaman. Her cousin had spotted bodies floating down the Queiq. Muna, from high school, was killed by a government airstrike on the Faculty of Architecture and Arts; she was in the middle of taking an exam.

First do no harm. The president was a doctor. A graduate of the School of Medicine at Damascus University—where Tasneem had studied. He would have taken the Hippocratic Oath. Did he value life? Other than his own? Here, in Merkel, a physicist, a former research scientist, was decency. *It goes without saying that we will help them and take in people who seek refuge.* It didn't go without saying. It was exceptional. Merkel was speaking to her.

Play. "... Recently someone told me of a Kurd who took German citizenship. He fled many years ago under very difficult circumstances, fearing for his life. He said that the most important thing about Germany is that his children can grow up without fear. That's perhaps the biggest compliment anyone can pay to our country, that the children of the persecuted can grow up here without fear."

Merkel tilted her head, furrowed her eyebrows, and continued. No razzmatazz, only substance. "That was one of the reasons, twenty-five years ago in the DDR, that crowds were drawn onto the streets every Monday. In 1989, hundreds of thousands demonstrated for democracy and freedom, and against a dictatorship that made children grow up in fear. Once again, people are marching on Mondays shouting: 'We are the people!' What they actually mean is: 'You others don't belong here because of your skin color, your religion.'"

The absence of bluster made her trust this woman. There were pockets of relative sanity. She was grateful to be living in one. She felt invisible threads joining her to the other commuters from all walks of life on this train. This was the system they sought when they marched in University Square; it would never come to her country as long as Assad stayed in power.

"So let me say to anyone who attends such demonstrations: Don't follow their call, because mostly what they have in their hearts is prejudice, coldness, and even hatred. And, my fellow citizens, how fortunate we are to have lived for almost twenty-five years in peace and freedom in a unified country."

Batul removed her earbuds. Her eyes were moist.

"This afternoon I want to show you a video," she told Anna when she stopped by her room in the morning.

At the end of her shift, she returned her cart, pulled off her gloves, and made her way to Anna's room. Anna was lying on her back, touching her hand to her cheek. She walked over to the bed. Anna's lips were blue.

"Batul! Hi. I'm ready to watch."

"Are you feeling okay? You look pale."

Anna pressed the back of her hand to her cheek. "I can't tell if I'm still cold. Do you mind ... could you check my legs?"

She lifted the duvet from the foot of the bed and placed her hand on Anna's ankle, above the cuff of her thick, wool sock. Batul touched her own forehead, then Anna's ankle again, then her calf. "You do feel cold. What happened? Do you want me to put an extra blanket on you?"

Anna nodded, and Batul began to unfold the blue woolen throw that the family had brought from home.

"They changed the schedule. I had my first session in the pool."

"Was it helpful?"

"Yes, I think so, a little. It was strange and a bit scary. I was lying on my back. They put a floating collar around my neck and pool noodles—you know what those are?—under my arms and shoulders and knees. The therapist—he was wearing a bathing suit, and I was wearing my bathing suit, and he was so close—not like in the gym where there is some distance—his skin was touching my skin, his hands underneath me—"

Anna, in a bathing suit, in the water. A man, in trunks, in the water with her, touching her back, under her knees, her shoulders. Wouldn't they at least use a female therapist? They didn't think of these things?

"... He told me to relax. Not so easy. I kept thinking—if the collar came off, or the pool noodle slipped, or he got distracted, my head could go under. He told me to make little motions with my shoulders. He dragged me through the water, very smoothly. This is supposed to train the muscles to reduce spasms. Really, it was too cold to relax. If you're not moving you're not making warmth, and I'm so skinny, I used to get cold swimming even before.

"After, when we came back, the nurse gave me a long, warm shower. I think I'm still cold. I see now why all the warnings and instructions from Dr. Eckert about body temperature regulation."

"What time were you in the pool? It was in place of the usual afternoon therapy?"

She nodded.

Two hours ago.

"I'll get you tea. To warm you from the inside."

She came back with the tea, which she mixed with a small amount of cold water. She held the cup. Anna drank through a straw and then closed her eyes, and after another minute, Batul could tell she was sleeping. She put the cup on the table, leaned over, and gently dislodged her glasses; her skin smelled clean, of soap, and faintly of chlorine. On the way out she stopped at the nurse station and told them she'd put an extra blanket over Anna, so they would pay attention and remove it if she got too warm. On the train home, she watched Merkel's New Year's address one more time.

TWENTY

When Tomás visited her, a week after her stroke, he had assured her that he'd reassigned her tickets. She was not to think about work, he said, except to know that everyone was rooting for her.

Before Christmas, she'd sent him a text. He replied immediately: *Merry Christmas to you too Anna!*

A few weeks ago she had texted him again: *Congrats!* That was after Real Madrid beat Schalke. He didn't reply. He might have missed it, or, she supposed, it wasn't a text that required a reply. Still, it left her unsettled. Was she still on his radar? She could close her eyes and picture her desk on the 23rd floor of the DDB building— snug amid a row of others like it, her photos thumbtacked into the padded walls of the low-slung partition, her water bottle (it would need a serious scrub) standing in its usual spot to the right of her monitor, the Post-it notes fighting for position around the edges of her screen. Or maybe they'd boxed everything up and given her spot to someone else.

Dr. Eckert was always talking about getting back to your life, getting back to work. She could see now that, for many of the people here, this was merely aspirational. Ingrid was not the only one who watched TV all day. Some, like Ingrid, were pensioners. But there were also patients no more than a decade or two older than Anna, in their prime, who made no effort in PT. And while Dr. Eckert made a lot of noise, she wasn't going to kill herself to stop a patient from going down the path of least resistance: moving into a group home, giving up PT, and racking up ailments by not taking care of their body.

Yesterday, Dad had finally talked to Herr Bergmann:

"What job will your daughter have?"

"Software engineer."

"Do you believe she'll be able to handle the demands of a big job like that? How many hours a day do you think she'll be able to work?"

"What did you tell him?" she'd asked Dad, Mom listening in on the extension.

"I said I wasn't sure."

"Mom?"

"I don't know, sweetie."

Why was she the only one who believed she was going back to work? Why couldn't Herr Bergmann get (or care?) that she burned to be independent, to be building stuff, to be relevant, to be back among friends in an office? Why couldn't Dad?

She'd been on the tram once, scrolling through her phone as she stood, one hand grasping a grab strap, when a man got on. Another man, in the seat next to her, stood and offered his spot. The new arrival laughed, said, "Sir, you're at least twenty years my senior. Please. Sit." She'd looked up from her phone and there was no question: one man was her father's age, the other her grandfather's. So which was accurate—the picture from outside or your inner self-image? And who got to decide? It was time to check in with Tomás.

She texted: *Hope all is well. I'm getting stronger. Looking forward to getting back to work. It's hard to say exactly when I'll be leaving here but certainly by the fall. Maybe we should start to talk?* Six months seemed fair warning.

She held her phone, waiting irrationally for an immediate reply. She wanted to read, *Great! Can't wait to have you back!* She tried to imagine herself in the office. Hard to square her old self—dashing from desk to desk, spinning her chair and sliding over to look at a friend's screen, operating at a million words a minute—with her present self. Tap ... Tap ... Tap.

She set her phone on the table next to her bed and rolled to the mirror. Not by manipulating a joystick, but with the muscles of her own two arms, her hands—or one hand, one wrist—pushing the chair's wheels. She loved her new toy. With her right hand she could grip the handrim of the right wheel and push, release, push, release. The occupational therapy team had fashioned a brace for her left arm to keep the wrist from flopping; using the inside-facing surface of the brace, coated in a high-friction material, she could rotate the left wheel by making contact with its rubberized handrim.

This manual chair matched her personality. It was exercise. It was small. Efficient. If her electric was like sitting on an easy chair positioned in the cab of a lumbering truck, this was her sports car, her body connected to the floor. She missed Turtle, which she drove fast. She could feel it in her mind—her left foot pressing in the clutch, her right hand slamming back the stick shift, her right foot flooring the accelerator. "How about me trying to sell your car?" Dad had asked back in December. Reluctantly, she'd agreed.

When she learned to drive again—and she would—it wouldn't be a stick. Sadly, it might not even involve foot pedals; more akin to driving her electric wheelchair, none of the thrill of *real* driving. Anyway—cars were going the way of her chair, not the other way around. Who knew, maybe she—and everyone else—would eventually sit in sedans and hatchbacks piloted by algorithms. Still, she was going to miss the beautiful growl of Turtle's engine, the exhilaration of her body being pushed sideways when she took curves at speed.

This thing was actually pretty mean at cornering. She could pull on the right wheel while pushing on the left and pivot on the spot. From her brain to her arms, from her arms to the wheels, the wheels to the ground—she could maneuver herself with precision, getting into spaces too tight for her electric. It was the closest thing she had to legs. And it was fun.

So most humans could walk on their own two feet and she needed this chair. So what? Birds could fly with their own two wings but every human needed a plane—or a helicopter, glider, parachute, blimp, hot air balloon, jetpack, ornithopter. Nobody felt bad about that. *Well, flying in the sky does sound exciting, but I would need to use a plane, and that's cheating, so I can't take joy in it.* Why shouldn't she have fun with her chair? Lots of technology was about augmentation. Sure, she was now down a few rungs on what the body could do unaided, but if you looked at it as an alien arriving on the planet might, it was a difference in degree, not kind. Plus she'd like to see Julia try getting into a tight corner with this thing.

Thinking about planes—did anyone watching the Wrights leap those few hundred meters imagine how fast the technology would develop? Think that, in their lifetime, they'd be able to board a routine flight and cross an ocean? With computers and networks, things moved even faster now, and with AI they would only accelerate.

True, statistically, people with high tetraplegia had only a thirty-year life expectancy. But that averaged in people who were older at the time of injury and people who failed to take care of themselves. Like that woman she'd met in the lounge who refused to use her cough assist machine and kept getting readmitted with respiratory infections. Or the man in the next room who would be here for months because, back home with his wife, they'd let a pressure sore go unnoticed and untreated.

That wasn't her. She would guard her body. She would learn how to insist on excellence from her nurses and aides. So she would see the final decades of the century, and even if she didn't heal on her own, it was inconceivable that there would not be new technology to help her, maybe to cure her.

At the top of her wish list: technology to repair her spinal cord.

Get the nerves talking again. It was just a matter of interpreting signals from one place and sending them to another. How could that not be invented in her lifetime? Say within a quarter century? Her muscles would be atrophied, of course, and her brain might be confused, but so what, she would train and train and—was it unreasonable to expect that she'd be walking again by fifty?

She stopped her chair in front of the room's one mirror. Seven months to the day since she was on that train. The things she could do now that were impossible that first month were incredible: make a fist with her right hand, independently control all the fingers of her right hand (except the pinky and ring finger still moved together), move her left arm at the shoulder and elbow, bend her right leg at the knee, bend her right foot at the ankle, wiggle her right toes, stay balanced in her chair, stay upright for four hours at a time, move herself around the hospital floor without a motor.

She raised her left and right arms, and watched to make sure they moved in sync. Slowly up from her lap, now level with the tops of the wheels, now level with her chest, now shoulders, the peak. Then slowly back down, watching in the mirror, instructing her left arm to slow to keep it level with the right. Again. And again. Two more repetitions. Her forehead was sweating.

She made eye contact with herself. She didn't hate what she saw. Mom had trimmed her hair. Her skin was clear. There was a bead of sweat on her nose. Her blue eyes were sharp behind the clean lenses of her glasses. Now that she could hold her body upright, if she were on a video call, the camera framing only her face and neck, she would look normal. *Yesterday I finished this, today I'll be doing that.* Colleagues seeing her projected on a screen in a conference room would see nothing unusual—the same smiling face in glasses they knew from before.

The mirage, though, would disintegrate in person. Here was something she still couldn't do: transfer herself in or out of her chair. Here was another thing: urinate on her own. Here was another: shift her position in the wheelchair (except when it happened by chance due to a spasm)—and she needed to adjust positions on a regular schedule, otherwise she would develop sores.

Sit still! That was what teachers said to kids. But what they really meant was stay in your chair, stop getting up, stop disrupting the class, stop distracting your classmates. Nobody ever sat truly still by choice. You shifted your weight from the left to the right side and back. You wiggled your butt. You leaned forward and back, pressing against the back of the chair. You fidgeted. You pushed up with your feet. You did all of this without thought; your body sensed when the flow of blood was blocked and corrected the situation without bothering to alert your mind.

No, you didn't know what it meant to sit still until you couldn't move. Where her body was placed, that's where it stayed. And since she had neither the arm strength nor the control to lift and shift herself, she needed to rely on others. It was something she needed to worry about twenty-four hours a day. It didn't matter if she was sleeping or awake, horizontal in bed or upright like now, she needed to make sure no one spot on her skin, no one part of her body, took her weight for too long. (She'd had a dream where she was sleeping, floating, weightless, in a cotton nightgown, no pressure anywhere on her body. If only. What she wouldn't do for one uninterrupted night of sleep!)

Anna started another set of arm lifts. Ping—from her phone over near the bed. Tomás? If she had her own team of aides, one of them would come with her to work. A nurse, at the desk next to her on the open floor, or relaxing in one of those enveloping purple armchairs near the espresso station. She couldn't see it. The nurses here were always harried, running behind, thriving, she suspected, on being busy. It was a mode of operation she knew well.

Her phone called to her, but she completed another five repetitions first. Then rested. Peter was always warning her not to overdo it. She looked in the mirror again, used her right hand to put the brace back on her left, pivoted herself around, and pushed herself back, listening to her wheels rolling over the vinyl floor.

Back at the table, she picked up her phone. The text *was* from Tomás. She hesitated, squinted, read. *Good to hear from you. Let me know once you have a better idea of the date.*

Her shoulders dropped. She forced a smile. What could she say without coming across as needy? *Will do.*

TWENTY-ONE

A steady, rhythmic rumbling. Chicken Abu Zakkour. Taking Anna to eat a potato sandwich. Showing her Aleppo. They would eat in the park. A classmate from high school would walk by. But where was this? Anna's legs over her own, her arms around Anna, about to pivot and transfer her from bed to chair, but this wasn't the bed. Rumbling. Murmured speech. She could feel Anna's ribs against her fingers. She breathed in her clean smell. Heat radiating off her skin. Her fragile torso. Her thin body. Where was the wheelchair? She always put it in position first. That was the procedure.

A man. On the other side of Anna. He shouldn't be so close. Now his hairy arms around Anna's back. A purple, silicone, tight-fitting cap on Anna's head. The man was shifting Anna's legs, taking them off her lap, putting them over his own. *Excuse me. Excuse me.* But no words came out. *Anna. Anna.* Whispers drowned out by the rumbling. She reached up. No hijab. In its place a rubbery cap.

The man held a yellow fixed pole and leaned in, toward Anna. Now he brought his head close. She sensed Anna knew him, she knew him too, but from where? His face was blurry, feminine. A blue lycra cap. "I'll transfer you." Anna smiled. Now he touched her cheek and traced the rim of her ear and slid his fingers underneath the silicone cap. Anna closed her eyes.

Bum-bump. Bum-bump. Batul's heart was speeding—two beats, rest, two beats, rest. She wasn't holding Anna's back. She was far away. Above. Watching this man with the hairy arms, still holding Anna, his fingers still under her cap, Anna's eyes still closed.

"I don't need you." Anna's voice. Directed at her. Echoing. *I don't need you. I don't need you.* The rhythmic rumbling. *I don't need you.* Bum-bump. Muffled talking. High-pitched squeal.

"Einsteigen bitte!" From the loudspeaker. *Please board.*

Her head was bent forward, her chin resting on her collarbone. Drool below her lip. She raised her eyes. An African woman with a kind, smooth face, seated opposite on the train, nodded and half smiled. The dream—her sick mind.

She stepped out at her station in a daze. The hairy-armed man. His fingers under her cap. The neurons firing should not have allowed such images. But they wouldn't leave her head, not as she climbed the four flights to their apartment, not as she waited for Baba to finish in the bathroom. Inside, she washed her hands three times, then cupped water direct from the faucet to her mouth. Swish and spit, then the whole procedure twice more. Finally, she cupped more water with her right hand, inhaled this into her nose, and pressed on the bridge with her left hand to push the water out.

She'd never had impure thoughts.

She inhaled and pushed out the water twice more, then washed her face. Three times. Each arm to its elbow. Three times. She wiped back her hair, staticky from the hijab, and rinsed behind her ears. She raised her feet to the sink, each in turn, and washed between her toes.

In her bedroom, she put on socks, draped a scarf over her hair, and unfolded the corner of her prayer rug. Feet together, eyes down.

She couldn't pray. Her brain was sick. Impossible. Only men had —she needed to think the word in English—erotic dreams. That's why women needed to cover up. That her subconscious would conjure up—and about a friend ... she couldn't let herself think it. Something was wrong inside her, because even now, under the harsh clarity of the naked fluorescent bulb screwed into her ceiling, she saw the dream.

She focused on her breathing, on her intention to pray. She raised her hands to shoulder level. *Allahu Akbar.* She clasped her right hand over her left hand and brought them to her chest. *A'othu billaahi min ash-shaytaan ar-rajeem ... Ameen ...* She put her hands at her side. *Allahu Akbar.* She bent at the waist, pressing her hands to her knees, making her upper body horizontal. *Subhana rabbiya al'azeem.* Glorious is my Lord the Magnificent.

She stood. She raised her hands to shoulder level again, palms facing forward. *Sami'a Allahu liman hamidah ... Allahu Akbar.* She descended to her knees, prostrated herself, pressed her forehead to the floor. She felt the texture of the rug on her hands, her forehead, her knees. *Subhana rabbiya al'ala ... Subhana rabbiya al'ala ... Subhana rabbiya al'ala.* Glorious is my Lord the Most High.

Now, scarcely letting the words form, whispering them in her mind, "Oh Lord, I know what I dreamed is evil, please take this out of my heart, please guide me. Oh magnificent Lord, please keep me on the holy path."

Allahu Akbar. She lifted her head and raised herself to a kneeling position, her back and head upright, her hands on her knees. *Rabbi, ighfir li.* Lord forgive me. *Allahu Akbar.* She prostrated herself again, touching her forehead to the rug. *Subhana rabbiya al'ala ... Subhana rabbiya al'ala ... Subhana rabbiya al'ala.* Glorious is my Lord the Most High. *Allahu Akbar.* She completed the second rak'ah. The third rak'ah. She rotated her head right. *As-salamu 'alaikum warahmat-ullahi wabarakatuh.* Left. *As-salamu 'alaikum warahmat-ullahi wabarakatuh.* Peace be upon you.

TWENTY-TWO

The beginnings of a pressure sore on her tailbone—no leaving bed today.

"Time for breakfast."

"There's a box with my name on it in the fridge near the lounge. A friend brought it. Do you mind getting it? There's a pastry in there I'd like to have with my breakfast."

The woman returned, empty-handed. "There's no box."

Who took her food? She'd watched Melanie label the front and top.

Later, she asked Batul to check. "Yes. It's right there. On the top shelf. With your name. Can't miss it."

Petty bitch. She kept it together until Batul left. These people abusing their power because you couldn't leave the bed, because you couldn't complain, because they thought your mind was broken. Fuck. Fuck that woman. Anna reached out with her arm and swiped everything off the table. Her fingers closed around a baby carrot and she flung it as hard as she could at the wall. It landed between the bed and the window. "TV off! Ingrid—don't turn it back on."

No answer. "Sorry, Ingrid." Next time she'd insist. Except it was pointless. She remembered a favorite expression of her eleventh-grade history teacher: Arguing with a fool is like wrestling with a pig —you get dirty, but the pig likes it.

TWENTY-THREE

Back in January, after her left shoulder and elbow woke up, she'd thought the wrist or fingers would be next. Over and over and over she'd been telling her wrist to bend, her fingers to curl, but two months had passed, and nothing. Her left hand was a floppy appendage at the end of two feeble dowels joined with chicken wire. Useless without the brace, and even then more a clumsy stick than a forearm and hand.

Two summers ago, she was scaling walls to train for that obstacle course. The strength of her arms and legs made it easy to pull up her skinny frame, and then extend an arm to help her friends up. Yesterday, in PT, Peter asked if she wanted a challenge. "Yes."

He'd lifted her out of her chair and laid her stomach-down on the mat. "Try to turn yourself over." She pushed with her right arm. She used her neck. She strained, her forehead covered in sweat. She tried bending her right knee, pushing with her left arm, twisting her body. She pushed with her right arm and her right knee and her neck all at the same time—*the bitch who said her box wasn't there*—push—*fucking Herr Bergmann*—push—*we should go our separate ways*—almost there—almost on her side—but she couldn't. She fell back to her front. Stuck. Lying like a dead salamander, her wet forehead and nose pressed into the foam. She breathed in and out. In and out again. Her pulse slowed.

The thing was, having experienced what it was like to be unable to move her fingers, to need someone to feed her, to be unable to sit upright, her current limitations didn't seem so limiting. Even if they had left her lying on that mat yesterday in a heavy pile, unable to complete a roll from belly to back, a skill last mastered at age six months.

That's not how Mom and Dad saw it. They'd finally reached Herr Bergmann this morning, and had called her afterward. "Did he file the paperwork? Can we start looking for an apartment?"

She heard her mother take a deep breath over the phone. "Your father and I think, if you're against living with us, you should consider the group home. You won't have to worry about working."

How come even her own parents couldn't understand? Think she would give up on her career and live entirely off the state? The thing she hated most about this place was having no control. She couldn't decide when to get out of bed, couldn't decide when to go to sleep, couldn't even turn the TV off without a fight. To have that be indefinite—to be written off—to be unable to build—she wasn't sure what was more terrifying—that she would or wouldn't adapt.

"Mom, you have to know that's not right for me. I'm too young. I haven't achieved anything yet. I want to work. I need to be around normal people. I'm not living in a nursing home."

"It's not a nursing home. It's a group home for long-term care. Sweetie, won't you feel safer there, with nurses around, where they know how to take care of people like you? It's what Herr Bergmann suggests."

People like her! Let Herr Bergmann—what was he, like fifty?—move into a nursing home and make self-portraits out of construction paper. But she was too tired, and her shoulders and left hand were in too much pain to argue. Maybe she was the crazy one. The way her parents were talking, it could be that they were right, if her condition stayed like this, could she commute, could she work, was it realistic to live in her own place?

Yes, she thought with renewed energy when she woke up this morning, and she would prove it. Lying in bed, she pulled up Google Maps. The nearest S-Bahn station was 1.8 kilometers from the hospital. She used to jog that far to cool down after a run; wouldn't have thought twice about walking that distance and back with Ursula and Rajeev to grab lunch.

She turned on satellite view, pinched with her thumb and index finger, and dragged, following the route. There were sidewalks the whole way. It looked like there were ramps at the intersections. And ramps where driveways cut through the sidewalk? Hard to tell, even zoomed in.

She would need to text Peter and tell him she was stuck in bed. Then take the elevator down as usual, but turn the other way. She felt her right eyelid twitch. She'd done riskier things. Not recently.

There were all these rules. One was that it was forbidden to leave unless you signed out with the name of the person accompanying you. Well, she wasn't a child, she hadn't committed a crime, the hospital wasn't a prison, the need-to-be-accompanied policy wasn't a law, and she was contemplating rolling along a sidewalk, not robbing a bank.

The nurse wheeled her manual chair toward the bed.

"Let's go electric today." Her mouth was dry. For sure she couldn't get there with her manual. Inside, where the vinyl floors were smooth and level, it was her legs. Outside, she wouldn't have the strength to push herself on rough ground, not to mention up an incline, or, scarier, slow herself when going down one.

The nurse looked at her. "Are you feeling okay?"

Fifteen minutes later, she was at the sliding glass doors in the main lobby, ready to be stopped and sent back to her wing. But no one approached. She exited into the daylight, and quickly turned right, toward the west end of the campus. As she left the complex and turned onto the sidewalk, no alarm went off, no security guard came running after her; the only difference was the sound her tires made—louder over the gritty cement than the smooth asphalt of the hospital paths.

She pushed the joystick all the way forward and increased her speed to the maximum, about the pace of a brisk walk. Her body was jostled—but only slightly—as she rolled over the seams of the cement slabs. The sidewalk was wide, making it easy to keep a safe distance from the curb on the right; she wished she was moving in the direction of traffic, but judged that crossing the street wasn't worth it. The air was cold on her face and hand—invigorating. And this—this was no big deal. She should have done it sooner. Eight months of venturing no more than three hundred meters from her bed had messed with her sense of what was possible. She'd formed her own psychological prison.

Cash. Too bad she hadn't thought to bring any. A döner kebab at the station—lamb, onions, pickled cabbage, lavash soaking up the yogurt sauce—each optional filling yay-ed or nay-ed by her, here, out in the normal world—

Scheisse. Construction ahead. She eased back on the joystick. The cement slabs of the sidewalk ended in front of her and dropped to an unpaved stretch. It looked like a drop of—hard to judge—two or three centimeters. Then about ten meters of gravel and sand, then a similar rise to where the paved part resumed. It was nothing—if she were running she wouldn't notice. That was before. The only outdoor surfaces she'd ever driven over were hard. She listened to herself—she'd set out to make it to the station—she'd covered less than a third of the distance—how timid had she become?—she wasn't giving up at the first obstacle.

She tapped on the joystick and moved forward a tiny distance. Then again. Then braced herself for the drop. She nosed forward. There! The front casters thudded into the sand, then the main wheels, and her body was jerked up. Not so bad. She gave herself a moment, breathed, and then pressed on the joystick. She rolled forward a meter, a second meter, a third meter. And then, suddenly, her chair turned left. The left drive wheel must have lost traction. She'd immediately let the throttle go back to neutral, but now she was stopped, rotated ninety degrees, and facing a fence, her back to the curb.

Tenuously, she nudged the joystick forward. She heard both wheels spinning in place. Her heart pounding, she pushed the joystick all the way now, but only for a second, frightened she would take off and crash into the fence. Instead, no movement at all. She pictured ruts in the sand dug by her wheels. It was like getting a car stuck in the snow, except she couldn't use a shovel. Or spread salt. Or blast the heater and wait. Or get out and walk home.

Okay, but say she was stuck in a car. The thing to do would be to rock it slightly and hope the tires could get purchase. She pulled back very, very gently on the joystick. Her wheels spun in place. As for rocking back ... the curb was less than half a meter behind her. If she pulled back hard and the wheels suddenly got traction—she'd go off the curb, her chair would tip backwards, her head would slam into the street, a car could hit her. No way.

Even as blood pounded in her head, she felt her face, neck and hand getting cold. Could she make this not humiliating? She listened until she heard a car, then turned her head to the right, raised her right hand as high as she could, and rotated her wrist so her palm faced out toward the oncoming car. She waved and attempted to make eye contact with the driver. No acknowledgement.

She tried again with the next car, a black Golf. The driver waved back. She could tell, from the look on his face, and the exaggerated wave, that he'd made a flash judgment: she wasn't all there. Come on —why didn't people think, "this person needs help, that's why she's waving." Don't conflate physical damage with intellectual impairment.

Ten more minutes and five more cars. None stopped. Batul would come immediately. But she'd also be angry and worried and make her swear to never go out on her own again.

She pulled out her phone, finally, and swiped it alive. Peter.

Three minutes later he was sprinting toward her. "What the hell, Anna? I thought you were smarter than this."

A week later, Batul, who knew nothing about her failed trip, asked how things were coming along with finding an apartment.

"I'm not sure it's going to work," Anna said, feeling like she was letting Batul down.

"But you're doing so well." Batul looked at her in her manual wheelchair, hands on the rims. "I don't understand. What changed? Why are you giving up?"

She'd tried talking to Herr Bergmann on her own. It was exhausting. Round and round he went, never giving logical answers to her questions. She'd received a copy of paperwork he'd filed a month earlier in which he'd checked the box saying she could transfer herself in and out of bed. This was obviously not true, and would preclude qualifying for a round-the-clock aide team. When she confronted him, he claimed it had been a mistake. She thought of herself as a good person, but she wished him all the worst in the world, wanted karma to come for him.

Most of the time she couldn't even reach him. He'd call back once for every dozen messages, and that one time, she couldn't answer her phone. No surprise there: *most* of the time she couldn't answer, and he sure as hell didn't care enough to call in the evening, when she was in bed and available. And telling her his mobile number? Out of the question.

"Is there someone else I can talk to?" she'd asked the receptionist, after navigating the phone tree and listening to elevator music for five minutes.

"No. Herr Bergmann is your case manager. You need to wait until he's back from vacation."

She'd tried researching the laws and policies herself. She'd asked her parents to push harder. "Honey," Mom said, "when you've been around as long as we have, you learn: the system decides, not you."

She wanted Batul to understand what she was up against. "Nobody thinks I'll be able to manage," she started. "The insurance company keeps saying I should live in a group home. It seems like they don't want me to work. I don't know. Sometimes I think it's all about what's cheaper for them. Other times I think they could be right and I'm fooling myself."

Batul looked straight at her with an intensity she'd never seen before. "Don't think that way. I know you, and you can't give in. When I was trying to get into university while we were in Turkey, there was all this paperwork, and everyone tells you it's not possible. But the thing is, it's easier for everyone to not be helpful, or to only pretend to be helpful."

Batul looked up, then back at her. "Here, I have Tasneem as my guide. Do you have any friends who understand how to navigate bureaucracy? Like a lawyer? You need someone to argue for you, someone who knows how to get things done in this country."

Julia. The one person she least wanted to ask a favor of. "I'm already a physical burden; I don't want to ask a friend for help with something I should be capable of doing myself." And it was true—if she could keep her energy up, stay awake later to do the research, find more time during the day to make phone calls and send emails—

"Anna, this is your future."

The next day she texted Julia. *Would you be willing to help me ...*

TWENTY-FOUR

Within a month, Julia had asked a lot of people a lot of questions. She'd drawn an org chart. She'd scared the shit out of Herr Bergmann and figured out that while he could screw things up by filling out forms incorrectly, he had no power to make things happen. She'd untangled what was decided by insurance, what was up to the Ministry of Labor and Social Affairs, what was up to the Ministry of Health, and who specifically at those agencies needed to approve funding. Julia threatened. She charmed. She probed. She escalated. She hired a lawyer.

"I can't afford that," Anna had told her.

"I'll pay out of my big fat commission from Caterpillar. We need a lawyer. Look, these bureaucrats, they're not assholes, ba—Anna, they're just lazy as fuck, they don't know you, and therefore they don't give a shit about you. We're going to change that. We'll get them to see the human. And we need a lawyer so they know we're not backing down. Otherwise they'll push papers around while they wait for us to go away."

"What if they feel antagonized and dig in?"

"I'm not worried. You have to think about it this way: Most

people just don't care all that much. They're going to do the easiest thing. Our job is to make it more painful for them to deny you your own nursing team than to approve it."

One lesson of these past nine months: Nothing came together with randomness and spontaneity the way it used to. When no one gave you the benefit of the doubt, when everything took ten times as long, when you depended on others, you needed a plan, and a backup plan, and a backup to the backup.

Which is why she was finally forcing herself to touch something she'd been afraid to poke at—the details of her return to DDB. She was still unsettled by what Tomás texted back in March: more or less that they would figure it out later. In her situation, postponing a decision guaranteed a worse outcome. This wasn't a normal return, like after being on parental leave. She would only be able to put in so many hours a day. And if her physical abilities stayed where they were now—something she now nearly accepted—she would need an aide with her in the office.

She dictated the long email to Tomás that she'd been composing in her mind, read it over, and hit send. He wrote back quickly. *Those are good questions. I owe you a visit. I'll stop by after work tomorrow if that works for you.*

She would have preferred a phone call, as suggested in her email. By voice it was easy for the other person—and her—to forget she was paralyzed. In person, that was impossible. Maybe that's why he wanted to visit—to see how she looked and start to imagine how she'd fit in.

Well, she didn't want to tell him not to visit. *After work.* The timing *should* be okay—after dinner, before the evening routine. She would have liked more time to plan, but she didn't want to send a signal that everything with her was now going to be complicated.

Looking forward to seeing you. Would 6:30 work?
Perfect.

The next day, thankfully, things stayed on schedule. By 6:15 she was waiting for him in the lounge, hoping the two people playing chess would finish their game soon. By 6:30 she was alone. Now it was 6:52 and she checked her messages again to see if he'd written to say he was running late. Nothing. *Are you still coming? Are you almost here? I may need to go to bed soon so let's reschedule.* No, she wouldn't text him.

7:03. The nurse came into the room. "Frau Werner." Shoot. This was the older nurse, with whom she didn't have the greatest relationship, who even after all these months refused to call her Anna.

"Time for bed. You need to go back to your room."

"I'm waiting for a visitor. Can you put me last today?"

"No, I can't. There's a schedule and we follow it."

If only. She would need to text Tomás to reschedule.

"You can do that after."

Half an hour later her teeth were brushed, her face washed, and she was in bed. She unlocked her phone, started to text—and just then there was a knock on the door.

"Anna?" Tomás's voice.

He sat on a chair between the bed and the window.

"Sorry I'm late. I brought you a decaf americano and a Pfannkuchen."

No way would she eat in front of him while she was lying down, and certainly not a jelly donut. "That was thoughtful. Thanks. Can you put them on the table?"

She asked about his kids. He told her about their trip to visit his parents in Madrid. She asked about work. He told her the team was behind on the upgrade. He asked her if she'd tried using her laptop. "Not yet." She told him about her schedule for leaving the hospital and how she would have an aide with her at the office. She tried to project certainty even though, despite Julia's confidence, nothing had actually been approved yet.

"Look," he finally said. "I'm so glad you'll be coming back to work, but I'm thinking we shouldn't put you right back with the old team. It's too high-pressure. You'd agree with that, right?"

Did she? She would need time to ramp back up, she would need to get her work done in new ways, but her old team was where she belonged, and where she already knew everyone. "I guess so."

"What I'll do is speak with HR and get them looking for something easier for you—something where, if you need to take time off or have slow days, it won't be a big deal. I was thinking support."

How was support a good role for her? Starting slow made sense. Starting in support made none. If she had a headset on, she wouldn't be able to use voice to control her computer, so she'd have to do everything by typing, which would be slow and would annoy customers. And what if a conversation went long and she needed to use the bathroom? "I—"

"Get some sleep. I'll put the wheels in motion. Sorry ... not intentional. By—September, you said?—we'll be all set for you."

"How'd it go?" Batul asked her in the morning. "Is he okay with you starting with a limited schedule?"

Anna had barely slept. *We shouldn't put you right back with the old team. You'd agree with that, right? I guess so. You'd agree, right? I guess so. I guess so. I guess so.*

"Was it firm or do you have a choice?" Batul asked. "Him reassigning you to this other department. Did you agree because you were surprised?"

"Yes." And also, lying in bed, she didn't see how she could push back, didn't see how he could perceive her as an asset to his team rather than a legal obligation.

"He misread you," Batul said. "He doesn't understand what you're capable of. Can't you email him, take back what you said, explain?"

Yes. She would do it today, after lunch, when she had time to lay out her argument. Before he put the wheels in motion.

His reply was again fast. *I hear you. Let's start you in support. Once you're back in the swing of things we can look into a transfer.*

Too fast. Didn't he need to think about what she'd said? Discuss with others? Also his tone. This was her career. *We can look into ...* Look into it when? As it was, she was getting rusty, and meanwhile machine learning was advancing: her Cambridge friend had shown her how researchers had trained a neural network to write captions for photos. You gave it a picture and it generated text like: "Two ponies standing in a grassy field." How was that possible? The only way to stay current was to be in it. Maybe it was naive (yet again), but she had expected to hear from Tomás what project she'd be working on—not to be hijacked by a demotion!

She took a deep breath. This is why she'd started early. Everything was harder—ten times harder, a hundred times—in this body. When their CEO visited, he'd said something about if there was anything he could do, if she ever needed his help, to get in touch. Well, she doubted he meant this kind of help. She was pretty sure he meant something medical, like to use his influence if she wasn't getting proper care. She couldn't see going layers above Tomás.

No. It wasn't that he didn't like her; it wasn't that he was malicious; he was busy and didn't see her clearly. She needed to reset the ideas he'd formed of what she was and wasn't capable of. And that wasn't going to happen by debating with him over email. Tomorrow she would email back and ask if they could talk again in person. And this time she'd plan better.

When her parents emptied out her apartment, they packed her clothes in boxes with mothballs. This she discovered back in the winter when Mom turned up with her swimsuit and she was hit by that nauseating, toxic, naphthalene smell.

"Why *mothballs*?" she'd complained.

"We put everything in the attic. You want your clothes getting holes?"

"But nobody uses mothballs anymore. Because they smell like this."

"Anna, honestly, it's nothing. You hang the clothes up for a few days and the smell goes away."

Which was why, when Tomás agreed to meet again, she called Mom and asked her to go up to the attic, dig out a professional outfit, and air it out so that the naphthalene odor would be gone by today.

Mom had brought, at Anna's request, two pairs of jeans. Jeans had been her daily uniform at work, and they said, in her mind, "software engineer." But the instant Mom removed them from the laundry basket she'd lugged in, it was clear they wouldn't work. Too dangerous. The denim was rough and rigid, the fit was tight—they would be a pain for her nurse to get on and off, and it wasn't worth the risk of those back pockets pinching her skin, causing friction, cutting off blood, even the pair without rivets.

She settled instead on loose black slacks—the same pants she'd interviewed in. She wore a white blouse with a collar and the gray zip up fleece with the DDB logo that Mom had had to search through all the boxes to find. Half an hour before she was due to meet Tomás, she asked the nurse to transfer her to her manual chair.

"You sure you don't want the electric?"

She was sure. To Tomás a wheelchair might be a wheelchair, but not to her. She felt like herself in the manual, she looked better, less disabled, it wasn't so big as to swallow her up, plus she wanted to arrive under her own power.

The where, at her suggestion, was the hospital coffee shop. They could sit at a table. He could have a drink. A donut if he wanted. The surrounding din would make their conversation more comfortable and casual. Doctors, nurses, visitors and other people who moved on legs would be coming and going. It would feel ordinary. Not all that different from the DDB cafeteria, minus the view.

"Do you want me to come with you?" Mom offered.

That would send the opposite message. This wasn't like talking to a doctor or Herr Bergmann. She needed Tomás to see that she was independent. And it reminded her of a story she'd heard from Ursula who'd done a phone interview where she could hear the candidate's mom whispering tips in the background. "Tell them you have a good work ethic." "Tell them you know Java." To Ursula's horror and amusement, the candidate lost it, hissing back, "Holy mackerel Mama! They don't USE Java." And even after that the mom kept whispering. "Tell them you'll start at a low salary."

Tomás was already there when she pushed herself from the elevator to the coffee shop—standing near the entrance, staring at his phone. She rolled up next to him and looked up.

"Anna! You look great. How are you feeling?"

"Good. Grab a coffee and put it on my tab, and I'll find a table." That "tab" had taken some arranging. As soon as he sat down, she asked about the upgrade project. This time they were going to talk shop. *Let the ball come to you.* Another of Julia's sayings.

The upgrade had hit some serious roadblocks. He mentioned a performance issue they'd isolated to an obscure third-party module, but which they couldn't figure out. She imagined the logic inside that module and could see how the developers, in adding support for double-precision floating point, could have inadvertently made a change that slowed everything down.

"Ask Rajeev to instrument the number of cache misses under load and compare the old and new versions," she suggested. "I bet that will turn up a clue." Part of this was performance, but in fact her mind was buzzing. Only deep in its recesses was a clock ticking, reminding her she would soon need to get back to her room.

"You know what?" Tomás said as he was reaching the last dregs of his coffee. "It may have been premature for me to suggest you switch to support. Let me think about this some more. There's still plenty of time, and we can keep talking. I'll come back again, even—it's easy, this place is practically on my way home."

TWENTY-FIVE

In bed, on her left, a horizontal rest before her afternoon therapy session. Yesterday her Grad der Behinderung had arrived. One hundred: the maximum disability level. This was the trigger that would allow the agency to start assembling her aide team.

"That's wonderful," Batul had told her this morning. "Even though it's strange to congratulate you for this type of one hundred."

Yes. When the man from the Ministry of Labor and Social Affairs came to interview her, he'd told Mom and her, in a tone that implied she was gaming the system and asking for services to which she was not entitled, that she would be evaluated again in two years and her grade might go down. "We'll be thrilled if the score goes down to zero," Mom told him.

"What do you think of me asking Batul to be on my care team?" she'd asked Mom.

"That's up to you, honey."

What if Batul said yes but hated it? What if—

Ping. A text. From Tomás. She took a deep breath.

Is now a convenient time to talk?
Free for next hour.

She'd thought about it and made peace with it. If this was to tell her he still wanted to transfer her, she would accept it. There would be plenty to learn from helping customers, and as she got healthier, she'd work her way back to engineering.

Her phone rang. She slid her earphone in. Ring. She moved her hand back to her phone. Ring. She answered.

"I'm going to get right to the point. You know how the upgrade project is way behind schedule?"

Yes. They'd talked about it last time. The team had been planning for it practically since she joined the company. The original goal was to complete it this year.

"What I didn't tell you when I was over there is the eyes on this, the pressure I'm under. I'm going to speak unvarnished here. It's straight from the CEO. I got called into his office. It was him, the CTO, the VP Machine Learning, and my boss. 'Get it done before Q3 next year or find another job,' he told me."

He'd never shared anything like that in their two years of one-on-ones. "Okay ..."

"They told me to put a new leader on it, someone not from a project management background. We need someone who gets our system, can read the code, and can talk about stuff at a technical level with the other engineers, who can call bullshit when they make up excuses for why bugs aren't getting fixed ..."

He was going to ask her to lead this? It smelled of desperation. Or of a search for a scapegoat.

"... You know, when I visited you in your room, I may have misjudged you. After we talked last time, on my way home I was thinking—wow, she hasn't been at work in nine months, she's dealing with this medical situation, and she still has command of all these obscure system details ..."

Sure, but going from totally sidelining her to handing her a higher-profile project than any she'd worked on before her stroke? Julia may have been right that he wasn't a good judge of ability.

"I told my boss about our conversation, I told him you were the engineer who designed the drift detection feature, and he floated the idea of you leading the upgrade. I checked around. People have a lot of respect for you." He paused. "Anna, you know, I may have underestimated you, even before the stroke. You were so young. But now, well ... Are you interested?"

Even last year customers were starting to ask about running large models on GPUs, something DDB couldn't support until all the systems were replumbed through this upgrade. It would be a classic swapping of the engine mid-flight. And screwing up, given their customer base, could result in the failure of an actual engine on an actual plane. Should she sign up for something so important?

Well, she did have the whole system in her head. She was good at talking with people—and getting better, Ingrid aside. She could see herself in a conference room with the other engineers, listening to them, working through technical tradeoffs, coming up with logical goals. She would get exposed to all the subsystems, including what it took to run production models on GPUs. And that she would now be slower at coding wouldn't matter as much.

It occurred to her that the reason she hadn't been promoted last year was because she'd expected the company to evaluate her in an unbiased manner, automatically detecting that she was operating above her level. Same mistake she'd made at the ER—thinking the system would do the right thing. In a perverse way, her paralysis was working for her, because now nothing was automatic and this—no, she—had forced Tomás to look below the surface.

"You can think about it, of course," he now said, retreating. "No need to decide right away." Though she could tell he wished she would.

Everyone here was always talking about her "number one priority": her health. If she said yes, and then the project started going south ... she knew herself well enough to know that, if she had to let anything slide, it would be self-care. She'd skip PT, get sloppy with monitoring her body. And what if she had no say in the matter? If another infection landed her in bed for weeks, no meetings, no laptop? But the alternative was worse: a future of safety, easy projects with loose deadlines that didn't matter. Sooner or later she was going to have to find a balance between managing her health and, well, living.

"No—I can tell you now. I'd love to take it on."

TWENTY-SIX

It was the first day of summer. Anna was in the front passenger seat. Dad was driving. Mom was in the back with Peter. "I'd like to see it anyway," he'd told her, and offered to come along on his day off.

She looked out greedily, making momentary eye contact with a man in a strikingly blue t-shirt gazing out of a city bus. On the next block, she watched a woman with a high ponytail and leather crossbody satchel riding a bike, her right hand on the handlebar, her left grasping the leashes of two floppy-eared, long-legged, rust-colored dogs trotting beside her. Also on the sidewalk: a couple leaning on a raised bar table outside a pizza stand, a man bent over tying his daughter's sneaker, a woman walking and texting, a dozen bikes and scooters parked against a rack, and kids waiting at a bus stop bearing an advertisement emblazoned with the soloists for the 2015-2016 season of the Berlin Philharmonic.

For her, for almost a year now, the chopstick taps of the octopus had been so slow, her whole world reduced to the hospital and its immediate sprawling, uninspired, almost suburban surroundings. But the metronome for all these other people had continued at its usual pace. In some three-dimensional vector representation of movement and activity over time, hers would be immediately distinguishable from everyone else's. Less than child's play for a machine learning model to pick her out of the population. These people had done stuff. They'd gone places. That couple would relish their pizza all the more because they had work tomorrow. The city had not stopped.

They pulled up in front of the building where Melanie had found an apartment whose landlord would allow renovations. Dad and Stefan were using all of their vacation time to do the work, and had been at it for three weeks. Now Dad unlocked and opened the door, and she pushed her way, tentatively, over the threshold. She soaked in the smell of sawdust and fresh paint as she waited for her eyes to adjust to the sunlight reflecting off white walls.

It was a wonder. The large shower area was unenclosed, the floor gently pitched toward a drain along the wall, with both the handle for an overhead shower head and a wand easily in reach. "We installed a thermostatic mixing valve," Dad said proudly. The water could never get to scalding temperatures, even if her aide accidentally turned the faucet all the way to hot.

The toilet was mounted on the wall at the precise height to accommodate her shower/commode chair. The sink was flat, also mounted on the wall, at a height and depth that would let her wheel her manual chair under it, reaching the faucet controls with her right hand. A large window next to a heated towel rack flooded the room with light, though the glass was rippled, to provide privacy. The tiles were all a pinky-beige, warmer than anything you found at the hospital, almost the color of her old bath towels, not yet unpacked from the mothballs.

"This is impressive," Peter said to Dad, peering in from the hallway. "What you did with the doors was smart." Not only the bathroom, but all the rooms had sliding doors. In her bedroom, Stefan and Dad had switched the mechanism for opening and closing blinds from the old-fashioned pulley system to an electric switch. A bunch of hooks lined the wall a little below eye level: a funny grabbing tool that looked like a long-necked turkey hung on one. She pushed to the wall and confirmed she could lift it off the hook, and replace it.

Dad's wet saw sat on the kitchen floor. They'd demolished the cabinets on the far wall, below the window, and were in the process of building a new, lower counter.

"What do you think?" Dad asked.

"I love it. I love every bit of it."

Later in the week, back in her hospital room, she looked at Batul. Behind her, squirrels—three or four of them—were chattering, screeching, chasing each other like mad through the deep green foliage of the oak tree, leaping from branch to branch, ascending higher and higher. "Everything is set."

Insurance had issued her a (refurbished) manual wheelchair. It'd been fitted, she was getting used to it, and she'd be taking it with her —her legs for when she left here. They also, supposedly, would soon approve funding for her electric chair. There were so many options and tradeoffs, but the one she had her eye on had a thirty-kilometer range, would be able to lower her all the way to a horizontal position, and could mount in the driver's position of a special van. (One day ...)

The plan was to move next month. She'd asked Peter to work with her on a technique for rotating herself from side to back so her future aides would only need to wake up twice during the night. They'd tried. Only under unrealistic conditions—when there was a single pillow behind her back, when there was no bedding in which to get tangled, when her legs were positioned exactly right—could she do it. "Work with your aides," Peter said. "I bet you'll find a way."

She'd been telling everyone about her apartment and how much she was looking forward to moving. What she hadn't admitted, and didn't dare tell her parents, was her recurring nightmare. She's in bed. A lumbering woman with broad shoulders, leathery skin, and straggly hair is rummaging through her cabinets, her back to her. The aide takes out her laptop. Tosses her clothes on the floor. Opens her shoebox with photos, runs her hand through it, turns it upside down.

"Please, no." She opens another shoebox, finds her hiding spot, pulls out the cash. Her phone. The aide has it. The aide pockets the cash. The aide is leaving the room. She can't breathe. So many hours since she was rotated. So many hours since her bladder was last emptied. "Please ... please ... I'm begging you ... take the cash, only give me back my phone. I won't tell. Please don't leave me trapped."

In the hospital there were lots of people around who knew what they were doing. Here screams would be heard. Once on her own she would be dependent on a single aide. Oil and water and stuck in hostile silence. Or worse, she "forgets" to wake up in the night to rotate her, she doesn't clean her properly, she touches her ...

Yesterday she and Mom met with the representative from the agency that was hiring her team. Unlike Herr Bergmann, this guy seemed thrilled—no talking around the hot porridge. She put her Julia glasses on—every team, every week was income. He explained the process, and told them to expect "stormy seas" and turnover in the first few months.

"It's quite personal and it's not always so easy to staff the team with compatible people. I can tell you, though, our aides will be eager to work for you."

"How come?" She was friendly? Talkative? Less depressed?

"You're light."

Of course.

"What about ... like if I'm in bed and need help ... if I can't reach my phone—"

"Oh, let me tell you, much easier than calling, this is what we do. We'll get you a wireless doorbell, plug the chime into the wall, you'll wear the button around your neck on a lanyard. Anytime you need help, you press."

Like an aristocrat in her salon, tinkling a bell, her little pinky stuck out, summoning her servant to bring black tea on a silver platter —she couldn't see herself pressing.

"If," Mom asked him, "Anna has a friend who wants to be one of her aides, how would that work?"

. . .

"Everything is set. Funds are approved." She looked at Batul. "The agency will start assembling the team." She thought about her conversation with Leo, him talking about the lifetime costs. "They want me out of the hospital by the end of next month. And ..."

Her neck turned red. She'd twisted these thoughts up so much that she couldn't tell if she was asking for reasons that were fair to Batul. She wouldn't ask Melanie to do such unpleasant, intimate things. It was one thing to imagine a nurse becoming a friend, and a whole other thing for a friend to become a nurse. You could talk about everything with your close friends, but you didn't ask them to wash you, or empty your bladder. There wasn't the detachment of an agency making the hire, and if things went sour, there was a path that wasn't possible with a friend.

Also Batul might be offended. Although, if the situation were reversed, she wouldn't be—she would take it as a sign of trust. She pictured herself in her bed, pressing the doorbell hanging on her lanyard necklace, summoning Batul. No—she could never— Batul was going to be a doctor, why—

"That's great news," Batul said, after Anna's *and* dangled into silence. They were both quiet for a moment. Then, "Would it be okay if I come visit you once in a while?"

They'd talked most weekdays for the past nine months. "You're kidding, right? I'm counting on it. And I want to keep helping you prepare. You can study at my place if you need somewhere quiet. I want you to think of my house as your house. But ..."

If she said no, she said no. Once, in eighth grade, she'd asked Sandra to help her with an English assignment, even though she didn't need the help. They'd sat on Sandra's bed, heads together, textbooks out. She felt pressure behind her eyes. There were a hundred reasons not to ask. You could talk yourself out of anything. "I wanted to ask you ..."

Batul nodded.

"Would you be interested, only until you start university, instead of working here ... in being an aide? I think the pay should be the same. That's what the agency said. It would give you more free time to study. Only some of the shifts would need to be overnight—would that be okay with your parents?"

Batul tapped her finger against her lip. She was figuring out how to say no. Or making up her mind. Debating if she wanted this type of responsibility. Thinking about the unpleasant aspects. Or if her family would let her.

"Are you sure they can hire me? Wouldn't I need to be certified? I'm not officially qualified ... there are lots of things I've never done." Batul looked out the door. "And here there are always nurses around. What if I do something wrong and there's nobody to help? What if I hurt you?"

She would be the last person to hurt her.

"You would need to get a certification. The agency person explained it. It's not difficult. A class of a few days and then a test. This is to be an assistant. The team will have four people. One will be a full registered nurse with all the education and special knowledge, and she will be responsible for teaching and supervising the others."

"I see." Batul breathed out, leaned forward, brought her palm to her chest. "Anna, here, you know, I use the meditation room in the basement—"

That was her concern. "Of course! In the apartment you'd be totally comfortable. And at the office, there are other employees who pray, there's a room for it. You'd be in good company."

Batul looked relieved, shifted back.

Anna moved her hands to her rims. "You know the reputation—quick to say how we think, not so quick to tell people how we feel." She rolled back and forward and raised her head and looked right at Batul. "You ... make me feel cared for and you make me feel like you see me, not my paralysis. I hope ... if you want to do this ... and it works out ... you would be helping me in new ways ... and in the beginning it will be uncomfortable for both of us ... please ... I want to keep being your friend and not become your patient." She took a deep breath and felt the pressure behind her eyes dissipate. She was glad she'd asked.

"I would like to. I will talk to my father."

TWENTY-SEVEN

Batul entered the number Baba had seen on the empty storefront in Friedrichshain and pressed the call button. One ring, two—she glanced up at Baba.

"Kraus, hallo."

"Yes, hello, I want to ask about the store on Grünberger Strasse."

"Where?"

Was she stressing the wrong syllable? She repeated, "Grünberger Strasse."

"Yes, what about it?" His tone was detached, as if, if this were in person, he wouldn't bother looking up from whatever he was doing.

"Can you tell me the rent and how many years the lease will be for?"

"What kind of business?"

"Food. Pastries. Like baklava." He didn't say anything for a second and she felt the need to demonstrate that they were a legitimate potential tenant. "Our family owns a well-known sweets shop in Syria and my father wants to open a branch here."

"Not interested."

Had Baba found a spot unsuitable for food? Or this was something else. "May I ask why?"

Now he spoke calmly, dispassionately. "I'm not leasing to an asylum parasite. We're not the world's welfare office. Germany is for Germans."

She was stunned, shaken, uttered a nonsensical, "Thank you."

He hung up.

"How much is the rent?" Baba asked.

"It's not available."

She'd been planning to ask him about Anna, but that now felt out of the question. Rami's arrival was a relief. "I talked to Omar," he said. "He heard, from a friend of a friend, that Yaman was freed and left the country. But nobody can get hold of him. I can't find him online. So maybe it's just a rumor. Maybe wishful thinking."

She'd wondered whether—had she known he'd been arrested with Rami—she could have gotten his Facebook profile taken down too, and whether it would have mattered. Impossible to know. She'd still never told Rami that she and Yaman had exchanged numbers, or that she'd tried calling him the night they were arrested.

In her room, she opened her laptop, but then closed it and lay on her bed. She was thirsty and hungry and the *Germany is for Germans* had sapped the last of her energy. The first week was always the hardest, and today sunset would be at 9:33, nearly the latest of the entire year. On her mind was the lemon tart. And the walk. Early last month, she'd poked her head into Anna's room, who surprised her: "Do you want to go for a walk later? To the shops near the station? I did it with my parents on Sunday."

During the rest of her shift that day she'd thought about the responsibility. Despite the sun beating down out there, it was still cooler than the weekend. With a blanket and hat, though, Anna would be warm enough. The route was the one Batul walked twice a day—sidewalks the whole way, no more detours from the construction, they could be there and back in about an hour.

When she got back to Anna's room, Anna was in her manual chair. "It's not exercise with the motor."

Sun warmed Batul's back, joining the scent of lilacs and hyacinths in shouting out the season. Anna wore leg warmers over her fleece pants; her soft leather ankle boots rested on the foot support; balanced on her lap, over a thin wool blanket, lay her wallet. Batul walked, slowly, beside Anna as Anna pushed. Still on campus, Anna stopped next to a garden bed.

"Need help?"

Anna shook her head, brought her index finger to her lips, then pointed at the mulch. A rabbit small enough to fit into Batul's hand was crawling out of a hole, its ears back, its little paw pressed to the ground, staring at another bunny—its sibling, she thought—hiding under a shrub, its ears raised. She and Anna watched, not moving, the bunny now paused halfway out of the hole, sniffing the air, tiny vibrating whiskers visible in the sunlight.

She gave a little push to help Anna make it from the hospital path to the sidewalk. Then Anna pressed her brace against the left rim to convert her momentum into a fluid turn. They started down the few blocks that connected the hospital to the station.

Batul spotted a man who looked familiar walking in their direction. A doctor—though he seemed younger in street clothes. He nodded at her as they passed. Probably thought they were patient and caregiver, not friends who could complete each other's sentences in two languages.

She watched Anna's arms pushing the wheels forward, reaching back, pushing forward again. The people around them had no idea. They would think she was a normal wheelchair user, paralyzed lower down, or not paralyzed at all, say with a broken leg. They wouldn't understand that what they were witnessing was a feat of unimaginable willpower. For a second she imagined crouching down and whispering how proud she was of her.

As a gentle breeze began to rustle the leaves on the trees, Anna slowed, her chair pivoting to the left, her breathing more audible.

"Do you want help? I'm sorry I keep asking."

"Yes, please. And I like that you ask. It means you care."

Batul stepped behind the chair, but so as not to lose the feeling of walking side by side, leaned forward, her head parallel with Anna's, who let go of the rims and rested her hands in her lap. She could smell Anna's shampoo and the birch trees planted between the sidewalk and the supermarket. A group of nurses on their way to the hospital reconfigured themselves into a single file. As they passed, smiling at her and Anna, Batul straightened her back, and, unusual for her, made eye contact with each. She wanted nothing more than to keep walking like this for hours.

Close to the station. "Do you want a coffee?" Anna asked.

"Do you?"

Anna nodded. They went into a little shop. "Two coffees, one slice of Zitronenkuchen, and one—" Anna looked at her. "What do you want?"

She looked at the cakes behind the glass, pointed, "I'll try the other lemon one, the tart."

Anna joked with the woman behind the counter. At the cash register, Batul reached for the euros in her pocket. "No, it's my treat." Anna took cash out of her wallet, put her hand forward and up, just reaching the woman's outstretched fingertips. "Please keep the change."

They sat outside, across from each other, no part of Anna's chair visible, her left wrist in its brace resting on the edge of the table. Anna leaned forward a few degrees, looked at her, smiled. "This is fun."

There were—used to be—countless open-air cafes back home, and she'd been with her medical school study group, and with her cousins, but never once like this, with just a single friend.

"You want a bite?" Anna asked.

Batul nodded, then offered the same. "I used to have such a sweet tooth," Anna said. "It's somehow gone away, thank goodness."

A woman roughly their age, in white slacks, walked briskly by. "That's going to be you soon."

Batul looked at her slice of cake. She should have been close to finishing her degree and well into clinical training. Years lost. She tried to tell herself: This was real; that was not.

"What's wrong?"

She was always positive for Anna; Anna knew she was human. "I skyped with my grandfather yesterday. I'm no longer so sure."

"About what? About going to medical school? What did he say?"

"No. He always asks how my studying is coming along and when I will apply, and says he's proud of me. It's just ..." She swallowed. "It's just he always encouraged me, and stood up for me with my uncles, and the situation there is so bad ... you can't imagine, I can't imagine. Why should I have a bright future? Why do I think it's a possibility? Who am I to make plans? I asked when I will see him again. 'Soon, my beautiful granddaughter,' he used to say. But yesterday, for the first time he didn't answer."

"Batul." Anna stared into her eyes, silent. But then, again: "Batul, here's what I know. Your grandfather is going to be in the front row at your white coat ceremony. And so will I."

She *was* going to get in. No excuses. She got up from bed, went back to her desk, and reopened her laptop. Two hours later she was in the kitchen helping Mama. They broke the fast with dates and yogurt and then prayed Maghrib together as a family. During the meal, energy restored, no longer so shaken by the call, she announced, "I received a job offer today..."

PART 3
SUMMER 2015

TWENTY-EIGHT

Moving toward the bank of elevators, Anna stopped at Rajeev's desk. "Hey. It's a good question about swapping out that module. I'm not sure. Let's discuss tomorrow."

"Okay, boss," he said, eyebrows raised.

She rolled forward. "Anna." Ursula. She stopped again, pivoted left.

"Thanks for talking that through with me. I found the problem. Had to do with the CUDA version."

"Oh, great. See you tomorrow." Pivot clockwise. Roll forward. Sofia was waiting for her at the elevator.

This week Anna had upped her days to four hours, two of which, today, she'd spent in front of her computer. She was so into it, her mind so completely transported into the intricate logic of the script she was writing, that she forgot she was in her wheelchair. When Sofia came to adjust her position, she experienced a series of millisecond jumps—from being immersed in code, to remembering she had a body, to remembering it was paralyzed, to reacquainting herself with the pain in her shoulders that never went away.

She'd joined Ursula and another engineer for lunch in the cafeteria. They talked normally—not like a month ago, when a person might mention a yoga class or hike and then blanch and go silent. She'd also, today, reviewed a pull request, helped Ursula rubber duck an issue, and met with Tomás, who told her she was doing a good job.

Normal. It was all so beautifully normal. Her new routine did not feel so different from her old one. Now with Sofia on the train heading home, reflecting: humans were collaborative animals, builders deep down—accomplishing stuff with other people is what we are meant to do. Dr. Eckert: You will be able to lead a full life, you will adapt. You are still you.

A chime sounded from the loudspeaker and a clear voice came through: "Zurückbleiben bitte." Two teenage girls with backpacks, one with her head covered, got on, chatting, and found places to stand across from her and Sofia, both holding the same pole. On Batul's first shift as her aide, a month ago, she had taken off her hijab, unveiling a whole new layer of herself. She looked so different without it, with thick, wavy hair framing her face when it fell over her shoulders. Anna had tried to resist staring.

"Some people," Batul had said, "are stricter. I think it's fine because there are no men here. But my mom would leave it on because you're a different religion, and, you know, you might describe her hair to a man. Of course that's ridiculous."

"What's ridiculous?" Batul's hair was dark brown, and without her hijab, she seemed both older and younger. "That a non-Muslim woman would be more likely to describe your mom's hair to a man? Or that I in particular would tell someone? Like I'd be deep into some technical thing with Rajeev, and then I'd say, oh, something else, you know Batul?, yeah, I saw her mother's hair over the weekend—it's dark, cut short ..."

Batul did not laugh. "It's not something to joke about. You are trustworthy. That's what I meant. Believe me, it happens. I've heard stories of women describing the hair of their friends to men."

But who cares, Anna wanted to protest. She'd dropped it then, frustrated with Batul because it seemed so nonsensical, and then immediately with herself, because what business did she have judging. Who was she turning into—her sister-in-law?

She rolled into her apartment, said bye to Sofia, and—ooh—a delicious, charred, smoky aroma. She followed Batul's gaze to a spread of what looked like falafel balls, a yogurt sauce, grilled slices of eggplant, and a salad of tomatoes, cucumbers, and parsley. She must have come directly from the testing center, hours early for her shift.

They started eating. Her with chopsticks. Batul also with chopsticks. These little balls had an earthy warmth, a hint of cinnamon—definitely not falafel. "So ...?" Anna asked. She'd been scoring so high on the practice tests. Today had been the real thing.

"I'll know in a few weeks."

"But how do you *think* it went?" Was Batul turning German, refusing to speculate?

"Good, I think. One of the listening passages I couldn't follow a hundred percent and I had to guess between 'superfluous' and 'sensible.' Otherwise I was pretty sure about my answers. And Anna, if it weren't for you, I would have struggled so much, especially with the listening and speaking parts."

"Batul! I don't believe that for a minute." Did she still not get it? When they first met, sure, the German was to help her prep, but they were so far beyond that. "And the essay? What was the prompt?"

Batul finished chewing. "A quote by ... I forget the name ... about how when you know the culture of another, you stop seeing them as a stranger."

"Did you have enough time?"

She nodded. "I argued it was the other way around. When you know an individual from a different culture, you stop seeing their culture as strange."

Anna picked up another ball with her chopsticks, rolled it in the yogurt sauce, and popped it into her mouth. She looked over at all the bowls and pans in the drying rack and her eyes fell on the bottle of wine on the counter. She could count on one hand (her right one) the number of times she'd drunk since the stroke. Melanie had brought it over last night. Between them they'd had a glassful, if that.

Batul turned, and saw where she was looking.

"Would you pour me some?"

"Are you sure?" she asked, eyeing the bottle.

She nodded. "Yeah. Just a little."

Batul stood, slowly, took the bottle from the counter, and looked down at the drawer. "How do I ... do I need ...?"

"It's open already. Pull the cork out."

Batul brought the open bottle to the table—

"The gla—"

"Yes?"

"Never mind."

She finished her water and Batul poured the wine into the glass. Anna chewed a slice of eggplant, then sipped. Batul told her about the reading passages—one on Clara Schumann, one on factory robots for car assembly, and a third on veterinary medicine.

Anna drank more. She lifted a diced cucumber with her chopsticks, looked over, and saw that Batul also was in the middle of lifting a piece of cucumber to her mouth. Their eyes met, Batul raised a single eyebrow, and she knew with certainty they were both thinking the same thing—how unlikely and yet utterly natural for this woman from Aleppo and her paralyzed German friend to be sitting in a Berlin kitchen and talking about canine abdominal surgery while eating cucumbers with chopsticks.

"Do you know what it means to *rubber duck*?"

Batul glanced up. "Yes. When there is an accident, and on the other side traffic slows." Batul swiveled her head, looked at the fridge for a moment, then turned back. Her waves followed an eighth of a second behind her skull before settling back on her shoulders. "Because everyone is staring."

"What? Oh, no, that's *rubbernecking!*" She pointed at her own neck with her chopstick.

"Oh, *duck* ..." Batul shook her head.

"From the bathtub toy, those little ducks that float around. You know the song from Sesame Street—the kids' show? Rubber duckie you're the one, you make bathtime lots of fun ..."

Batul laughed, a deep, full-throated sound. She laughed so much more here than she ever had in the hospital. "Iftah Ya Simsim—we had that show, too."

Anna took another sip, wondering now why Batul's laugh had turned almost giddy. Rubber ducks weren't *that* funny. Perhaps it had more to do with the exam being over. "In this context, though, it's an engineering thing. You're stuck figuring out a bug, so you turn to a little rubber duck on your desk—well usually just in your head—and you explain the problem step by step, as if the duck could understand, and, amazingly, you figure the problem out."

Batul looked at her with a half smirk. "Like the Association of Salad Bars?"

"No, this is a real thing!" Why again had she brought this up? "Like I was Ursula's rubber duck today. She was stuck all morning; all I did was listen and she figured out that the problem was related to the version of the library we use to talk to GPUs."

"Rubber duckie, you're ..." A vague memory of their kindergarten teacher showing Sesame Street in English. Smiling Ernie, bubbles, soapsuds, the whole class singing along. "Rub-a-dub-dubby."

Batul stood and moved their plates to the sink.

"Rubber duckie I'm awfully fond of you."

She reached for the glass of wine, and watched as Batul returned to the table with a baking dish of baklava. She'd never seen it like this before.

"You made this?"

"You think the granddaughter of the owner of Nawwar Halab would *buy* baklawa!"

"Even the layers?"

"The phyllo? No, that I got from the grocery store. It's hard to make the sheets uniform without the rolling machine we have in the shop."

Batul used a knife to wedge out a parallelogram-shaped piece of pastry from the dish and tip it onto a dessert plate. Anna lifted it tenderly with her chopsticks and brought it to her mouth.

"Oh my god, Batul."

The flaky dough and nuts soaked in syrup—she could taste pistachios. And a flavor she couldn't place that was subtle and fragrant and made her think of that first time Batul had wrapped her arms around Anna, transferring her from bed to chair in the hospital.

Batul picked up her own piece of baklava with her fingers, took a bite, and put it back on her plate. When she finished chewing, she announced, quietly, "I took part in a demonstration."

"The counter-protest in Kreuzberg?" Anna was surprised—not that Batul would be against the far right, of course, but she couldn't see her taking time away from studying, holding up a sign, standing in a crowd of German strangers.

"No, not here. A long time ago. Back home. Against the regime. With Rami. I never told my parents. It was the moment in my life that I felt most alive."

"I thought you said you were at home when he was arrested?"

"I was. That was later. This was earlier, in the beginning."

"The beginning of the uprisings?"

Batul nodded. "You can't think of this like the protests you see here where it's safe, where there is no risk. In Syria, there is no place for dissent. The Assad family controls everything. And anyone can be an informant."

"It sounds like what I heard about from my parents."

Batul took another bite of the baklava, set it down. "Let me tell you how we thought. In January 2011—this was only two months before the first demonstrations in our country—Al Jazeera was always on. We were watching tens of thousands of Egyptians marching in Tahrir Square. My father made a comment, that this could never happen in Umayyad Square, impossible—"

Anna felt her face go briefly blank.

"It's in Damascus. Like our Tahrir Square. I remember thinking, yes, Baba is right. I thought that Syrians would never dare do anything publicly against Assad. Anyway, I don't mean to say I was thinking a lot about this. I was busy with med school. I just want to explain that what was happening in Egypt and Tunisia was all over the news, and everyone in our circles thought—never in Syria. Except we were wrong. Because in March, people started going into the streets."

"What did you think then?"

"I thought—yes, I want to live in this Syria without corruption, without nepotism, with more opportunities, with freedom, with legal protections. Yet, to be honest, I thought it was good for others to demonstrate, but for me, I had too much to lose and I was too scared ..."

She sipped her wine and watched Batul's face. Like all her stories—genuine.

"... Rami got a call from a friend saying there was going to be a demonstration. I told him he shouldn't go, but of course, he wasn't going to listen to me. So once he was going I decided to go too. We—"

"You thought it would be safer for him if you went together?" She finished her baklava.

"I don't remember. Yes, that it would be safer, and also, I might have thought—this was my chance to be a part of it. In hindsight, we know, things turned horrible, but back then, if the government fell, if Assad stepped down, if democracy came, did I want to say all I was doing the whole time was studying?"

"What happened?"

"I covered my face. We went. We got lucky. While we were shouting with all our lungs for freedom and dignity, we got a warning that the Shabbiha were on their way. You've heard this term?"

She shook her head.

"Thugs loyal to Assad. Brutal people. Not the official military. They go to the protests and beat up the demonstrators. Like later, when Rami was at the Faculty of Mechanical Engineering, the Shabbiha—they came first, before the soldiers. For us, that day, as soon as word went through the crowd, everyone stopped marching and chanting and sort of drifted away. There was no violence. Only optimism. And relief."

"I'm so glad."

Batul picked up her piece of baklava and took another bite with her front teeth. "I know you think I'm such a rule follower."

Yes. She did think that a little. But so was she. And relatively—from all she'd learned about her this past year, it was Batul who was more of the rebel. "I don't—"

"I see how you look at me when I say certain things. I need you to know that I hold convictions, but I'm also capable of following my own thoughts."

"Nobody who knows you well could think otherwise." Although, she admitted to herself, she did sometimes think otherwise.

Later, Batul was behind her, close, brushing her hair. She felt Batul's fingers amid the bristles. She could have glanced to the left, to see the scene reflected in the mirror, but instead closed her eyes for a moment, losing herself in the tactile sensation, relishing the proximity, imagining she was seated by choice. Batul came round to stand in front of her, brushed a few errant strands of hair away from her face, behind her left ear. Anna could smell Batul—a soap and shampoo no longer masked by the cleaning products Batul had used at the hospital. She looked up at her nose, her smile, and imagined blacking out everything except her eyes. Would she recognize those in a crowd?

Batul put down the brush, ran a washcloth under warm water, and lifted it to scrub at a spot on Anna's cheek that Anna had missed earlier. Her face was so close. Anna studied the shadows cast by her cheekbones. She shifted her gaze and met Batul's eyes. In them she saw warmth. Anna's hand, resting on her lap, shivered. Could she initiate? Batul never would. Anna moved her neck forward and let her lips graze—

Batul jerked her head back. Her cheeks blushed fast and furious. She said nothing, then reset, continuing to dab at Anna's face.

Anna's own face flushed, too, and her heart dropped. Disgust. At being kissed by a tetraplegic? At being kissed by a woman? At being kissed? At being kissed by her? Should she apologize? Explain herself? Tell her this thing that in a year of friendship she'd managed to never bring up, but was sure by now Batul understood?

"I'm sorry," she said. "I'm sorry."

"Let's get you to bed."

TWENTY-NINE

Batul lay in her room, or rather, the room for whoever had the night shift. "Yes, the care team is entirely women," she'd assured Rami, Baba, Mama. "No, Anna is not married, she doesn't have a boyfriend, her father does not live there, her brother will not stay over, there will be no men there."

"But what will you do in the middle of the night?" Baba had asked.

"I'll study. I'll sleep. I'll set my alarm and get up three times to rotate her."

They never could have imagined that what she thought about, over and over and despite herself, wasn't some phantom visitor but Anna herself. She was hyper aware of Anna's every physical change, every battle through pain, every impulse—or thought she had been, before this evening. She'd told herself this was good care, like how Anna talked about Peter.

The extent to which her own mental state depended on Anna was only now dawning on her. On the days she wasn't working, receiving a text from Anna made the world bright; no communication left her anxious. She'd never before been so interested in another person that she could start thinking about them at three, pick her head up, and it was four. Never before read the messages from one person over and over again. It might have just been Anna—someone who, more than even Grandpa, believed in her. Someone who wanted to know what she thought about *everything*, and whose tilted head and teasing smile Batul could see with her eyes closed. Before, she always knew where Anna was—her room, the lounge, the gym. Now, when she was off, Anna could be anywhere, with anyone.

If, when Tasneem warned her against the distractions of men, she had had to articulate why it seemed of such little concern, she would have said that it didn't work like that. Men lusted after women. Women acquiesced because they wanted security. If medical school was more appealing than that security, she would have no problem turning away potential partners.

Stupid. She practically deserved this, thinking she was stronger than other people, cleverer, when in fact she'd just never felt what they felt. How arrogant of her to believe that the subject of so much human creativity through all of recorded history was contrived.

She was drawn to Anna. It was wrong. And it was safe. Because Anna would never be drawn to her, not in the same way, not with the same obsessive thoughts. Now with wine on her breath she'd done something shocking. Solely due to the alcohol? Or something else.

It didn't matter. She had iron self-control. This city was filled with selfish people whose first priority seemed to be personal expression. People with tattoos, shaved heads, weird piercings, strange clothing. She would never become like them. She had her priorities. She knew right from wrong.

THIRTY

Anna stared at Rajeev's question, the one she'd told him she would answer today, already twenty messages down in her inbox. Was it worth the two week delay to swap out that third-party module that had been giving them trouble? Well, if they did—

The moment when Batul—reacted—it was like that tall guy at the beer garden, after she watched the marathon, who went from talking about fueling and electrolytes to, with no warning, leaning in to kiss her, his breath the stink of alcohol and curry. She'd yanked her head away, but still regretted not saying, loudly, "What the fuck?"

Batul was at work. Washing her face. Imagine it was her—Anna—employed in a nursing home, leaning over an old man, tenderly pressing the corner of a warm washcloth to the edges of his mouth, peering close to get every spot— She was revolting. She squeezed her eyes shut.

Back home, with Batul on night shift again, Anna tried to keep things normal, light, and she could see Batul doing the same. She told Batul about an engineer they'd interviewed today, how he'd looked great on paper, how the recruiter was so positive about him, how he sounded confident in the early part of the interview, but how badly he did on the whiteboard coding exercise. She asked how Rami was doing in his new job. Batul answered, mechanically, and poured her more water.

What she didn't tell her: that during every second of that exercise, while she was sitting there staring at the whiteboard, pretending to be engrossed in the candidate's attempt to figure out the algorithm, she'd felt dead inside.

Finally, she couldn't take it anymore. "I want to apologize." She put her chopsticks down. "I'm so, so sorry about yesterday. I shouldn't have done that. It was wrong—I was wrong—for so many reasons. I want you to know ... if you feel you need to report me, you should, and I'll understand. You could get your BKM job back, I hope, or see if the agency needs you for someone else. I'm just so sorry."

Batul squeezed her eyes closed and then opened them again. "I don't want to leave your team." She shook her head. "It was the alcohol—that was my mistake."

Except it wasn't only the alcohol. Deep breath. Another. "I also feel you should know ... in case you don't already ... I do like women."

Batul's expression turned weird. Almost like she didn't understand.

"I shouldn't have poured you so much wine."

"You get what I'm telling you, right?"

"I'm not sure."

Was this *not sure* as in she understood but didn't want it said aloud? Well, she'd made up her mind. No more keeping things blurry. She was going to be German blunt. This was too important. If it pushed her away—no—that wouldn't happen.

"I'm attracted to women."

Batul turned red. Looked down. Said nothing.

"You've never met anyone who was attracted to people of the same gender?"

"There are no people like that in Syria."

"What are you talking about? Yes there are. At university, you didn't have female classmates who were into girls? Or guys who liked guys?"

Batul turned even redder. "No. Absolutely not." She looked at the ceiling, then back. "There was ... I did have a cousin of a cousin of a cousin in Damascus who went off to France, the rumor was to be with a man ... this was a long time ago, I heard about it from one of my other cousins, it was a big secret from their side of the family. I've never heard of a Syrian woman who wasn't interested in men."

Batul couldn't seriously believe this. She was too sharp. Too well-read. Anna could maybe believe that Batul hadn't realized that Anna was queer, but not that she knew so little about homosexuality. This was an act—but to what end? Anna's hand, gripping her right rim, squeezed the rubber-coated metal. "That's statistically impossible. I know certain things might not be in the open, might be illegal, might be against religious beliefs. But come on, you're going to be a doctor, you'll be seeing patients. You need to be objective."

Batul stared at her food and took a deep breath. She looked up. "I ... don't deny that there are men who are attracted to men and women who are attracted to women. But it's never talked about, and back home, even someone like that, they would never admit it, they would still get married. It's rare and it's wrong."

The pain in her shoulders made itself present. Pressure was building in her head. "Sorry, it's not rare." She was speaking louder than she intended. "A spinal stroke is rare. Being attracted to someone of the same gender is not. And there's definitely nothing wrong with it. I'm sorry, there's just not."

The glass Batul was gripping, Anna noticed, was ever-so-slightly shaking. Her eyes rose to Batul's face, and she saw her wiping away tears. Her anger disappeared. She let go of the handrim and, before she could stop herself, touched the back of Batul's hand.

"You could be right," Batul murmured, withdrawing her hand a tiny distance. Back home, even if a woman was interested in another woman, she wouldn't have the courage ... her family would disown her, it would be a big drama, it would go against—marriage in our culture—everyone is putting their noses, for the woman, it will be better to marry a man even if she doesn't like him, or men at all."

THIRTY-ONE

Should her first photo make it clear? She didn't want to pretend to be something she wasn't. Never subscribed to *fake it till you make it*. Lies had short legs. But—she swiped. Headshot. Swiped. Headshot. Swiped. Headshot. Making her first photo anything other than a headshot would break with convention.

But the second photo definitely needed to show her chair. The manual. An outside shot, on the street, her hands on the rims, her left hand in the brace. And then, as a third image, her at her desk, in front of her laptop. Nerdy? Yes. But it would convey that she earned her own living. And that work was important to her.

So say someone found her smiling face compelling. Her freckles speckled over a button nose, her glasses with the subtle tortoiseshell pattern on the thin, plastic frames, her straight, dark blonde hair. They'd tap on the profile, scroll through the other pictures. They'd see the photo of her in her wheelchair. If a turn-off, they could move on.

But someone might be intrigued, or not realize it was chronic, or how high up her paralysis started. She'd spell that out in her bio. She'd use her line about it being a wheelchair, not a coffin. She'd talk about how everything took her longer, so she only wanted to do things that were meaningful with people she cared about.

There were a lot of humans out there. Was it so absurd to think a warm, able-bodied woman somewhere in the city might be interested? This wasn't Peoria. Wasn't Aleppo. But it felt impossible. She couldn't see it.

Then again, she'd never understood why Julia was attracted to her. And paralyzed or not, who the hell knew why one person liked another? It was self-defeating to go into this, or anything, assuming failure.

It was Sofia who'd encouraged her, telling her how a previous client had had success with dating apps.

"Really?" She was almost embarrassed by her own incredulity.

Sofia, in her mid-sixties and head of the team, had been taking care of paralyzed people for decades. "Sunshine, yes. You have to be careful, but you're not made of porcelain. Life is for living!"

Sofia had also figured out a new way to transfer her in and out of bed, after discovering that Anna could lock her right knee. Together they positioned Anna's chair so that the right wheel was up against the mattress. "Make your leg stiff." Sofia pulled her up so she was standing, her nearly full weight supported by her own leg for a moment, then spun her ninety degrees and lowered her onto the bed. At first it seemed impossible, but after a week of practice they could do it in seconds, so much faster and more dignified than with the yellow banana board. Anna taught the technique to Batul and Iza and, just yesterday, to Mom.

The biggest miracle—declared impossible back at the hospital—was that she and Sofia had worked out a way to catheterize her without her needing to transfer out of her chair and into a horizontal position. It involved Sofia sliding Anna's butt forward, to the very edge of the wheelchair, putting her hands on the back of a chair positioned in front of her, placing her feet such that her body stayed in place, and Sofia sliding off her pants.

Sofia had been skeptical at first. "I'm not sure it will all come out."

"Of course it will! You've never siphoned an aquarium? It's physics. As long as the drainage bag is below my bladder, we're fine."

In a sixteen-month personal golden age of lifehacks, this was revolutionary. Now they could use the handicap bathroom in the office and be in and out in twenty-five minutes.

"Too bad you're into women. You're my son's type."

She made a face at Sofia.

"Yeah. My second son from my second marriage. He's a fireman. Big, big guy. Built like a fridge, strong as a bear. Has a thing for pretty blondes like you. And paralyzed women. Don't ask. Hero complex or something. He needs someone with your brains. Not like the ditz he's dating now or his bitch of an ex-wife. Ha ha. His father is no genius either. Not sure why I married him. Well, I do know." She winked.

"How many times have you been married?"

"Three times married, three times divorced. Unlike you, sunshine, I need a man, and not for his brains. I can tell you that. Not something I would have admitted to anyone in my village in Poland when I was a little girl! Ha ha. That's why I love this country."

Anna was shocked at how much interest she got. Almost frightened. *She* wouldn't have swiped right. Were there women out there with wheelchair fetishes? Could be about control, or seeking purpose, or wanting to prove to themselves that they didn't see disability. Or maybe these people were just curious. Whatever the reason, it turned out she could be—and needed to be—choosy.

She started messaging with one woman, Nicole. At first, she was just going through the motions, encouraged by Sofia. But reading Nicole's messages, re-examining her profile, she began to feel sparks of genuine interest. She was cute—dark hair, a tiny nose ring. And what was it with her and people in sales? Though Nicole had taken a roundabout path, starting a PhD in biochemistry before leaving it for a distributor of lab equipment and reagents. She loved to travel, loved people, loved reading, loved dogs (axolotls? Familiar but no opinion), loved to talk, loved to go out. Loved a lot of things. Her energy reminded Anna of Julia, plus the nose ring, plus a tattoo of a double helix on her bicep, plus, apparently, the ability to be attracted to someone who was paralyzed, minus the polish, yeah, not at all like Julia.

She was straight with her—this would be her first date since her stroke, she had to be super careful with her body, she was nervous, she wasn't sure she was ready, her nurse had encouraged her. "Anna wheelie,"—*wheelie?*—"I'm the most accepting person you'll ever meet. No pressure. No taboos. We'll talk. I'll be proud to be your first post-paralysis date! I'll help you get back out there." Anna decided not to mention that there wasn't much of an "out there" to get back to: she'd only ever dated two women: Julia and her first girlfriend, in that last year of uni.

Now that she was up to five hours a day in the office, the date needed to be the weekend. "Low key, low pressure," Nicole had said. Right. It would have felt high key, high pressure even before. They were going to meet at eleven today, Sunday, and go for a walk. Unfortunately, Iza and Batul had swapped shifts.

"What? Why?" Batul had asked when Anna told her the plan. "You don't know this person. What if it's not even who the photos were of?"

"We did a video chat."

"What if someone else shows up? What if they steal your money and take your phone? Or threaten you? Or aren't careful—jostle your chair, or push you into something, or spill coffee on you, or leave you stranded? How will you protect yourself? I should go with you. Or ask Stefan. Or Melanie."

She'd had all those same thoughts. "No. I'm sure as hell not asking my brother to come with me on a date. I'm not going to live in fear. Something bad could happen, yes, but something bad could have happened before. I need to try things." She was reassuring herself as much as Batul.

"Yes, but you don't know her." Batul's hand shook. "Please, Anna, I'll come with you. This woman doesn't need to know we're friends. She'll see me as your aide, another foreign healthcare worker. You can't go for a walk in the park alone with a stranger you met online. Please."

She could feel Batul's nerves, almost panic, reaching her in waves.

"Batul. It'll be okay. I need to do this. You'll come with me to the park. We'll make sure it's the same woman I've been speaking with all along. I'll keep my phone in my pocket. After an hour you'll meet me and we'll have lunch. Okay?"

Within ten seconds she could tell it wouldn't work. Her heart wasn't in it. She could also feel Nicole staring at her left arm and the way it moved. Still, it was good to get practice. She wasn't going to make an excuse to get out of it. Especially not after her whole speech.

"Nicole, this is my friend and aide Batul."

Nicole, in her cargo shorts and t-shirt, started to extend her arm, unclear if she was planning to shake Batul's hand or hug her. Batul stiffened and Nicole put her arm back down and nodded her head instead. "Good to meet you."

"You two would enjoy chatting." She looked up at Nicole. "Nicole knows a lot about lab equipment." Nicole nodded, but also made an expression like *why would she care?*

Then she looked at Batul. "Batul is studying medicine. Reads a lot of scientific articles. That's how I know what a reagent is." Batul didn't jump in, so she kept going. "She only started learning German last year and now she's fluent enough that she can explain things like gene editing, which happens to be what we were talking about over breakfast. You probably know about that, right?"

Nicole nodded. Batul still hadn't said anything, so it was a little funny for her to be bragging about her German.

Silence for a moment. "Should we go?" Nicole asked.

"I'll wait here," Batul said, setting her bag down on the bench, finally speaking. "Please protect her—especially when you go by that field where they play frisbee."

"I can push you."

"No, thanks." They got to the spot where a gentle incline started.

"You sure?"

"I can manage."

She turned her chair to the diagonal. Push, strain, bring arms back, push, breathe. She made it to the edge where the path met the grass. Engaged the brakes. Breathed. Breathed. Released the brakes. Rotated the left rim back with her brace, pushed on the right, now on the new diagonal. Pushed, sweating, braked again at the edge. Five zigs and six zags and they were back on level ground. She wiped the sweat from her brow.

"You're incredible. I'm impressed!"

She smiled.

Fifteen minutes later they were in an open field.

"Want to take a break? Sit on the grass?"

The day was warm and bright and the grass looked so inviting. She would need to trust Nicole to lift her out of her chair, and to get her back in.

"I'm very good at following instructions from my days in the lab," Nicole said as if reading her mind. "Just tell me how to hold you and how to move you to the ground. I'm like twice your size—ha ha—so don't worry about me hurting myself or anything."

"Okay. Let's try. I won't be able to sit up. You can lie me on my back." She double checked that her phone was in her pocket.

They were both on the grass, looking up into the sky. She should have brought a blanket. Little stones could be digging into her butt or the undersides of her legs. She'd need to ask Batul to look her over with a microscope. Suddenly this was all too much. She pushed the thought to the back of her mind.

"I love days like this," Nicole said.

"Mm-hmm. This is the first time grass is touching my skin since before." Back when she was training for that obstacle course, she'd thought nothing of jumping into mud, didn't worry for one instant that gravel might pierce skin. Hard to believe how little she used to stress about her physical environment—

"... Do you know it? It's fantasy. I'm almost done with the second book. There are like five or six in the series."

"Not sure." Ugh. "Is it good?"

"Amelia goes between the enchanted realm of Elaria and ..."

She bet Batul was enjoying herself, sitting on that bench, head bent, reading on her phone, looking up as people walked by, alone with her thoughts, breathing in the smell of freshly cut grass.

"... only in Elaria can she unfurl her wings, but she's scared to because ..."

There could be a column of red ants marching up her tailbone. Or a beetle climbing into her pants, its six legs skittering along her calf. Her favorite doctor had told her a horrifying story during her last week in the hospital. This was the doctor who'd been paralyzed below the waist in a motorcycle accident a decade earlier, and, after rehabilitation, joined the spinal cord injury department as a senior physician.

"Haven't seen you in a while," she'd said to him. "Vacation?"

"I wish."

"What?"

"Uhh—this you might not want to hear."

"Now I'm curious."

"Well, okay, Anna, you're my only patient who I'm confident could handle it." He wheeled forward and pointed out the window. "We live in a little bungalow in Falkenberg—I'm sure you know the type—with a big vegetable garden. My wife was at the supermarket, I was inside watching TV, our son was outside weeding, the back door was open, there was this wonderful breeze blowing through the living room. 'Papa,' our son came rushing in, 'I think an animal slipped into the house.'

"'What? What animal?'

"'Not sure. I saw it from the corner of my eye. Like a squirrel or a hedgehog.'

"'I didn't hear it,' I told him. 'Are you sure?' He looked around. Didn't find anything. Went back out to the garden, closed the door. I went back to my show and forgot all about it. That night, in the early hours of the morning, around three or four, it was still dark, my wife screamed.

"'Zaubermaus'—that's what I always call her, you will see in a second, my dear Anna, that that was exactly the wrong term of endearment for this moment—'what's wrong?'

"'I felt something on my foot.'

"I switched the light on and looked down. The sheets were soaked with blood. My wife pulled the top sheet away. Blood was pumping out of a gash on my leg. Then we saw movement in the corner of the room: a huge brown rat. It had been gnawing on my leg; my thigh was covered in bite marks. I bandaged the wound and we rushed to the ER. Luckily I was current with all my shots, and I got more shots, and these last few weeks I've been recovering, doing everything I can to encourage healing."

She'd had nightmares the next few nights, but she didn't think anything like that could happen to her. Her right leg would feel the rat and she'd wake up. And if it were her left leg, she might not feel those incisors, but the leg would spasm, and the rat would be scared off. Even when they cut her left toenails, odd signals were sent through her nerves, so she always needed one person to hold her foot still while another used the clippers, except the one nail technician who was very skilled—

"... and then Amelia finds the sorcerer but decides not to get her wings transmogrified after all. Pretty good, right?"

"Yes."

"Yes?" Nicole slapped the grass, playfully. "Repeat back one thing I told you about it!"

"Wings ... yeah. Sorry. I guess I'm not so into magic."

"I can respect that. For me, I like the escapism. Like Elaria is pretty appealing compared to visiting cold biomedical labs and meeting with procurement managers in windowless offices."

A speck of a plane passed overhead. Neither of them spoke; the silence was comfortable. Nicole brought her head close and she could smell her unfamiliar scent. Then she kissed her on the cheek—she'd thought the lack of attraction was mutual. Nicole turned and raised herself on her hands and knees and brought her face close. She avoided her eyes and stared at her nose ring. Nicole kissed her on the lips. She didn't respond and Nicole got the hint.

"Sorry, can we go back?"

To her credit, Nicole was both gentle and careful when she lifted her and put her in her chair. Twenty minutes later they were almost back to the bench.

"What was your aide's name again?"

"Batul."

"How does it work? Does your insurance cover your care? Did they find her?"

"Yes, insurance pays, funded by the government, and I also contribute. I have a team of, right now, four people, and someone is always with me. The head nurse and the other two women came through an agency. Batul, though, it's a little unbelievable, she was a janitor in the hospital, a temporary job, while she got ready to apply to medical school. She started in Syria but had to leave. We've known each other for a year—"

"She has feelings for you. And you have feelings for her."

Her neck got hot. "Why do you say that?"

"The way she looks at you. The way you look at her. The way she treated me! It's obvious."

"She's straight."

"Yeah. Me too."

The next day she had lunch with Markus. Shortly before her return, the team had interviewed him, and Tomás had made an offer. But he'd only started last week, after moving back from California. He'd been working for Facebook there, building an internal tool for measuring the scalability of the machine learning algorithms behind the news feed. Facebook was a totally different type of company, of course, but their scale was huge, and a similar testing tool would be required for DDB to cut over to the upgraded platform.

"How'd you decide to move back here?" Anna asked. And then: "Actually, how'd you end up over there in the first place?" He'd also gone to TU Berlin, three years ahead of her. She'd never heard of anyone getting hired directly out of university by a US company for a US office.

"My wife's American. We met when she did a year abroad here, and after I graduated I moved over there. Then, after our son was born, we started thinking about moving back. We wanted the quality of life here, and to be closer to my parents—hers don't help at all—and I thought he had a better shot at ending up bilingual."

"What's his name?"

Markus took out his phone and showed her a photo. "Mason."

"Oh, he's beautiful. I like it. Markus and Mason."

He chuckled. "Yeah, that was on purpose, my wife is Megan." He swiped. A selfie, the three of them, his arm around his wife, the baby in a carrier on his chest, in front of a wide tree trunk. "That's in Sequoia National Forest." He swiped again. Megan holding hands with Mason, older in this photo, on a narrow, rocky trail, steep, jagged, canyon walls rising on both sides, like an alien planet in a movie. "Death Valley. Our favorite national park. We camped there for two weeks in March at the base of a sand dune. Incredible hikes." March—when she tried to get to the station on her own. Another photo. Lush, green, Megan pregnant. "This was before Mason. Spent three weeks in Hawaii. Went all over."

"Did you like Facebook?"

"Yeah." He didn't elaborate.

"The number of items to be ranked times the number of users looking at their feed every second ... I guess the numbers get very big very fast."

He nodded.

"Plus I'm sure the data scientists were always adding more and more features to the models. The number of signals in that environment—like a user pauses their scrolling for an extra quarter second on a photo and hey, could be a sign the user cares about the person in the photo, so that's a signal you should feed to the model."

He nodded again.

"How did it work—the testing tool you built?"

His answer was vague. She assumed because the details were confidential. She wished he would just say that.

THIRTY-TWO

Batul turned the key, let herself in, and set the groceries on the kitchen table. She looked at her phone. Four hours until Anna got home. The last time Batul had come this early, it was because she needed uninterrupted study time. Today, and in some ways for the first time since they left Turkey, she would put the books aside.

She unwrapped her hijab, draped it over the sofa in the living room, and stuck the pin into the fabric on the back of the sofa. She rolled up her sleeves, washed her hands, laid out the cutting board, and dug out the food processor.

When the pan on the stovetop was hot enough, she began sauteing half the ground lamb. She split a yellow onion in two, root to stem, discarded the peel, and started dicing the first half, the flat side flush against the cutting board, the tucked-in fingers of her left hand guiding the blade.

She stirred the meat. Once it was browned, she moved it to a bowl and added the onion to the pan, turning down the heat and leaving it to caramelize. When done, she added the onions and pine nuts to the bowl, combined, and set the filling aside.

She turned on the faucet and held the cutting board under the running water. She had prayed, over and over, to remove the obsession from her mind. What she was contemplating now—she couldn't think about it in Arabic. In English, even, her brain seized up as soon as words formed. She switched to German.

I need to tell you ... She wouldn't be able to say it. It was wrong. Her hands, now wiping the board dry, shook. And what if she did say it? Anna was going on these dates. She didn't see her that way. The— that— it was the alcohol. Anna regretted it.

What did Batul even want? Where could it lead? Telling her would end their friendship. These images—of spending the rest of her life with her, of taking care of her, of her beautiful eyes and freckled face—wrong. She needed to wipe them from her mind. Except a compulsion was telling her to act.

She slid the cutting board into the drying rack and pushed her thoughts into safe territory: Anna's story about her doctor's leg, cellular regeneration. While chopping, if she slipped and sliced off a sliver of skin, it would heal. Epidermal cells died and replenished at a rate of millions per day, unlike neural cells which could stretch to a meter in length and lived your whole life.

She washed the dry bulgur, squeezed the water out with her bare hands, and combined it with the other half of the ground lamb, still raw, in the food processor. Another onion, this time grated, went in too. Batul turned to the sink, let the water run until it was cold, and filled a glass. Concentrate. She turned on the food processor and began to drizzle in water as the mixture gained mass. More. More. Not too much—the dough would become unworkable. A little more. Stop. This was the consistency.

She filled a bowl with ice and water, waited a minute for the water to cool, then plunged in her hands and soaked them in the painful, numbing cold. Compulsions could be controlled. She slowly removed her hands. She grabbed a small hunk of the bulgur mixture and rolled it into a ball between her palms. Once just firm, she hollowed it out with her right index finger, then spooned in the filling from the other bowl. She wet her fingers again, then pinched the edges of the bulgur shell to seal the seam. Anna was going to love these.

I need to tell you ... She couldn't.

Bulgur. Wheat. A memory. High school. She's making these same stuffed kibbeh with Mama, Auntie, and her older cousin, and she's trying to explain something to them. The day before, in Life Science, the teacher's sister had visited. She's a plant virologist who specializes in crops that grow in arid regions. If a virus infects a plant, she tells the class, it can be transmitted to its offspring, so seeds need to be screened before they are distributed to farmers. She passes around photos of PCR gels from five samples and asks the class to use the images to say which seeds are infected with which viruses. This is what she's trying to explain now, to her family. How PCR works by amplifying segments of DNA. But no one is even pretending to listen, and Auntie keeps interrupting—too thick, it's going to be too doughy, thinner, don't make a tear. Keep them uniform! Look at your cousin's.

Her attention on the bowl in Anna's kitchen, she scooped the last spoonful of filling and sealed the last shell, surprised at her luck in getting the ratio right. Then she put a pot on the stove and started browning the lamb shoulder for the stew. She looked at the table with the few remaining groceries: the quinces, the pomegranate juice, the canned tomatoes, the jasmine rice.

Anna asked from the table: "Did you get your score?"

Batul was at the counter, ladling the stew into bowls. She nodded.

"And ...?"

She studied the piece of lamb she was cutting in Anna's bowl, making sure everything was bite-sized. "Full score in all sections."

"Batul! I'm so proud of you."

She felt her neck turning warm and a mixture of pride and fear percolating up. It was only a test, one of many steps. She brought

Anna's bowl to the table. "Thank you for all your help." Then turned to retrieve hers.

"Stop it," Anna said.

Now seated, she kept her expression neutral as she watched Anna dip her spoon into the bowl and bring the broth to her lips.

"Holy shit." Anna took another spoonful. "What's in here? It's sweet and sour. Lamb. Garlic. Mint? Is that mint? I've never tasted anything like this." She set down the spoon, picked up the chopsticks, brought a piece of kibbeh to her mouth, bit into it. "Oh my god. Batul. It's so good."

Batul looked at Anna's blue eyes through glasses steamed by the hot stew. Her stomach felt like when a minibus goes over a dip in the road. She wanted to reach across the table and wrap her fingers around Anna's. She wanted to cook for her for the rest of their lives—such a strange thought.

Anna tasted the stewed lamb. "It's so tender. This is Syrian?"

She nodded. "A classic. From Aleppo. Lamb stewed with stuffed kibbeh and quinces. It's ... time consuming. I've helped my mom with it before; stuffing the kibbeh, that's the hard part, the dough is difficult to handle: it's bulgur and ground meat, it doesn't bind like flour. To be honest, it's my first time making the whole dish on my own."

"I can't believe these flavors. It tastes—I can't place it—like not from the Middle East, almost Asian, with the sweet and sour."

"A reminder of connections in the ancient world. We were part of trade routes that extended all the way to China. You can imagine how spices, recipes, ideas, changed hands."

Anna stared forward, like she was picturing a map. "Overland? By camel?"

"Yes. It's fascinating to think about timescale, because those ancient times were yesterday compared to when the camel crossed from North America to Asia, but without the camel, there wouldn't have been trade routes through the desert."

Anna focused on the ceiling for a moment. "Not even yesterday, more like a minute ago." Then looking at her bowl, pointing with her chopsticks, "What is this?"

"That's the kibbeh I was talking about. The shell is made from bulgur, ground lamb, and onions and the filling is also lamb and onion, but with different spices, and also toasted pine nuts."

"It's incredible."

I need to tell you ...

Later, evening routine complete, Anna sat at her desk in the corner, working on her laptop. Batul pulled up a chair. She looked at the colored lines of computer code on the screen, green and red indicating additions and deletions. Then she looked at Anna's face, her eyes focused, her lips pressed together, the horizontal colors reflected in her glasses, her mind making sense of each line of code, her middle finger pressing the down arrow, the lines scrolling and coming to rest, her eyes scanning these new lines. The shape of her unpierced ear. The down arrow again: press, more rows, press again. Why this compulsion to risk a declaration that could lead nowhere? Press. That would push them away from each other, or move them toward something she knew to be wrong? Press.

Anna shut her laptop, turned to Batul.

"Are you okay? You're shivering."

"I want to talk ..."

Anna looked at her more closely. Batul could almost hear the click click in her brain as her concentration shifted away from the code she'd been scrolling through. "About what will happen when you start school? It's been on my mind a lot too."

"No ... I ... I ..."

Anna put her hand on her leg. She was aware of where each finger made contact with her jeans. She could smell Anna's peppermint mouthwash. "Are you worried?" Anna asked her.

She was cold, yet her palms were wet with sweat. Her armpits, too. She breathed in. She felt Anna's fingers leave her leg, watched as she pushed her glasses back up her nose and tucked a lock of hair behind her ear. Batul breathed out.

"I think about you all the time. No matter where I am, you're there with me, I'm talking to you, hearing your voice. And when I'm really with you ... you make me feel optimistic—like mornings when the sun is orange, and its first rays scatter through the imperfect glass, and the inside glows golden, and anything can happen." A day would never go as perfectly; she might never again work up the courage. "I love you."

Anna stared back at her, silent. What had she done? She studied the contours of Anna's face. A constellation in her freckles. A fingerprint on the edge of her glasses. Now conviction behind two earths.

Anna blinked. "I feel the same way. I have for a long time. Batul, I didn't think ... It wasn't the wine." Now unblinking, this impossible face, uncharacteristically serious, seeing into her, "I love you."

A little girl reading a book in the back, the dense air thick with the golden butter, toasting almonds. Their stare. Still unbroken. *I love you. I love you. I love you.* A sustained, amplified cry echoing off limestone. Enveloping warmth. Belonging. Home.

Anna reached her arm forward. Batul felt Anna's thin, calloused fingers against her own. She'd had no idea touch could feel this way—the joy coursing through her, the trembling. She wanted to stay like this. The wheelchair, the desk, the room, the rules faded. Only Anna, her hand, her smell, the electric warmth between their fingers.

Later, after she moved her to bed, she sat on the edge, leaned over, and kissed her on the temple. "Good night, Anna."

Anna slid her hand over hers on top of the sheet, on top of the mattress. "Good night, Batul. I'm so happy."

She turned off the light and closed the door. She couldn't quite believe it—any of it. That she had gotten up the nerve. That it was mutual. Anna loved her. She was afraid.

THIRTY-THREE

Two weeks later she and Batul went to Il Casolare. This was the restaurant a few doors down from her apartment, where she could usually find a spot where her back would be to the wall, and where the tables had legs that left room to get her wheels underneath.

"Anna! My favorite person!" Luca, the bald, ruddy-faced British-Italian waiter who'd moved to Berlin for his wife ten years ago. "So good to meet you!" he crowed when she introduced Batul. And then, to Anna, "The usual?"

She looked at Batul. "Do you want to share a salad and a margherita pizza?"

Batul nodded and Anna nodded at Luca.

When their salad came, Batul pulled a pair of disposable chopsticks from her bag, ripped open the paper wrapper printed with the name of the Chinese takeout place near the office, and broke apart the two sticks.

"Is everything ready?" Anna asked.

"Yes. I'm going to submit online and mail the hard copies tomorrow."

They stopped talking, both now eavesdropping on a couple

arguing about money in English, and then the argument got drowned out by laughter from the table next to them. Two men who looked to be in their late twenties walked in and found seating at the bar. One kept looking over at her, and then at Batul, and then back at her. Her left hand, in its brace, was on her lap, and from his vantage point, he likely couldn't see her wheelchair. Batul turned to see where she was looking, and then turned back. The man, who looked a little like Stefan, raised his beer glass. Anna looked away and smiled at Batul.

Here they were, the two of them, across from each other, surrounded by conversation, among packed tables, warm lighting, the smoky, burnt-wood scent from the oven and the smell of baking dough. She felt the guy's eyes still on her. She put her chopsticks down and placed her hand over Batul's, who started to pull away, but then stopped and let her hand remain enclosed by Anna's.

"Not everyone is so welcoming," Batul said as Luca left the table after setting down their pizza and asking Batul where she was from. Batul began sawing at the pizza, then paused. "This was while you were still in the hospital. My father found a shop for lease in Friedrichshain. He told me to call. The landlord asked what type of business, said he wouldn't lease to us, that Germany is for Germans."

Anna shook her head, whispered, "'Deutschland den Deutschen.' He used those words? It's disgusting." Not said: her own sister-in-law, she suspected, had the same slogan echoing in her head.

Batul went back to cutting the pizza into small pieces. She moved them to Anna's plate, then cut a slice for herself. "It wasn't the first time and it won't be the last time I hear something like that. I can even understand the sentiment. What shook me is he wasn't in a crowd, riled up, chanting; and it wasn't like I overheard him talking to someone else; it was directly to me, in this calm, matter-of-fact tone, as if he was telling me the store had been taken already, or it wasn't possible to install a commercial oven. My father was ready to pay him rent. He didn't know anything about us."

Anna shook her head. "I can't understand people like him. We don't hide from our history. We're taught what happens when you divide people into us and them." She sipped her water. "There's a guy I know who's been resharing posts from the AfD. This new political party."

Batul raised her eyebrows. "From DDB?"

"A friend from school. He went to Leipzig for university and now he works at Commerzbank. I don't know how he could believe that stuff."

"Us versus them is human nature," Batul said. "There are always people who have something to gain by stoking division."

Anna closed her chopsticks around a piece of pizza. Division. Grouping. A thousand dimensions could barely approximate the variety of human experience. She bet that in such a space, the point for Batul and the point for her would be close, much closer than, say, between her and the guy at the bar. But the twisted genius of these people Batul was talking about was to get everyone fixated on a single dimension. Ignore the rest of the dimensions, it's just about religion or race or the latitude and longitude of ancestors a certain number of generations back. People got blinded and forgot that an infinite number of other boxes could be drawn, or none at all. "You're right."

After they paid and left the buzz of the restaurant, they could hear an amplified acoustic guitar. They followed the music to the bridge where a woman, her hair in dreads, a silver ring linking her nostrils, leaned into the microphone she'd set up on a stand on the cobblestone sidewalk. "I ... eh ... think everyone knows this next one," she said in Spanish-accented English.

She picked out the first chord one note at a time, then the second, then the third, and then Anna recognized it. Her voice was gritty and sandy, her pronunciation charming, she stretched out the lyrics. Anna loved this song. Batul put her hand on her shoulder and she leaned her head against Batul's side. The temperature of the air, the sun setting behind the wrought-iron railings, the feel of Batul's ribs against her cheek, her smell. She shut her eyes, absorbed, memorized.

. . .

The following weekend Dad came to pick her up. He lifted her and moved her to the front passenger seat of their station wagon. This was the second time she'd be spending the night back home.

The little bumps in the road as they drove out of the city exacerbated the throbbing in her left shoulder. Batul would be sitting somewhere, laptop out, using Tasneem's account to read a journal article; or in the kitchen helping cook; or out at Hermannplatz picking out ripe tomatoes.

"How is it?" Dad asked, his eyes on the road.

The threshold. Her muscles tired at the end of long days, her left arm feeling like it was inside a heavy work boot, she hadn't had the strength to push her chair from the living room to her bedroom. Last weekend, Dad had come over with his toolbox and sanded down the threshold. "So much better."

They passed the TU, entered the roundabout, and took the third exit, both silent until they merged onto the motorway. Then Dad reached over and lowered the radio.

"Honey, I want to apologize."

She looked over. Both hands were back on the wheel and he was looking out the windshield.

"I should have stood up for you with Herr Bergmann. I thought a group home was best. Now I see you living on your own and working and you're your old self again. You were right all along."

She wiped her eyes, moved her unbraced left hand to touch Dad's arm. "It's okay. You take anyone, leave them in bed, trap them with a roommate, take away their control, undress them like it's nothing, and even they forget who they are."

An hour later they stopped in front of the house. She looked up and saw that Dad had scrubbed off the moss she'd noticed last time growing on the reddish-brown clay roof tiles. He slowly reversed into the driveway so the passenger side was close to the three cement steps that led up to their front door. He got her wheelchair, unfolded it on the landing, lifted her—not exactly correctly, with too much force under her shoulders, but she didn't want to say anything—carried her up the steps, and put her in her chair. He held open the door, she pushed herself inside, and he went around to the garden.

"Anna!" Mom took off her rubber gloves, bent over, and hugged her. She could smell the soap her mom always used, the glass cleaner she'd just sprayed onto the coffee table, and through the open window, the lighter fluid Dad was squirting onto the charcoal.

"Where's Stefan?"

"They'll be here soon. What're you smiling about?"

She hadn't told Mom yet.

"I'm seeing someone."

Her eyes widened. Then, "That's wonderful. The woman with the DNA tattoo? You gave it another chance?"

She shook her head. "Batul."

Mom's eyebrows came together sharply. "Batul. I see the way you look at her, hear the way you talk about her." Was it so obvious? "But, do you really think this is okay? She's your aide. And isn't she quite ... devout?"

"The aide is only a temporary—"

"Is this something she wants? Are you sure she even knows what she wants?"

"She said she wants this, too, Mom, and I can't—"

"And sex?"

Just like her mother to go there. It wasn't something she could discuss with Batul. She didn't know what was possible with her body. And she didn't know if, down deep, anyone could have a raw, physical attraction to her or would ever act on it. None of which had stopped her imagination.

"It's not that type of relationship—"

"You know, I'm glad you like girls. Because with a man it would be like you were his sex doll."

"Mom! Please!"

. . .

The next weekend, she met Batul's family. Batul had relayed what her mother had said: "You talk about Anna all the time. Invite her over for dinner. It's the least we can do after how she helped you."

"Mama, she can't: no elevator."

It was for the best. As curious as she was about Batul's family, she didn't want Batul to start seeing her through their eyes.

"But," Batul had said, "what do you think about them coming here?"

Batul's mom moved with the same flowing gait as her daughter. She kept her hijab on the whole time, as did Batul. They brought a feast—grape leaves wrapped around lamb and rice, miniature eggplants stuffed with nuts, shells made from ground lamb and wheat like what Batul had made—except with hard-boiled eggs inside!—a salad of beets, parsley and onions, dough that puffed into pita bread in Anna's oven, and, for dessert, a creamy flan made from semolina, with sugar and cinnamon sprinkled on top.

Rami was bearded and reserved. Anna watched his face carefully when he walked into the apartment, and saw disgust—unclear if it was directed at her paralyzed body alone or him picturing his sister taking care of her. His German was limited, but his English excellent. He opened up when they started talking about work. He was now a backend developer for a company that organized academic literature. As they talked, Anna sensed him reassessing her, and when she corrected his understanding of how cosine similarity was used with word embeddings, he laughed, and she saw respect in his smile.

Batul's dad was warm, with Batul's eyes. He didn't speak English or much German. Batul translated. The winter days in Berlin were too short, but on balance life in Germany was better than Turkey, and as much as they hoped the war would end, they didn't think they'd be able to go home anytime soon. His plan was to start a shop and he was looking to rent space in Friedrichshain or Neukölln. The rent in Neukölln was lower, the long-term business prospects in Friedrichshain greater—by his estimate. The al-Jaberi name alone would bring business—he was sure—but perhaps not enough. (Anna knew all of this already, but Batul translated faithfully, either out of respect for her father or because of Rami.)

Batul's mom, who also didn't speak English or German, kept putting more food on her plate. Batul translated: "Dear, if you like this food I can send some with my daughter when she comes to work. The dishes from our city are famous, you know that?"

"My sister is also a great cook," Rami said. "She likes to hide it, but one day she's going to make her husband very happy."

Wanting to change the subject, though unsure, even as she spoke, whether she should bring up this topic, Anna asked, "What did you think of what Merkel said?" Her feed had been filled in recent weeks with images of refugees arriving at the train station in Munich. And of Germans standing on the platforms, holding up welcome signs and passing out bottles of water.

"Wir schaffen das?" Rami asked. *We have managed so many things. We can do this.* Anna nodded and Rami said something in Arabic to their dad, who looked at Anna and placed his hand over his heart. "Sehr gut." *Very good.* Then more Arabic, then he pointed, and Batul translated.

"For people escaping danger, and who had a much more difficult time getting here than our family, this is unbelievable. I am grateful to your chancellor and her leadership. I am proud that my children are contributing to your country."

Later, with Batul's father in the bathroom, Rami looking at his phone in the living room, and Batul ferrying dishes to her mother who was washing them, Batul touched her right shoulder. Just then, her mother turned and asked a question in Arabic—did they have a scrubbing brush?

More tea, more conversation, and then, goodbye. Batul closed the door, turned the deadbolt, leaned against the doorframe, massaged the back of her neck, removed her hijab. In the bathroom, Anna studied her face in the mirror. She loved how Batul squeezed her eyebrows together when she was concentrating, even on putting the right amount of toothpaste on the toothbrush. Her nose was elegant, triangular—bolder than Anna's own squat button; and those eyes—she *would* recognize them anywhere, even on a shrouded face in a crowded square. They were eyes that compelled you to listen, conduits into a mind that ran faster than her own.

There was time before bed and they sat next to each other in the living room. She rested her head against Batul's shoulder. She listened to the hum of the refrigerator and distant voices through the open window from people drinking at the bar up the block. "Your mom is sweet."

Batul didn't respond, maybe wasn't listening. She felt Batul's muscles contract. Then, still saying nothing, she half stood and pivoted her own chair so they were facing each other. Now sitting on the edge, "Thanks for being good with my family."

She reached for Batul's hand and they stayed like that. Then she leaned forward, touched her nose to Batul's neck, and breathed in her skin. She raised her head and looked into Batul's eyes. The tips of their noses pressed together. They inhaled and exhaled. Inhaled. Exhaled. Batul looked away. Anna slid her hand out of Batul's, pressed her palm to Batul's cheek, gently turned her face back, traced her lips. Warm air passed through the window and circulated; Batul let Anna's thumb linger. Then Anna closed the tiny distance and kissed the corner of Batul's mouth. Anna tilted her head and pressed her lips to the center of her mouth. She could taste the salty sweetness. Batul kept still, then kissed her back, softly, barely audibly, then, in slow motion, backed her head away. Her neck and face and ears were red.

"Batul," Anna whispered, swallowing, wanting her to come close again, tiny bubbles still rising and popping in her brain from where their lips had touched. But it was getting late, and Batul put her in bed, pecked her forehead, and turned out the light. She replayed the whole evening—Batul's parents arriving, the meal, sitting next to each other in the living room, the little kiss—over and over and over. She was so lucky.

. . .

"Forget about the performance issue for a second." Rajeev wiped his mouth with his napkin, waiting. Anna continued, "Tell me instead if you understand this. A camel wanders into Istanbul ..."

The joke was convoluted, involving the camel, a nuclear submarine, a Turk, and a Russian. Even after Batul had explained all the background, and the double meanings of certain words in the original Arabic, Anna still hadn't been sure she got it. That hadn't prevented the two of them from winding up in fits of giggles. "You know, because people always think there are subs crisscrossing the Bosphorus, and in Arabic ..."

Rajeev didn't get it at all. "What? What are you talking about?"

"Sorry, Rajeev. You were saying, your first idea is to cache ..."

A group of men and women from the sales team walked into the cafeteria. She spotted Julia, who was wearing her white V-neck tee. Anna waved. Julia waved back.

THIRTY-FOUR

Batul rotated Anna, tiptoed through the dark hallway, climbed into bed, closed her eyes. Too many thoughts pounding. Last week her cousin's husband's brother was killed, found under the rubble after a barrel bomb attack by the government air force. Putin was going to prop up Assad. Still Grandpa refused to leave. Or even shutter the store. She hadn't yet heard back on her application. She couldn't grasp a concept in the paper she was reading. Anna, earlier, engrossed in her laptop, pushing her glasses back up her nose.

Batul unlocked her phone. *The linear relationship ...* Her eyelids shut for a moment. Her application. Why hadn't she heard? For this type of research, where so much signal was collected, why not use machine learning? Couldn't the techniques Anna was always talking about decipher relationships that scientists might otherwise miss? She kept reading. *Characterized by a context-invariant positive, linear response to running speed ...* Her eyelids shut again.

"It's about the entorhinal cortex." Sitting in the armchair, she looks up from her phone, at Anna in her manual chair on the other side of the room. "It's fascinating. Think of this area of the brain, in here," she points to her temple, "as modeling the spatial environment. They found neurons that they call speed cells, and these cells form a circuit that represents the speed at which the mouse is moving."

She hears a motor whir and then Anna is next to her, looking at a figure in the journal article, their heads adjacent. "Like the accelerometer in a phone?"

"A little, but we're talking about speed, not acceleration. I assume an animal knows where its limbs are so its brain can determine speed directly without integrating—"

"You assume that?" Anna's breath is so close to her ear, poking fun of her. Now—

Chime. Chime.

She turned over. Untangled her arm from the sheet. Groped for her phone, found it next to the pillow, turned off the alarm. Two o'clock. She rolled out of bed, washed her hands, went to Anna's room, and, trying not to wake her, rotated her from her left side to her back. Ten minutes later she was back in bed. *Characterized by a context-invariant—*

She read the words without processing them. Awake, asleep, here, at home—the kiss. Those few seconds. Her on the armchair leaning forward. She'd thought she'd wanted to. Outdoors, on that bench, the week before, her head buried in her phone, she'd heard the rise and fall of a conversation, the creak of wood, then a chuckle, looked up, and on the bench across from her—one woman nuzzling the ear of another. She'd looked back down, but a force made her lift her head again, and then they were turned into each other, their mouths linked, the taller woman's two hands cupping the face of the other, and she'd stared.

With Anna, after, she'd felt sick to her stomach. Yet she wanted it to happen again: Anna to touch her cheek, stare into her eyes, trace her lips, kiss her. She saw the women on the bench, but it was Anna and her. In her dreams, snapshotted by her consciousness at the sound of the alarm, she and Anna were lying next to each other, her arms around her, her face tucked into the back of her neck, her mouth on her skin. She'd prayed to remove these images. They kept returning.

THIRTY-FIVE

They got back just as the temperature turned too chilly for her cotton sweater. Her arms were sore from all the wheeling. After the evening routine, Anna pushed herself to a position next to her bed and set the brakes. Her body was exhausted. She had pain in both shoulders, her neck, her left arm, and most acutely, her left hand.

Batul came over, took off Anna's glasses, set them on the nightstand, sat on the edge of the bed. But then, instead of lifting and pivoting her, she reached forward and tucked a strand of Anna's hair behind her ear. "I wish every day was like today," she said, and it seemed like she wanted to say more.

They'd gone to the city's old airport, taken out of commission around the time Anna was starting university, reopened a few years later as a public park, a place she and Karoline used to run sprints. Batul, walking beside her on the flat, wide runway, had said she missed her. Anna breathed in the brisk air and pushed herself forward. They hadn't seen each other in nine days, since before the prior weekend.

"Sorry, Batul, can you help me into bed? I think I've been in the chair for too many hours. My shoulders—"

She caught a flicker of an unexpected expression on Batul's face. Disappointment? Batul moved her to the bed, put her on her left side, positioned pillows around her. *Lie down with me.* It would be comfortable. They could rest their heads next to each other. Keep talking. Look at each other with their eyes in the same orientation.

Batul leaned over and kissed her on the temple. "Good night, rohi."

"Good night, rohi."

Batul stayed standing beside the bed, her weight shifting from one foot to the other. Anna looked up and saw her biting her lower lip.

On the runway, a woman in lycra had cycled past at high speed. Coming in the opposite direction, a little boy of five or six pedaled proudly ahead of a couple holding hands, the man pushing a stroller. In the distance, to the right, tiny people flew kites. To the left, behind the old air traffic control tower, swirls of orange and yellow clouds.

"Could I lie down next to you?"

Her recurring daydream. She saw the brilliant, hued sky in her mind, turned her head and looked into Batul's sideways eyes—and nodded. Batul, in her jeans and sweater, placed her palm on the edge of the mattress and began to lower herself.

"Do you want to wash up first?"

She straightened back up. "Yes."

She heard the door to the other bedroom open, and close, and open again. Then the door to the bathroom, the toilet flushing, water running from the faucet. In a few minutes, her face would be across from hers, they could touch noses, talk through their eyes. The faucet went off, then back on, then off again, then on again, then off. Then silence. The bathroom door hadn't opened yet. She was having second thoughts. She was staring at herself in the mirror. Maybe she was flossing her teeth! Anna had been so tired, but now she was alive, buzzing, her mind noticing each passing millisecond.

"Did you ever fly from here?" Batul had asked while they were walking.

Anna's eyes had been tracking the little boy on his bike, making sure he saw her, not wanting him to get too close.

"No. The first time I was on a plane was the summer after my second year at uni and by then it was—"

The little boy was now meters away, coming straight toward her. Okay, he was turning around, back to his parents. He was rotating the handlebars ... too much; he toppled over. Batul rushed the few steps forward, helped him up, combed his hair to the side with her fingers, said something soothing in Arabic. How did she know?

The muted whoosh of the bathroom door sliding open. Then she was back next to the bed. In the light seeping in from the street she could make out her long-sleeved cotton pajamas. She wanted to hold her. Hug her. With her right hand, she patted the mattress next to her. Batul sat, put her phone on the nightstand, then stiffly lay down on her back with her head on the bare sheet and pulled the blanket over herself.

Anna reached out, touched the back of Batul's head. "I love your profile in silhouette." She combed Batul's hair. "Are you comfortable?" Batul nodded and she felt the movement transmitted through the mattress. "I feel so lucky," she told Batul.

The little boy on the bike had reminded her of how she'd taught her niece to ride last spring. How they'd stopped for ice cream at one of the kiosks. Mia telling her then about the axolotl in her classroom, the first time Anna had heard of them. "Why," she'd asked Batul, while they were still moving down the runway, "can't we regenerate like axolotls?"

"I'm not sure." Batul stopped walking and closed her eyes. Anna recognized the expression—the first time she'd seen it was when they were talking about tractors. "I'm a four-legged mammal a hundred million years ago." Anna imagined a mouse in the grass with a smoldering volcano in the background.

"A predator bites off one of my legs, but I scurry into my hole before he gets the rest of me, and, for the sake of argument, my blood coagulates fast enough. Now what?" Batul opened her eyes.

"Now you're in trouble."

"Right," Batul said. "I'm alive, but I can barely walk, so I can't find food, and I can't run away from danger. I would die before regrowth could help me, so no evolutionary advantage."

"Wouldn't the same be true of amphibians?"

"No."

"Ooh." Anna saw it. Legs for walking, tails for swimming, salamanders able to thrive on land or water, time bought for limbs to regenerate, evolutionary advantage therefore conferred.

Batul scooched a little closer, rolled onto her side, and lay her head on the same pillow. They stared into each other's eyes. She'd imagined this. The reality was better. Batul was here. Next to her. They were under the same blanket, sharing this small horizontal rectangle in the universe. The clean sheets. The fall air. Her girlfriend.

She moved her hand from Batul's head to her back and felt her shoulder blade against the tips of her fingers. Batul snuggled closer. She hugged her, squeezed with all the might of her arm, and Batul put her arms around her, held her, pressed her lips to her forehead, stroked her hair, slowly, slowly, over and over. Her muscles relaxed; she let herself be swallowed up in the embrace. Calm. She could stay like this forever.

"Remember those ponies?" Batul whispered.

"Mmhh."

Batul slid her head down the pillow and looked into her eyes. "We're like them."

She smelled her. Her skin. Her sweat. Her warm breath. She was whole. Loved. "May I kiss you?"

Batul nodded, almost imperceptibly.

She looked at Batul's cheekbone and the tip of her nose and the groove above her mouth. A car passed outside. She pressed her lips to Batul's and they stayed like that, their closed lips touching, breathing through their noses, cheeks on the pillow. Then she kissed the corner, the middle. She touched Batul's lips with her tongue. Batul kissed back, tentatively, gently, tiny, tiny quivering sparkles. She kissed her again, and, unexpected, Batul opened her lips, and their tongues touched, and the oxygen between them changed. This connection. Her mouth. Her lips. Her tongue. A lifetime passed. Or no time at all. Shivering. They were one person. Smiling eyes. *I love you.* Batul —everything. Batul—beautiful human. Anna knew who she was—the person who belonged here with Batul. If this were the end, all would be okay, and tears came to her eyes.

Batul broke the kiss, backed away no distance at all, held the side of her head, touched her thumb to under her eye where her skin was wet, and kissed her tears. Then she tucked her arm in between their bodies and took her hand. Comfort. She belonged to Batul. They belonged to each other. She kissed Batul's lips again. Batul kissed her. Their noses touched. They breathed the same air. This was all she needed.

Batul's hand, holding her own, shifted down, so slightly, and— like a shock—her fingers, scarcely making contact, tickled the delicate bones on the inside of her wrist. Now Batul walked her fingertips along the wrist, up, down. The oxygen changed again. My god. What was happening? Could she know what it was doing? Her nerves had rewired. A wave of pleasure coursed up the inside of her arm. Another. Without thinking, she bit Batul's lip. Another wave. She felt no pain in her shoulders or her left arm or her left hand. All had narrowed.

Please. Please. Her mind was on fire. She wanted Batul to kiss her harder. To kiss her neck. Her collarbone. Images long absent played in her mind. She wanted Batul to tear her pajama top off. To touch her breast. Her heart was beating faster. Sweet was gone. This athletic body which used to run sprints and could not walk—could it orgasm? She'd assumed; hadn't asked; but it seemed possible; in a different, diffuse way. My god. Batul's fingers on her wrist. She wanted Batul to kiss her right nipple. She wanted to feel her tongue.

Her teeth. Sucking. She didn't care that she was paralyzed. She didn't care about anything. Her brain had become hostage to biology.

Batul let go of her hand. No. And brought her hand up and placed it over her cheek, the pads of her fingers on her temple. She untangled her own hand from the sheets, raised it, and touched Batul's earlobe. Batul took a sharp breath and she felt Batul's body convulse. Could it be that at this raw level, where the truth came out, Batul was not disgusted by her body, wanted her too, even in this way?

She would make her feel good. Did she understand? What did she know of her own body beyond what she saw in the shower? Beyond what she'd learned in anatomy? Had she ever touched herself? What was in her mind? Could she know what her own body wanted? Could she imagine what Anna wanted? She moved her hand from Batul's ear to her neck, from her neck to the top of her chest. Batul took another sharp breath. Yes, even in this broken body she could give pleasure. Through the thin fabric of Batul's pajama top, she touched her breast, her nipple was hard—

Batul recoiled. Slid out of reach. Everything collapsed. Pain returned.

"Sorry. Sorry, Batul."

"You can't do that."

"I'm sorry."

A bicycle passed, rattling slowly over the cobblestones. A bottle shattered. Batul reached back, took her hand, interleaved their fingers. A car. Someone singing drunk. Batul rotated and wiggled closer. She buried her head in the back of Batul's neck and breathed in her scent. She loved her. They could take it slow. It didn't need to be sexual. Ever. Gradually, her mind calmed. The light in the storefront across the street was switched off. They fell asleep spooning, sharing the pillow.

THIRTY-SIX

Sofia asked a man exiting the shop on Warschauer Strasse to hold open the door. When he did, she reached down, folded up the anti-tippers, tilted Anna's chair onto the rear wheels, lifted the front wheels over the low-rise step, and pushed Anna forward. Now on the landing, Anna took over, rolling herself into the shop, then pausing, listening for the click that meant Sofia had lowered the anti-tippers back down.

She'd heard about this place from an American work friend. The smell of brewing coffee greeted them, as well as stacks of bagels—poppy seed, salt, black sesame—on shelves behind the purple-haired barista. The sweeter stuff, from chocolate chip cookies to cream cheese brownies to cinnamon babka, was displayed behind the long glass case atop the counter. Anna turned herself left. Shelves and shelves of books.

Earlier this morning, Sofia had come to the apartment to take over from Batul. "Morning, sunshine. You look beautiful today." After her exercises, Anna had been planning to get on her laptop and read the spec Ursula had sent her on Thursday. But she found, as she looked into the mirror and reached for her right shoulder with her left hand, still feeling Batul's fingers brushing against her arm when she'd said goodbye, that she was craving something more. She wanted to eat a chocolate croissant, to take pictures of oak trees dressed in red leaves, to stop on Admiralbrücke and listen to that Spanish woman playing the guitar. She wanted to be surrounded by people—not alone at her desk, Sofia knitting in the other room.

"Sofia, let's go to Friedrichshain."

Now, less than two hours later, she pivoted again and asked the other, non-purple-haired woman, "Do you have a science section?"

The woman looked to her right. "Up there ..." Her voice trailed off.

On shelves up a steep half-flight of stairs.

"I can get it for you. What book are you looking for?"

"I don't know. I was planning to browse. It's a present for a friend who loves science and medicine." She glanced over at Sofia, unsure if she was listening, wondering if she'd guessed. Sofia looked at her. And winked.

"Ah," the woman said, "I know the perfect book. Just a sec."

She came back carrying a hardcover with a drawing of a crab on the cover. Anna looked at the title. "I wasn't thinking cancer."

"Trust me," said the woman. "It's incredible. I read it last year. The author—he's a scientist and a doctor, and he draws on both perspectives. He includes stories about his patients but it's mostly about medical research. He writes about all these seminal discoveries and connects them back to the original journal articles. You get an appreciation for how science and medicine come together, like how we've investigated our own biology for thousands of years and learned so much, but there's always more, which is why still today cancer hasn't been cured. It's one of those reads that changes how you understand the world. In my all-time top ten for nonfiction."

Okay! She'd lucked out. "Do you have cards?"

Back home, that evening, her phone buzzed.

Running late. Can Sofia stay an extra hour?

Batul had never been late before. When she finally arrived and thanked Sofia and closed the door, Anna rolled toward her. "I got you—"

Batul followed her glance to the desk, where the book lay, wrapped, then back at Anna.

Something was wrong. "Rohi, what is it?" They'd gone too far. "I'm sorry if yesterday—"

"I ..." Batul, turned, looked around as if disoriented, finally made her way to the armchair and sat. "You remember I told you about Yaman?"

Yaman ... Yaman ... "The imaging technician?"

"No. Not that Yaman. Yaman al-Hakim. Rami's friend. Our friend from when we were little. He was also studying computer engineering, and was arrested at the same time as Rami."

Did they get bad news? "Yes. Sorry. I remember now."

"He's here. In Berlin."

"Oh—I thought maybe ... How long has he been here? Is he doing okay?"

Batul didn't answer immediately, and in the pause, Anna's shoulders stiffened.

"He's in good shape, physically—"

Anna saw Batul's gaze fall to the wheels of her chair, or maybe the blanket on her lap. "His family hoped ... we all hoped. But, well, losing contact with someone for so long, usually it means ... we couldn't imagine. I tried not to imagine. He was held for three years. And then—Rami thinks when his father collected enough funds or found the right person to bribe ..."

"Three years?"—2012, 2013, 2014—"Does this mean he was out a year ago? He didn't send word earlier?"

"No. It seems ... it seems he got out, and when he found out our family had moved to Germany—"

Oh no.

"At first he stayed at home in Aleppo. To recover. Then he crossed to Turkey and Greece and then came to Germany. He made his application for asylum here. It was recently granted."

"But why did he wait so long to get in touch?"

"Because ..." Batul stared past her. "He didn't want anyone in my family to question his intentions, to think he was doing it for residency ..."

"Doing what?"

"He came to our home. He wants to marry me."

Her left arm twitched.

"He said the thing that kept him going was ... thinking about our future life together, imagining our children."

"You didn't see him in all this time and he just says this to you?"

"I haven't seen him yet. This was yesterday, while we were here. My mother told me this morning."

She'd always said her parents were unusual; they supported her putting academics first. They'd turned down that guy in Turkey. But this wasn't a stranger. "What did they say? What did *you* say?"

"There was nothing to say."

"What do you mean?"

"He's a friend. Rami and I, we both looked up to him when we were little, and now he's survived what Rami went through—not for a week, for *years*. My parents want me to accept his proposal."

Her left arm spasmed again. She gripped it with her right hand. "What did you tell them?"

"I told them ... I will have coffee with him. But Anna—"

Not *rohi*?

"I need to accept. It's the right thing. My parents will expect it and they are right to expect it. After what he survived—and he's promised to support my studies. And ... it's what I want."

Rapid breaths. It was not what Batul wanted. "You need to tell your parents."

Batul shook her head.

"Tell your parents about us." Anna had a brief flash of sitting with Julia in the hospital. "Tell them we've become ... close. Maybe this stuff is never talked about openly, but they weren't born yesterday, they will want what's good for you. Not married to someone you don't love. Can't love."

Batul shook her head again. "They won't see it that way." She looked down. "I don't see it that way."

"But—"

Batul's phone chimed. The call to prayer. Batul looked toward the aide's bedroom, where she normally unfolded her mat, then turned back to Anna.

Anna focused on the rim of her right wheel. If she were more of a planner, she would have thought ahead, could have seen this coming, been ready. If she had listened to Batul more carefully. Down one path, shame, if not for Batul, then for her family. Not just a daughter with a woman for a partner, but an invalid. Down the other path, family, security, devotion, grandchildren. She *had* heard this. But she'd thought she had time.

She raised her head. Batul was crying.

"Rohi," she uttered. Batul turned away. "Don't call me that."

"Tell Yaman. Tell him you're in a relationship. He'll think it's another man." This was more promising. "He'll withdraw his proposal."

Batul shook her head. "He'll tell Rami. And Rami will go to the ends of the earth to figure out who it is. The truth will come out."

Anna's heart was beating faster and faster. Her face, she could feel, was flushing, and her tone of voice became harsh. "You need to tell your family you're a lesbian. If you don't, Batul, what kind of life will you have?"

"I'm not ... *that*. I never said I was."

Anna closed her eyes, tried to slow her breathing. "So you're just going to marry him?"

"I don't know. I need to think. But probably."

If Batul knew that this—that they—could never work, why had she let it go so far? Anna needed to get out of that room. She wanted to sprint kilometer after kilometer until she was exhausted and could think—or didn't have to. Or she wanted to stay here, grasp Batul's two thin arms and shake her until she saw reason.

THIRTY-SEVEN

"Ceylon-Zimt," Batul said, choosing without thought.

"What is that?" Yaman asked.

Still looking through the glass, "Cinnamon."

"You want that too?" Yaman asked Rami.

"No, only a coffee for me."

"If you like," said Yaman, "find a table, and I will bring everything."

She overheard snippets of conversations in German and English as she followed Rami to an open table in the corner. She could tell that Yaman had picked this place with care. It was upscale, bright, with a view of the canal; boisterous enough that if Rami switched spots he wouldn't be able to overhear them; and western enough that they could speak in Arabic without everyone around them listening in.

When they got word that Rami was arrested. When Baba declared they were leaving Turkey. When Mama told her that Yaman had asked for her hand, and told her to have a getting-to-know-each-other meeting this week, and that Baba would look for a restaurant for the reception, and she was relieved. These were pivots. Life moved along at one speed, and you thought you could predict the next day, but you could not. Sunday began with throwing up in the bathroom, being unable to calm her mind before praying Fajr, rehearsing telling Anna they could never lie down next to each other again; by the end of the day she was planning to marry someone she scarcely—

Yaman placed the biodegradable cup containing her chocolate wafer-topped scoop of gelato on the table, and handed Rami his coffee. Her eyes tracked him as he went back to get his own ice cream. He was tall. Taller even than she remembered. He wore jeans and a sweater. His back was straight, his gait smooth and confident as he navigated between tables. He didn't look like someone who'd been confined to a prison cell for three years.

"I'll sit over there," Rami said, when a couple on the other side of the shop stood to leave. She wished he would stay.

"Remember FIFA 98?" Yaman asked.

FIFA 98? The video game? She and Rami used to play it when she was in fourth or fifth grade. Strange thing for Yaman to bring up. Her finger twitched. "D."

"What?"

"D. To shoot."

He laughed. "Yeah. That's right. I was so jealous of your family for that PC. There was this one time, I was starting a game, you pulled my fingers off the keyboard, told me it was your turn."

She could picture that old computer in the study, the translucent plastic dust cover Baba was always sticking back over it. She could remember fighting with Rami over taking turns, could vaguely remember Rami's friends playing on it, too, but had no recollection of Yaman specifically.

"I thought about that a lot while I was in prison."

She dug her bamboo spoon into her ice cream and let it sit. She was unsure what to say. It had taken weeks for Rami's bruises to heal and much longer for him to stop thinking about those soldiers on the bus. Yaman was confined for years. He wanted her to ask. This was her opening. *Was prison difficult? How did you survive? What were the conditions?* "How did you manage?"

After a brief pause, he answered cursorily. "I survived and I'm very happy to be here and not there. But it's maybe not the best thing to talk about. I'm sorry I mentioned it."

Okay. "What about after?"

He wrapped his hand around his cup. "Batul, ever since I learned your family was in Berlin, I imagined today many, many times, and always it was exactly as now—I am recovered, you are beautiful, we are in a civilized place with fresh air and sunshine and people around, you and I are sitting across from each other, Rami is nearby, and, very important, I have my residency ..."

She listened to his low-pitched Arabic. His words were directed at her as if they were in a dark room, a narrow cone of light shining down on her. This conversation was important to him. She believed that, while in prison, he *did* remember the two of them playing on the computer. He wasn't fabricating a connection.

"Rami told me why you waited to get in touch," she finally ventured, wondering if she was being too forward. "What if you had arrived and I was engaged to someone else?"

"I had faith, Batul," he made eye contact, "that you would wait for me."

She shifted back in her chair, dug her nails into the cushion, held his gaze a moment longer, and then looked down into her ice cream. It wasn't arrogance. He believed— They'd exchanged phone numbers. It was a precaution, no more than that—although not easy to recall the subtleties of a conversation from four, nearly five years ago in a whole different world, when she was a whole different person.

"... so I got to Greece ..."

She'd tried his phone multiple times after Rami was arrested. He could have seen the calls. Or later, an officer, taunting him, threatening him, thumbing through the missed calls—*see these people who are calling you—you will never see them again.* If Anna were suddenly missing she would call her every minute.

"... I wanted to get to Munich so I could request asylum in Germany. I went to this camp, which was in an old school building. The intake people wore gloves—like I had a disease. Every classroom was filled with cots, and all the cots were filled with people. Lots of Syrians, but also people from other countries. They interviewed me for seven hours." He paused, no sign of the exhaustion he must have felt at the time. "It was similar for you?"

She shook her head. "No, we—"

"There were two people. One asked questions in German and the other translated into Arabic. I told them I could do it in English. They insisted on German, with the translator. 'Where are you from? How did you get here? What are your grounds for applying for asylum? Were you involved with the rebels? Were you detained? Where? For how long? What took place?'"

Her face burned at the thought.

"I answered their questions. And then more questions. I think they were comparing answers from one person to another and building up a database of locations and practices. After a week in that crowded school, they sent me and two brothers from Homs to live in a house in a village in the far north."

Yes, she knew that BAMF dispatched asylum seekers to live all around the country while its bureaucrats decided on applications. Rami said it was to deter people from applying, but she questioned his cynicism. With so many people arriving, there was a shortage of housing; and the government's argument that they wanted people settled everywhere, not just in a few big cities, made sense to her. What she didn't understand was why it took so long to process applications. Did they really think people were making up these horror stories out of thin air? And if they were, would a little desk research catch out the liars? Meanwhile, people complained about the drain on the economy: Well, let refugees start working sooner. As far as she could see, there were plenty of jobs.

"What was it like up there?"

He tapped his spoon on the edge of his cup of ice cream, still full and softening in the sun radiating through the window. "Cold. I couldn't understand why they sent us there. The village was empty. Were we there to talk with the horses? To be stared at by the few old people hobbling around with walkers?

"I'll tell you a funny story. Maybe not so funny. But in the end it made me feel better about this country, although that's not so important, because I came here for you. Even if you were in Antarctica, Batul, I would have found my way to you." She swallowed. Wished he were teasing but saw no sign of it in his solemn face.

"It's the second day after we get to the village. It's been snowing the whole time. I don't have boots or a winter jacket. But I need to get out of the house. So I dress as warm as I can—two pairs of socks, my sneakers, two sweaters—and open the door. There is so much snow on the ground, more than all the snow from all the winters back home. I step onto the landing, pull the door closed behind me, push my body against the blowing snow, feel it pricking my eyes."

He pressed his spoon deeper into his ice cream. "By the time I get to the village center, my toes are freezing. There's one store. It's where me and the brothers went two days before to stock up. Now I go in, not because I need anything, only to get out of the cold. I walk up and down the aisle looking at what things are called." He looked at her. "Oh, how's your German?"

"It's improving."

"Yeah. It's a pain. That's for certain. For a software job I'll only need English. One good thing. A lot of words are similar to English. Like *yogurt* or *butter*."

She nodded. With so much time alone in that village, he could have worked his way through a book or two in German. She bit into her chocolate wafer.

"Anyway, this whole time, I'm reading the labels, looking at prices, warming my hands in my pockets, and not a single other customer comes in. The owner—he's seventy at least—is at the counter and he keeps looking over at me, saying nothing. I'm surprised he doesn't greet me, smile, even if forced, ask if I need help, grateful to have a few new faces in the village, people without cars who can't drive the ten kilometers to the supermarket." This did not surprise Batul.

"But what can you do? I nod to him, leave the store, and keep walking. About a hundred meters from the store, inching my way along the middle of the road, where there's less snow, I hear an engine behind me and step to the side. I'm not even paying attention, just focused on my sinking sneakers, which are soaked by then, when a police car pulls up next to me …"

Batul had anticipated this turn in the story but what surprised her was Yaman's face as he spoke. She saw a flicker of fear cross it, like the lights of a police car turning a patch of snow blue, and like this were happening now, not last winter. Her mind flashed to Rami on the bed back home, bent forward, demonstrating how the cable ties were fastened around his wrists.

She tried to focus again on what Yaman was saying. "… I can't understand what the officer is telling me, I tell him—Englisch, bitte?—and he switches over and then asks for my ID. And now I'm panicking, like this is a trick to deny my asylum, or I need to pay some bribe. And he says, 'Where is *haz-uh-noos*? You take?' And now I'm totally confused, I'm not sure if he's speaking in English or German. Haz-uh-noos? Then he starts acting out some crazy thing, and finally I ask if I can use my phone, and we figure out that he's accusing me of stealing a bag of nuts! Hazelnuts! But by this time, he sees I'm either the best actor in the world or innocent of the crime, especially with me pulling my pockets inside out, patting myself down. So he apologizes and reverses all the way back to the store."

"Did you ever go to the store again?"

"No choice. Anyway, the snow melted, the fields turned green, the brothers and I joined a pickup football game on Tuesdays and Thursdays in the next village over, I made friends with a few Germans and a guy from Nigeria. One day, after a match, a German friend gave us a lift back to the village. I was standing in our yard, listening to horses neighing, drinking from my water bottle, staring at the glowing bricks. One of the brothers shouted, 'Mail! From Bundesamt für Migration. Yaman, it's for you.'

"My hand was shaking. I slid my finger under the flap and pulled out the letter. 'You have been granted humanitarian asylum status.' I hugged the brothers. I thanked Allah. I let out the breath I'd been holding since I crossed into Turkey. I thought—now I will go to Berlin and find you! Can I get you a coffee Batul? Do you want another ice cream? Cinnamon?"

She was still seeing the envelope, the house, the village. He was smiling, looking at her empty cup. It took her a second. "Yes, coffee, thanks. No more ice cream."

He had an exuberance she wasn't expecting and didn't remember, a resilience, an ability to find the positive. Like Anna, but without her sense of curiosity. He would be her husband. He was articulate. Handsome. Smart. She could get along with him. They would pray together. In time they could grow close. Sitting here now, watching his tall frame standing in line to order her a coffee, she saw that when they were married, the situation would be correct. *Rabbana give us joy in our spouses ...*

She'd rehearsed. Their time in Gaziantep. Baba's decision to come to Germany. Her job at the hospital. Meeting Anna. Getting hired to be on her aide team. The language exam. Her application to medical school. A straightforward description of the last few years, the logical progression as to why she worked as an aide and why she had overnight shifts. She would be careful.

He rejoined her at the table. *We went to Turkey first—*

"Remember the baklawa at your grandfather's shop? The walnut ones?"

"Yes," she said, nodding. How could she not?

"I dreamed of it so many times in prison. To have just one bite of one corner."

She nodded again. He looked like he was waiting for her to say more. Maybe he did want her to ask?

"When we're married, Batul, and living together, I hope you can make them. It would make me so happy."

She shuddered, then caught herself. She too dreamed about the sweets from Grandpa's shop. She *should* want to make him happy. And she loved baking. She nodded. "I will."

He beamed. Be smart. "You know that I applied to study medicine here, right? I'm expecting to hear any day. My parents talked with you about waiting to have children until after I've earned my MD, yes?"

"Yes. Batul, I will be your husband and I will do everything for you. I will get a good job and support you so you can concentrate on school. And I am in no rush to start a family. We will wait. There will be time in the future for children."

THIRTY-EIGHT

Anna knows this room. The low windowsills. The microwave. The chessboard. Familiar. In the hospital. The lounge. Batul's here—a triangle of sunlight on her shoulder. Tasneem, too. And Yaman. Otherwise empty. It's never this empty during the day.

Tasneem looks at Yaman. "That wasn't easy for you to hear."

Anna glances down. This is her chair, the one issued by insurance, but the brakes are configured like her old hospital chair. They've changed the brakes on her. Without her asking. Who would do that? She's distracting herself—the weight of his silence—she's unable to look at his face. She wraps her right hand around the rubberized brake handle and squeezes.

She forces herself to raise her head. It's so bright—the sun is in her eyes, and it's reflecting off Yaman's watch and bouncing around the walls, and the whole room is overexposed. She squints. Tasneem has her finger on the queen. A moment ago there were no pieces on the board. Yaman is staring at the green and white squares, his chest is heaving, he rubs his eyes with the fingers of both hands, more light bounces around. He lowers his hands and turns from Tasneem to Batul. His bottom lip quivers. His eyes are wet.

"Your smile has been in my heart forever. But ..." His hand shakes, scattering light, his voice trails off, his Adam's apple rises and falls. Then, with more conviction, "But I am thankful you told me. When you are for years in detention it teaches you about friendship. What you two have is special and I have no right to take it away. Batul, more than anything, I want you to be happy."

Batul lets out a breath and bows her head in Yaman's direction. Anna loosens her grip on the rubberized brake handle. Batul reaches over and touches her arm. Anna gives a quick, tiny shake of her head and pulls her arm away.

"Anna."

Another tiny shake of her head.

"Anna. Anna." What? "Time to rotate you." She opened her eyes to the dark. It was Iza, touching her shoulder. She could still hear Yaman's words, see the light glinting off his watch, feel Batul reaching for her.

"Positive about this?" Mom asked when she got to the apartment in the afternoon.

"Yes. I said we were coming."

"You look beautiful, sweetie." She'd borrowed the dress from Melanie, who was a thirty-six, which made it easier to get on. It was a sky blue ribbed knit sweater dress, zipperless, buttonless, with a turtleneck top, long sleeves, and a pencil skirt that fell just below her knees. She wore black wool leg warmers, her usual black leather ankle boots, and a silver necklace with an onyx pendant, also Melanie's—and Melanie's idea.

The reception was at a Turkish restaurant. Fluorescent light reflected off plastic tablecloths. She and Mom sat at one of the five large, round tables for guests; others had been stacked in a far corner to make room for dancing. The room vibrated with a driving rhythm from a big bluetooth speaker: drums and a piercing, reeded instrument.

Before her stroke, her tentacle on the sky octopus moved quickly. Tap, tap, tap. Wake up, do a hundred things. In the hospital, it became sloth-like. Tap. In bed, wide awake, wait two hours for the food service worker with her breakfast. Tap. Wait to be transferred from bed to chair. Once in her own apartment with her own aide team, she'd become accustomed to a new tempo that was still slow but more or less under her control. Then, six weeks ago Yaman appeared, and, tap, tap, tap, everything started happening so quickly. It was like she was driving, and someone put a paving stone on the accelerator. She couldn't dislodge the thing or press on the brakes hard enough to slow the car.

"I don't know what to do," she'd told Mom then. "It's all running off the rails."

"Honey, I know you care for her, but I told you this was a bad idea. You can't know the pressures that come with her situation. She's a smart woman. I'm sure she's weighed everything. She's chosen a path and you need to accept it."

She couldn't accept it. Tasneem. A common name with two common spellings. But she knew Tasneem was enrolled at the Charité, and that was enough to find her last name. A phone call to the office of the registrar in her most bureaucratic voice and she figured out her current clinical rotation. She rescheduled her meetings for that day and told Ursula she wouldn't be around for lunch.

Sofia said, "Don't do this, sunshine. It's a bad idea."

"I need to."

They left for the U-Bahn stop, waited for the elevator, waited for the train, and got on to the first of the two lines it would take to get there. She knew Batul listened to Tasneem. From the photo, Anna saw that Tasneem, too, covered her hair. But it was also Tasneem who'd encouraged Batul to apply for the janitor job and to get to know Germans. A sign, she thought, that Tasneem had a foot in both worlds, that she might see what Batul could not.

They rolled into the Ward Building. If there was one place where she looked like she fit in, where she and Sofia could get around without drawing attention, this was it. (Although, in truth, she often felt invisible.) They made their way to the right floor, the right department, asked one person who didn't know, asked another who pointed them down a hall, and there she was, walking to the nurses' station with a folder tucked under her arm.

"Yes. I'm Dr. Marouf."

"May I speak with you in private?"

They found a table in a niche in the hallway. Sofia went to get a coffee.

"You are the woman Batul takes care of, right?"

"Yes."

She hadn't been all that confident she'd actually find Tasneem or get the opportunity to speak with her. Now that she had, she wasn't sure how to bring it up. "I came to ask you for ... advice ... for help. I couldn't think of anyone else who would understand her situation. She admires you. She talks about you a lot."

"She talks about you, too."

She felt her cheeks flush. "Did she tell you about the proposal? The marriage proposal?" It wasn't her business to be telling Tasneem. She was crossing a line. She was about to cross a bigger one.

"Marriage? Who? Someone from back home?"

"Yes."

"I knew this would happen. She is interested?"

Anna nodded.

Tasneem read her expression. "You're worried you'll lose her? She won't be able to take care of you? You'll be losing a friend—" Tasneem kept watching her. "No. You are more than friends ..."

Anna made a tiny nod.

Tasneem looked down, tapped her fingertips a few times on the table. "I never would have guessed." She looked directly at Anna again. "Who is the man?"

"He's friends with her brother. They've known each other since they were kids. He was arrested at a demonstration. He was detained for three years." Now it poured out of her. "I think she feels an obligation because of her family and because of what he went through. She'll be miserable. This isn't only about me. I've tried to explain it.

Once she goes down this path, I'm sure, he'll have expectations, she'll compromise, it will interfere with medical school, her own aspirations—" Tasneem grimaced, pressed her lips together. "What?"

"She didn't tell you?"

Anna shook her head.

"She wasn't accepted."

What? When did Batul hear? She wanted to go find her and hug her. Tell her everything would be okay. Make a plan. "How do you know?"

"She told me. Yesterday."

Things were happening too quickly. "Her scores were perfect. I checked and double checked the translations of her transcript and letters of recommendation. I confirmed everything was in order down to the dot on the i."

"Yes, her scores and transcript were excellent. There are only so many slots, especially for foreigners. Luck is a factor."

"She can apply again. She can apply to more places. I'll help her."

Tasneem reached forward and touched the back of her right hand. "I may not look it," she gestured at her head, "but I'm a little less conventional and I've been in Germany longer. It's good you came to me. It's also important that you not tell anyone else—this would be dangerous for her."

"But you will speak with her?"

Tasneem looked at the table and then back up. She wrapped her finger in the edge of her scarf and tucked in a strand of hair. "Yes. I will. I'll be discreet. But I don't think she will change her mind. She has her ideas of right and wrong. It is very different, our culture, and it's not so easy to undo what was drilled into you from when you were little. For me ... I'm trying to imagine ... if I were like that ... no, I would hide it, I would never act, and I couldn't disobey. It's her parents, her brother, her aunts, her uncles, her cousins, her grandfather with his famous shop. To go against them—it's impossible."

. . .

The music filling the restaurant made her think of the music videos on that ancient TV at the hole-in-the-wall kebab place near her old apartment. The men danced in a circle. Yaman—suited, bearded, smiling—was the tallest. His legs pumped up and down. His arms swung, holding his now father-in-law's hand on one side and Rami's on the other. He didn't move with the perfectly coordinated steps of whichever relative was leading the line, swirling a napkin in the air, but she could tell Yaman had a sense of rhythm and the athletic grace of someone who must have spent countless hours juggling a football as a kid.

My god—she'd had so many opportunities to dance and she'd been so inhibited, timid and unsure of her movements, needing to drink to get out there. If her legs worked, and this were any other wedding, she would be up there circling around no matter how awkward she felt.

There was Batul. In a white wedding gown with a matching hijab. She too was dancing, holding hands with her mother and her cousin from Gothenburg, in a line with the other women, including Tasneem. Batul was swaying, moving her feet in a pattern Anna couldn't quite follow, or even see clearly because of the floor-length hemline. She looked uncomfortable. Or maybe that's what Anna wanted to see. So much makeup. Unnecessary. Hard to read her expression under all that.

Mom leaned over and whispered. "She looks miserable."

That octopus appeared again. Now its long tentacle was tapping her chopstick in time with the bassline blaring from the speaker. Tap. Tap. They'd planned the wedding so quickly. With such short notice, Anna had imagined fewer guests, a quiet reception, more like dinner with family and friends—not that they would rent out a whole restaurant.

The men's line passed in front of the women's. Yaman stole a glance at his bride. What was in his eyes—love, lust, desire, possession, joy? A mixture of all, she thought. In her imagination he'd looked a little scruffy, a bit like Rami. Not in reality, or at least not now. His hair was gelled back. His beard was dark, trimmed, with a perfect edge. When they slept together, she would feel his beard against her soft cheek. She would touch his slicked-back hair. She would place her open palm against his face and look into his eyes. Stop!

Anna picked up a feta-stuffed pastry, moved it to her mouth, chewed. She looked over at Batul again. God she looked good, even with all that caked-on makeup. Her movement was refined, subtle, gliding almost. Even if she weren't the bride, all eyes would be drawn to her. For just a moment she let herself think that it would be her alone with Batul later. They would talk about the guests, she'd ask Batul where she'd learned to dance, she would place her hand on Batul's waist, above her hip, and feel her ribs through the satin fabric of the gown.

She felt blood rushing to her face. Yaman, or Rami, or Batul's parents could look over, see her staring. Would they understand? Yes, it was obvious, Tasneem had guessed right away. Except it was also so far from anything they would think. She was, from their perspective, the female friend, the paralyzed employer, the non-Muslim patient— it would be too many leaps to imagine what they felt for one another.

Her thinking, over and over, despite what Tasneem had said, was that Batul would come to her senses. She would realize that marrying Yaman would be a disaster for her and for him. Now, watching them, him with the men, her with the women, she understood it would not be a disaster. She was the delusional one. Two healthy bodies. The same religion. From the same city. The same culture. The support of family and friends. Good wishes from hundreds in Syria, Turkey, Egypt, and Sweden who wouldn't have been able to make it with even a year's notice.

They fit. She watched Batul pivoting, swaying, still dancing as the line circled round and round the restaurant. She glanced down the line at Tasneem, who smiled at her, then brought together the hands of the two women on either side of her, separated from the chain, and came over.

"This is Tasneem Marouf," she told Mom. "Batul's friend. A doctor at the Charité."

Tasneem touched her shoulder. "I love your dress. You look very pretty. Come dance. You can eat later."

Dance? You know what? She would.

Tasneem took Mom's hand and brought her to the line of women circling around the restaurant. Anna rolled her chair forward and found a spot in the middle of the open area. She caught a strange look from Rami, but she didn't care. She raised her right hand to shoulder level and swayed it left and right in time with the driving rhythm.

Batul came over and put a cloth napkin in her hand. She felt Batul's warm fingers. She held the napkin up, between her thumb and index and middle fingers, copying the man leading the line. She waved her wrist with the cloth draped over her arm. Then Batul took the bottom part of the napkin, and now time slowed, and Batul danced around her wheelchair, grasping the edge of the napkin, her legs moving up and down. They stared at each other.

Then the line of women snaked by, Batul's mother grabbed Batul's free hand, and Batul let go of the napkin and took her cousin's hand. Anna kept her arm up, waving the napkin, absorbed in the rhythm, watching Batul, Mom, and Tasneem circling the restaurant.

PART 4
WINTER 2015–2016

THIRTY-NINE

Batul lay in bed, resenting the radiator, which rattled and threw off too much heat for the little room. Yaman had drawn the curtains, closed the door, and turned off the light. Her body was rigid. He climbed in and propped himself up on one arm next to her, his face hovering close to hers. There was a soapy, antiseptic, medicinal smell, which masked an oily scent from his hair gel, and under that she could almost taste the sweat from his underarms, laden with the turmeric and garlic from dinner—her first time cooking for the two of them.

"I would kiss your soul," he said.

"Abous rohik," she parroted back. They had no connection. Her soul. Did he already feel so close to her?

He ran the tips of his fingers over her temple and then along the side of her head and neck. She didn't want his hands touching her hair. She didn't like that next he would trace his finger along her shoulder.

A valve closed in a distant pipe and echoed through the radiator. *Stay calm.* She forced her arms to remain by her side, to rest on the sheet, palms open, willing her muscles not to tense, willing herself to not hug in her arms and hands.

"I would kiss your soul," he said again, in a whisper, and pressed his lips to her forehead, his mustache scratching her skin. He touched the bones of her neck and her collarbone. "You're so beautiful." She closed her eyes. *Stay still. Don't move your head. He is your husband. You are his wife.*

They were under a sheet. She felt his weight shift and his hands tugging up her nightgown. She squeezed her eyes. She turned her palms down and dug her fingers into the mattress.

He climbed on top of her. He pushed his pajama bottoms down. She felt his bare skin against hers. She hadn't looked or touched yesterday. She didn't want to look or touch today. She looked at his chin, then left of it. Reapply? Futile. Being married changed the equation—universities elsewhere suddenly seemed possible; she could go alone, or he might move with her. His weight on her. The sensation of him pushing against her. Her legs tensed.

He wasn't inside. Of that she was sure. She needed time. If he could go slower. If he could be lighter. If they could get used to each other. The thrusting got faster. His hand crushed her left breast. His breathing got heavier. Garlic. Sweat. Hair gel. Now even faster. Now warm liquid against her thigh. He rolled over and fell asleep. Tomorrow she would wash the sheets and hang them to dry before she went to Anna's.

Kneeling, she rotated her head right. *As-salamu 'alaikum warahmat-ullahi wabarakatuh.* Left. *As-salamu 'alaikum warahmat-ullahi wabarakatuh.* Peace be upon you and God's mercy and blessings. She cleared her mind, silently said *Subhanallah* thirty-three times, counting automatically on her right hand, then *Alhamdulillah* thirty-three times, then *Allahu Akbar* thirty-three times. Slowly she stood, stepped off her mat, folded over the corner.

She could hear him turning off the shower in their tiny bathroom. She looked at his rug in the basket. He'd used it the day of their wedding and the day after but not in the month since. Many times, she had been on the verge of asking him why he didn't pray. Each time, she'd stopped herself. He was present; he saw her praying; he could have volunteered why he was not.

The alcohol, though, she *had* confronted him about, mostly because she'd been so surprised that the words came out before she could stop herself. It was two weeks ago. She'd been in bed reading on her phone when he came home. Even after he washed up, she smelled it as soon as he climbed in next to her. "Have you had beer?"

"Yes," he said, as if it was the most natural thing in the world.

"Alcoholic?"

"Yes."

"But—"

"Are you my sister? I started when I was in the north, with my German friends, after football. It's good for socializing."

"But you can't drink."

"En kunta fi balad faf'al ma yaf'al ahluha"—if you are in a country, do as its people do.

"No. Husband. That is not who we are."

"There are worse things."

"But—"

He'd stared at her, his jaw set.

She'd begun to wonder if his time in prison had affected him more than he let on. Three days after he'd come home stinking of beer, she'd made him walnut baklawa.

"What did they give you to eat?" She hadn't been planning to ask this either.

"Let's talk about something else."

The most detailed report she'd found online came from a Turkish aid agency. The appendix contained transcripts of interviews with former detainees; these accounts made the slaps Rami received on that bus seem like horseplay.

She'd read it through in one sitting, ignoring studying for TestAS, which would help with her new applications, knowing that if she looked away she wouldn't be able to look back. Interviewee F had been imprisoned for two-and-a-half years. He'd been arrested with his cousin, and the two were still together a year into detention. That's when the jailer gave the man a rusty screwdriver and told him to dig it into his cousin's back and "gouge a deep cut from shoulder to hip." He refused. The jailer raised his gun to the cousin's head and told him to do it or he would shoot. The man lifted the screwdriver and pressed it to his cousin's back. "Deeper! Break skin!" He did what was required. Later the wound became infected and the cousin died in his arms.

Yaman—to survive that for three years? His prison must have been different. He had no scars, for one. Or none she'd seen. Yet exposure to even a fraction of that cruelty—of course that wasn't something you moved on from in a year, or in a lifetime.

She'd tried again last week. "Did you know any of your fellow prisoners?"

"No," he'd said, quietly.

Now, still standing beside her rug, she heard what might have been sobbing coming from the bathroom. She wanted to ask through the closed door, "Are you okay?" Instead she went to the kitchen and brewed coffee. When he joined her, smiling, his hair was combed, his beard neatly trimmed, his back straight.

"Good morning, habibti. It smells great!"

She poured his coffee, then her own, and sat across from him at their folding table. Who was her husband? This proud, positive, vigorous man? The man who had just been sobbing in the bathroom? The angry man with beer on his breath? If she were ever to hear him call her *habibti* and not feel a weight in her stomach, if they were ever to understand each other, she needed the glass partition to crack.

"Are you okay this morning? When you were in the bathroom, I thought, maybe, I heard ... you sounded upset."

Watching his face, a moment of denial, then a shift. "Yes, I'm okay now. When I cleared the steam from the mirror I saw my father, and with that, a ... memory."

She stayed silent, not picking up her mug.

"In ... in there ... not so long before I got out, I became friends with this kid Ghaith. In the cell you weren't allowed to talk, and it was dangerous, you didn't know who was who and who was reporting what to the guards, but sometimes you could whisper, and Ghaith and I started talking. He was seventeen. From Damascus. He told me his father's mobile and I memorized it, and he did the same for me.

"'If you get released,' he said, 'please call him, tell him I am alive and I am here.'

"'I will.' We swore to each other."

He paused. She waited, frozen.

"Do you hear the birds?"

She nodded, barely moving her head.

"When I heard nature again it was deafening. Birds chirping, insects, wind. You can't imagine how sweet the air smelled. I was blindfolded. They put me in the back seat of a car, and as it drove, I checked—yes, I knew Ghaith's father's number, and I told myself, if this wasn't a trick, and it was freedom, not the end, to which I was being driven, I would call him the moment I got home."

He stared past her. "They dropped me in the city, told me to count to one hundred, and drove away. I counted. To two hundred. Then I took the hood off. I approached a man—an ordinary man walking down an ordinary road. He called Baba. When I got home, I ate and I got clean. But I didn't call Ghaith's father. I told myself I would do it the next day. But the next day I didn't call either. And the day after that I didn't call.

"But why not?" How not, she wanted to ask.

He could not meet her eyes. "When you are out of that place, you never want to think about it again."

He looked down into his coffee. "For weeks I didn't call. I didn't let myself think about it. And then the guilt became too much, and I remembered that we'd sworn to each other, but by then I couldn't remember the number. Ghaith's father could have known he was alive. Where he was. Could have tried to buy his release."

She reached her hand across the table and put it over his. "I'm sorry."

He put his other hand on hers. "I told him about you. That you were my friend's little sister. How beautiful you were. That you tried my mobile after I was arrested. How when I got out we were going to get married. Now we are married. And Ghaith is still there, or somewhere else, or dead."

Her hand was still on his.

"Habibti, I need to tell you something else. The interviewing isn't going as well as I said."

FORTY

Exhausted. Unable to fall back asleep. Anna shouldn't have told her to leave. She should have given in. Given it time. Six weeks ago: Batul's head on this pillow, her nose millimeters away. Two days ago: the wedding. Earlier today: her shift.

At the office they couldn't talk. The train home wasn't the time to bring it up. Back in the apartment she couldn't bring herself to. Until if she waited any longer Iza would arrive.

Batul looked stunned. "A new aide? To replace me?" Her surprise, and the arguments she put forward, made Anna wonder if she'd imagined the past half year. "I check you more carefully than anyone else. Izabela gets sloppy."

And then: "Please. I'm going to worry about you too much if I'm not here."

It would be so easy to give in. "Don't you get it? You're not my aide. You're not my friend. I love you. I still love you. I will always love you. To go from what we had ... to this. I can't do it. I thought I could, until the wedding. I can't. I can't be around you, hearing your voice, talking about everything like before, watching you push your hair out of your face, feeling your presence when we're at the office—and then knowing you go home to him."

She swallowed. She began to stretch her arm forward to hold Batul's hand. But Batul moved her hand out of reach, and in her eyes she saw fear and anger. For the first time, Batul raised her voice. "Don't *you* get it? Do you ever stop and think about what I believe? I accept the whole you. I've done everything to support you. Why can't you accept the whole me? We said I would remain on your team. I need this."

But Anna had stayed firm and now, in the dark, she was replaying everything. Even before, she'd prided herself on seeing all sides. Yet Batul was right: when Batul's beliefs came into conflict with what she wanted, Anna couldn't accept them.

Or maybe she was being too narrow. People had these types of relationships. Especially in other places and times. Is that what Batul had been hoping for? Why should she draw such stark lines? She wanted to feel Batul brushing her hair, the pads of her fingers smoothing her eyebrows. When she left, after Iza arrived, their hands hadn't touched, and Batul hadn't crouched and allowed Anna to hug her.

Peace could be found in resolution. She'd ripped off the band-aid. The universe had plunged her into a new situation and said, "Deal with this you little human." She'd been here before and she *could* deal with it. It was pointless to fixate on what might have been. She was the roly-poly toy. She'd been tipped over yet again. She would right herself. She had to.

"I'm sorry," Ursula told her at the office the next day, "I'm way behind."

Shit. She'd been counting on Ursula to finish her part so they could hit their next milestone. If she skipped her exercises, skipped the massage with her physical therapist, skipped the cough assist machine, worked late tonight, put in extra hours tomorrow and the next day, she might be able to catch them up. Exactly what she'd sworn not to do. Her body had to come first, and as it was, she'd barely slept last night.

"I need you to find a way to get it done by the end of the week." She looked at Ursula, unsure what she would say. Argue that slipping by a week didn't matter. That it was impossible. Point out that she wasn't her boss. Anna had never made such a forceful request before.

"Okay. I will. I promise. I'll get it done."

Two weekends after the wedding, Stefan drove her and Sofia to Potsdam for Natalie's birthday party. It was her first time mingling with strangers in her wheelchair. She couldn't quite follow (or care about) the Russian Orthodoxy-centered conversation. However, she had a long and fascinating exchange with Natalie's graphic artist ex-boyfriend.

"So you also grew up in Dessau?" he asked. Which led to the connections between Bauhaus and sans-serif fonts, and then to whether algorithms could capture the essence of a school of design, which prompted her to tell him about this new neural style transfer network where a photograph, say of a city, could be recreated in the style of a specific painting, say *The Starry Night*.

"Copying the color palette?"

"No, well, yes, but much more." She pulled up the paper on her phone and they looked at a photo of the Neckarfront in Tübingen transformed into the styles of Van Gogh, Picasso, Kandinsky, and Munch. He zoomed into the pseudo-Picasso and studied the brushstrokes. A stream of air escaped his lips in an almost-whistle. Then, after handing her phone back, "This means AI can be creative."

"Yes, I think so."

The following Saturday she was supposed to go with Melanie and Elias to the aquarium. The night before, Iza spotted a tiny area of redness on the skin above her tailbone.

"Does it blanch?"

"Hard to tell."

"Take a picture."

It was so faint, nearly indistinguishable from the surrounding skin, and they could position the cushion a bit differently to adjust the pressure point, and being with a boisterous toddler at the aquarium was so much more appealing than staying home. "Let's look again in the morning."

She compared the photos. It was equally faint. No worse, but no better either. Respect your body. Remain vigilant. "I can't come," she told Melanie. She stayed in bed, on her side, scrolling through her phone. Buzz. Iza opened the door. "Ah-na! Ah-na!" Elias, with his big eyes and wild, curly hair, ran to the bed. "This is for you." He handed her a stuffed orange axolotl, also with big eyes. "Mommy says you can't walk."

"Your mommy is right."

She asked Iza to transfer her to her manual chair. She chased Elias around the apartment, him screaming, her unable to catch up to him. She let him play with her grabber, then they unpacked the lunch Melanie brought over. "What is this?"—poke bowls—they sell that at the aquarium?—"That's inconsiderate!"

By Sunday night the skin near her tailbone was clear and Monday she went to work. The following Saturday, Dad, Stefan, and her niece came over carrying two boxes and changed out her desk for an adjustable-height one. She pressed the button. Whirr. The surface moved up. Whirr. It moved down. She plopped the axolotl onto the far right corner where he could guard her mouse.

The next morning, a text from Batul. After no contact for a month. *Are you home? Could I come by? I'd like to ask for your help.*

Her hand shook. To double check the German on her new batch of applications, she guessed. A little bubble of joy—because that could be done over email.

Yes, she texted back.

She asked Iza to dress her in the light blue cashmere sweater Mom had given her for Christmas. The doorbell buzzed. Iza let her in. Batul placed a container with baklava on the kitchen table and made tea, as if that were still her job.

"What about Rami's company?"

"He tried. They're not hiring. The opposite."

This wasn't the conversation she thought they'd be having. "Where else did he apply?"

"Sixteen other places. He started looking as soon as he got his status. He didn't tell me. I think he wanted to surprise me once he had a position. Or he didn't want to admit he was struggling. So far he's had one phone interview—"

"He did it in English, right?"

"Yes. English. I've been trying to help. I made him a profile on LinkedIn. I've been researching companies. I've been writing cover letters, where we say that he completed all of the required computer engineering coursework before his studies were interrupted. I'm not sure the best way to explain the gap in his CV."

She could see why he was having a hard time. She'd been in plenty of interview debriefs. She knew what companies like hers looked for in a candidate and Yaman wasn't it. He didn't have experience. He didn't have a degree. He'd studied for three years at a university whose name meant nothing to employers here. And of course he didn't speak German. Even among recent immigrants there were more compelling candidates out there—people who didn't have a multiyear gap on their resumes, people who had degrees, had done internships, had worked for places familiar to the recruiters who screened resumes.

But still. Why was Batul researching companies and writing cover letters? Yaman should be doing that. "What about you? You're giving up? After all your work? After all our work?"

"No. Of course no. I'm preparing new applications. I have to be realistic. The chances of my being accepted as a medical student are so low—"

"What? Why assume the worst?!" This was not Batul. Where was the resolve? This was him. The asshole. She could picture it. *If it wasn't meant to be, it wasn't meant to be.* "You're going to get in. I believe in you. I know you. You can't—"

"Anna! Listen to me. I'm going to apply for a bachelor's program instead. I'll earn a degree in biology or biochemistry here in Germany. Then I'll have a new set of options. I could even go for an MD-PhD program in the US. I've talked this all through with Yaman. He would prefer to live in the US anyway and this would be years from now. By then he'll have work experience and I'll have a degree. It will be an entirely different situation."

Oh. She'd misread. Her resolve wasn't shaken: Batul had moved on. Leaving Germany? Moving to the US? "Degrees in the US are expensive."

"MD—yes. Not MD-PhD. I can't afford to waste more time waiting to be rejected by medical programs. This is my best chance. I'll get a bachelor's, and I need Yaman to get a job."

Here she'd thought she'd given up. She was charting a course that —three years for a degree here, an MD in the US was probably another three or four years, with a PhD would be much longer— charting a course that would have her studying for the next decade to become a doctor, and she was going to drag Yaman behind her. Where did she get the strength?

One thing she knew—Batul would succeed. And when she did, earned that white coat, what in retrospect would Anna be? A blip for a year. A curiosity. Someone Batul had helped, and who in turn had helped her with her German. *Tell me about this job in Berlin before you started university—you were a home health aide? Yes. I cared for a paralyzed woman. What did you learn from the experience?* Well, it didn't matter, because she would do anything for her, including helping Yaman get a job.

And as she thought about it, despite his lack of a degree or experience, he probably *would* be an asset to a software company. Rami said Yaman was the classmate others went to when they were stuck with their programming assignments. Always a good sign. Plus nobody needed to remind her not to judge an alloy by its name. For

Yaman, the thing was to get past a resume review, past a phone screen, and do a proper interview at a company that valued technical skill, and had enough of a global workforce that German didn't matter. A company like hers.

"You want me to get him an interview at DDB."

Batul nodded.

FORTY-ONE

Back at the hospital, in the weeks after Tomás asked her to lead the upgrade, Anna had mapped out a sequence of goals, the lily pads they would use to cross the pond. The most important, other than crossing the finish line, was when all the disparate parts would come together in a full-scale test environment. The truth lies on the field, as the expression went, and Anna knew it would only be at this point that they could really tell.

The team hopped onto this penultimate lily pad five weeks after Batul's visit. Now, a whole week later, and six days after she'd been expecting it, she messaged Markus asking when he was going to post the load-test report.

End of week.

Not to be pushy, and also not to create the expectation that she'd babysit his deadlines going forward, she waited until Tuesday morning to check in again, going a little crazy in the meantime. Wednesday morning he replied: *Here you go.*

She clicked the link and was taken to an internal wiki page he'd authored an hour ago. She was confused by the row and column labels, and the more she looked, the less sure she was of what she was looking at; easier to discuss live. She had another hour in the office, saw he was free, and sent a calendar invite.

Sorry. Feeling a little under the weather and heading home. Meet later in the week?

She started to move the invite to tomorrow, but saw the calendar now showed him out of office all day, and she was fully booked Friday. By the time they met, on Monday, in one of the smaller conference rooms, her irritation levels had risen in step with a voice questioning whether she had a right to be irritated. "What's this column?" she asked after he opened his laptop. "What are the units?"

After twenty minutes she still wasn't following. Her left shoulder was killing her, and Iza was standing outside the door, a reminder that she'd blocked the next half hour to use the bathroom. At this point it would be faster to read his code.

"Oh, good idea. I have to get it together. I'll send it to you tomorrow."

"Isn't it in a repo?"

"No. Best practice from Facebook. Never commit these internal load-testing scripts. Is that not how we do things at DDB? I'm happy to change."

While they were emptying her bladder, she thought this through. No way was that the standard practice at Facebook. Either she'd misunderstood or he'd misunderstood. No matter for now, she forced herself to decide. She would wait for the code and see for herself what those numbers meant; that was the nice thing about code—it could be traced.

At home, that evening, though, she couldn't stop thinking about Markus. She was responsible for getting this upgrade done; the load testing was critical; she didn't have time to double check or, worst case, redo his work; and instinct told her the report was bullshit. If she was going to be good at her job, especially given her circumstances, she needed to trust herself. She logged on and scheduled a meeting with Tomás for the next morning.

"Is the load-testing tool Markus's only project?"

He paused, maybe trying to figure out why she was asking. "Yes."

She took a deep breath, stared at the open laptop in front of her. She could wait until Markus sent the code. She'd never done this to anyone before, deserved or not; she didn't know if Tomás would listen to her; and if Tomás told Markus, Markus would know it was her. She pulled up the report, took another deep breath, and told Tomás.

Tomás rubbed his eyes. "You know he only has another week until the end of his probationary period? If there were concerns, you should have brought them up with me weeks ago. It's not fair to him …"

So that was the game Markus was playing. Running down the clock.

"Also he seems great. I mean, do you know how selective Facebook is?"

Anna said nothing.

"Listen, I've been doing this a long time, and it's important to understand that people have different working styles. It's to the company's advantage to accept that, even embrace it. I'll tell him to commit his code going forward—or you should. Assert your leadership."

No. The woman who lied about her box not being in the fridge. The lazy therapists who pushed neither themselves nor her. Her instincts *were* good. "Do you believe," she asked Tomás, "that at Facebook they tell the engineers not to commit internal scripts?"

"It's possible."

Trust intuition. Project certainty. "Come on. This is the point of the probationary period. You've got wiggle room now—so use it. I guarantee you'll regret it if you don't."

FORTY-TWO

They'd fallen into a rhythm. He went to work; he came home. They ate dinner together. He talked about what he was working on, his colleagues, what people said in meetings. She prayed; he did not. She went to bed. Sometimes he went out. Other times he stayed up late, on his laptop.

Last week, on Monday, she'd received the first email, followed by two more on Tuesday. She'd been accepted into bachelor's programs at three institutions. The one with the best biochemistry faculty was in Heidelberg, five hours away by train. "Congrats!" he'd said, not asking where. She still needed to bring up her plan to live in student housing during the semester.

She made kebab hindi for dinner. "I met with my boss today," he told her, lifting a spoonful of rice, sauce, and a meatball. "He said I'm doing great. He told me not to worry about passing the probationary period. He also asked if I'd be interested in joining the DDB football team. It plays in an intercompany league." This was her animated husband. No sign of the Yaman from two months ago. He'd reconnected with friends from back home, made new ones, joined a weekly basketball game, and apparently would now be playing football too. "How'd you meet so many people so quickly?" she'd asked him.

For dessert, she served the pistachio mabroumeh she'd made in the morning. "Better than from back home," he said. Then he asked something she wasn't expecting. "Habibti, do you want to pray together?" She nodded. She did wudu. He took a shower, which he never did at night unless he was coming from basketball. He stood on his mat, and she stood behind him on hers, and followed him in prayer. He raised his hands to his ears, *Allahu Akbar*.

He didn't bring his laptop to bed. "Why don't you put your phone away?" Now she understood. She slid down, lay her head on the pillow, stared at the ceiling. With his long arm he reached under the covers and began pulling down her pajama bottoms. She brought her knees in, took them the rest of the way off, folded them, tucked them under her pillow, and stretched her legs back out.

He climbed on top. She closed her eyes. "You're so beautiful." In the park, reading, a gentle breeze, warm earth— He brought his mouth to hers and pushed his tongue to her teeth. *Open lips. Open lips.* They stayed sealed. He rolled off, slowly. He lay next to her also looking up. She felt the thoughts radiating from his brain. "We're married," he said softly. "We're supposed to do this. You don't need to worry."

"I'm sorry."

"You don't need to be sorry." He turned onto his side, buried his face in her neck, placed his hand on her breast under the blanket and sheet but over her pajama top. She felt his erection against the side of her leg. "If it takes time, it takes time."

Relief. "Yes. We need to get used to each other."

He didn't say anything for a minute. His hand stayed in place. He was still breathing into her neck, the bristles of his beard scratching her skin. "Who's your closest friend?"

She no longer had— Tasneem was more mentor than friend. If only she'd never told Anna how she felt. If they could go back to how things were in the hospital.

"Did you fall asleep?"

She shook her head. "Anna, I suppose."

He pulled his hand away from her chest and turned his body back to facing the ceiling. "Anna! I meant a married friend. Someone who could give you advice in this ... area."

"Oh." There wasn't anyone. Her cousin? *What do you do for Samer?* She couldn't.

He shifted his head back to his own pillow. She sensed his thoughts running fast, anger in his stiff posture, but he didn't say anything. She waited, ready. That valve in a distant heating pipe closed. Someone walked across the floor in the apartment above. When, after a while, he didn't roll back on top, she took her pajama bottoms from under the pillow and slid them back up her legs. "Good night." No response.

In the morning, when she came out of the bathroom, *The Emperor of All Maladies* was lying on the bed. Yaman was studying the card which she'd left tucked into its pages. She froze. *Put that back!* "It's a great book," she said. "You'd enjoy it."

She prayed and made breakfast. He greeted her in the kitchen, grabbed his bag, and left for the office. The pan on the stove rattled when he shut the door.

She washed the dishes and wiped the table. Would he have understood the German? Alles liebe—all my love—that's how she'd signed the card. Not an unusual way to end a note. Quietscheentchen, nur mit dir—rubber duckie, only with you. The lyrics to a children's song, an inside joke. Rohi—that was the problem. Why would Anna call her *my soul* in Arabic?

She shouldn't have left it in the book. She made the bed and got dressed and still her stomach was churning. She called Anna. No answer. She waited. She texted. *Can you talk?* No response. She called again. No answer.

Would her keycard still work? Who would have thought to deactivate it? She put on her jacket and headed to the bus stop.

FORTY-THREE

Before her stroke, there were times when she would be eight kilometers into a long run, look at her watch, see she was hopelessly above her target pace, her body tired, the weather shitty, and the thing to do was—not stop, keep going, no matter what.

These last two months had been like that. Her foot had spasmed so violently when they were cutting her nails that the scissors sliced her skin. There were so many middle-of-the-night thoughts chasing each other around that she often stayed awake the entire time between rotations.

Meanwhile, they'd found enough problems in testing, and she'd been out enough, that the project had fallen three, and now four, weeks behind schedule. "Would you rather I find someone else to take over for this final push?" Tomás, under her continued pressure, had fired Markus on his last day of probation, and now seemed to resent her for it. She'd committed; she would get it done; she was scared that if she took the easy way out this time, she would always take it in the future. "No," she blocked. "I'll manage." She kept rolling —putting one figurative foot in front of the other.

This morning had been especially rough. Pooja, who was on

overnight for the first time, had positioned the pillows strangely and she woke up with more pain than usual in her shoulders. Then the morning routine took too long. Pooja had torn open the package, taken off the red cap, and set the catheter down on the sheet. "What are you doing?" She made Pooja throw it out and start again. They'd been running late enough that she decided on her electric, which should have helped them make up the time, except the elevator in the station was out of order; they had needed to go the opposite way and switch direction at the next station. And so she'd arrived at the office late, and by the time she rolled into the conference room, people had been sitting around waiting for ten minutes.

Now this was the third time she heard her phone buzz—she'd forgotten to switch on Do Not Disturb. Sure, looking at your phone during a meeting was rude, but for most people, there was an acceptable etiquette around it. A quick glance, followed by turning the phone over and setting it screen-side down on the table, an apologetic look around, making it clear you'd never lost the thread of discussion. For her, this was impossible. Every motion would be observed.

Anyway, in the seven months since she'd been back, she'd become convinced that being forced to quit the habit of reacting to every ping was good. She'd gone from proud multitasker to proud monotasker. Her Pavlovian conditioning had been undone, and she was the better for it. Still—why did it keep buzzing?

"So are you happy with the approach we decided?" Rajeev asked after everyone else had left the room.

She studied the back wall of the conference room. It had a special surface that let you use dry erase markers, and over the past hour, Rajeev had scribbled over a good three-quarters of it. This was his plan for moving all the machine learning models to the upgraded platform. "Let me look a little longer. Let's talk after lunch."

Rajeev left her alone and she backed away from the table so she could take in the whole diagram at once. Pretty amazing how everyone now trusted her with these judgments. The plan was careful and solid but also had so many steps. Were they all necessary? It would push them further behind schedule. What would—

Buzz. Right—she'd wanted to check. She reached her hand into her pocket, put her fingers around her phone, pulled it out, tapped the screen. Batul? Two missed calls, a text asking her to call. Her pulse jumped—why did she let herself react? Likely news about her applications. She would call back in a few minutes—

She heard the door opening behind her. She tucked her phone between her lap and the velcro seat belt, placed her left wrist in the U-shaped controller, and pushed it to rotate herself. Yaman. The front-end engineering team was a few floors up, and in the two months since he'd joined, she'd only seen him twice—once at an all-hands, and once in the cafeteria.

Everyone was tall when you were in a wheelchair, but she'd forgotten just how tall he was. It was hard to believe he'd spent years in an underground cell. With his trimmed beard, Oxford shirt, pressed slacks, and leather loafers, he was better dressed than most of the engineers. He looked like he was in sales, or an executive—someone going places.

She suspected he found her vaguely distasteful. Nothing personal or even about Batul—more like because of her disability, because of how physically weak she was. You always got a different sense of your self-image when it was reflected back through others. Under his gaze, she felt ugly.

Or it was all in her mind. He *had* thanked her, profusely, for getting him the interview and helping him prep. And back at the wedding, if she was objective, he was gracious. He'd come by her table, asked if she was enjoying the food, introduced himself to her mother, said he was thrilled they came.

"Yaman, hi," she said, forcing herself to the same friendly tone she used with other colleagues. She looked past him, out the glass door, at the couches in the coffee lounge—empty at the moment—where had Sofia gone?—and beyond, out the windows; in the distance, the TV tower at Alexanderplatz pierced the sky.

He strode forward, letting the door close behind him, and sat at the head of the table. She rotated and moved herself back to the open spot where she'd been earlier, next to him but at ninety degrees. There was a little bit of Batul in his scent—and a hint of cologne.

"Is Batul okay?" She took him in as she waited for a response. He *was* handsome. He had the face and the build to be a model—for suits, underwear, beard trimmers, fancy watches. Batul must be proud when other people saw her with him, and at night she might sleep folded into his tall body, his arms around her, making her feel safe.

"She's fine," he said, but dismissively. He looked at her more closely than he ever had before. "She talks about you all the time."

Anna smiled automatically, but quickly, instinctively, stopped. He wanted something. "She took such good care of me."

"How did she take care of you?"

Where was Sofia? *That's private. It's none of your business.* Did Batul tell him about ... anything? Was that why she'd called?

She was talking, suddenly, almost before she knew it. "Your wife" —good to emphasize—"was a wonderful aide and friend."

"Did she ever climb into bed with you? Did she ever lie next to you?"

Why did Batul tell him? Fear and also, deeper, hope rose in her. "I need to get back to my desk." She started reversing.

"Anna," his voice became quiet and his tone pleading, "she said she sometimes climbed into bed with you, to comfort you. I only want to know if it's true."

Sometimes? It was once. She stopped, looked at him, and nodded her head—

Suddenly, rage in his eyes, an instant transformation. "You whore."

Her pulse shot up. She pulled hard on the throttle as her left leg spasmed. He grabbed her armrest.

"Let go."

The wheels were spinning. She looked at his bicep, his hand. His grip did not slacken. "You fucked up her mind. You brainwashed her."

"Yaman, let go." De-escalate. She let the throttle go back to the neutral position. The sound of the wheels spinning against the carpeting stopped and the room became quiet. "Please, this is crazy, and I have another meeting."

"I've seen things done to people," Yaman glowered, ignoring her. "It doesn't take much for white to become black and black to become white. You're sick. Can't control your own shit, and what's going on in that mind all day?" He pointed at her forehead, though kept his other hand on the chair. "Sick, sick stuff. I knew her since we were kids. She was normal. A good girl from a good family, the brightest girl in school. And you ruined her. You fucked up her brain. You made her not want me ..."

With this last fading utterance, she heard resignation and sensed confusion beginning to supersede the anger. For a millisecond she considered if he was right. It was an old story—the nurse developing feelings for the patient. It wasn't mutual, genuine, beautiful. It was Batul eager to please, sensing and molding herself into what Anna needed. Stockholm syndrome.

"Yaman," she said, in a quiet voice, looking down at his hand on her chair. "Please let go."

He did, then put his hands in his lap and slumped back.

"Do you want to know the truth?"

She watched him. For a moment he didn't react, then he gave a tiny nod.

"I didn't *do* anything to her. She may be programmed a certain way." His face remained expressionless, but he was listening. "I'm sorry ... speaking from experience, it's not something she can control. You can't make—"

An explosion of limbs. He slammed the table and almost simultaneously grabbed her left arm.

"Help!" she screamed and tried to push his arm away with her right hand. He brought his face close, centimeters from hers. It was enraged. Raw, animal. She breathed in his coffee breath mixed with his sweat and cologne. She could see the individual hairs of his beard. "Fuck you."

"Help!" Her left leg was spasming again. Now her left arm, a wild spasm, her wrist, stuck in the U, yanked the throttle back, all the way. He was still gripping her arm. The velcro opened, the chair slid out behind her. Her body crashed into the carpeting. Her head banged on the frame. She was on her back looking at the ceiling. She couldn't tell how her legs were positioned.

"Sorry. Anna, sorry—" Yaman was kneeling on the floor next to her, his face a blanket of horrified fear, putting his hand out to help her up, as if—

"What the hell?" Ursula's voice. She was next to her in a second. Yaman rose, turned, ran.

Ursula crouched down. "Are you hurt? What happened? Should I help you back into your chair?"

She tried to catch her breath, to slow her heart. Breathe. Breathe. "No, I need to be checked at the hospital."

Ursula looked around, a helpless expression on her face.

"Please call an ambulance. Find Sofia."

FORTY-FOUR

Batul got off the elevator on Anna's floor, swiped her keycard, pushed open the door. Rajeev, in the first row, closest to the elevator, looked up from his screen. "Hi, Bu ... Bushra. Haven't seen you in a while." She nodded at him. Anna would not be happy about her showing up like this. Who was with her today? Sofia? Izabela? A new person? She scanned the lines of desks—

—a movement, out of place, far to her right, out of Rajeev's field of vision. She turned. Yaman. He was at the other end of the floor, back to her, walking down the aisle between the interior wall and the desks. If he was looking for Anna, then he was on the wrong side, because her team sat over here, on this side of the elevators. She started in his direction. "Yaman," she whisper-shouted. An engineer looked up from his two screens blankly, then returned to his work. "Yaman." He either couldn't hear her or didn't want to. He kept moving, then stepped into the stairwell door.

She moved briskly—but not so swiftly as to disturb anyone else. People here used the stairs all the time to move between floors within DDB, but of course she and Anna had only ever taken the elevators. Once in the stairwell herself, she paused. She didn't know if Yaman's group was up or down. She listened. Footsteps echoed off the cinder block walls. From above. She began climbing. "Yaman?" The footsteps got faster. "Yaman?"

She followed. The sounds grew fainter, and four or five flights up, she couldn't hear them at all. She stopped, caught her breath, continued to the next landing, and tapped her keycard. The light flashed red, the door stayed locked: This floor belonged to another company. If she couldn't get in, neither could he. One more level, same. A final level up. Same. Now the roof.

She squinted in the sun as she emerged, blind for a moment. She scanned the rooftop, but didn't see him. She let the door shut behind her and circled to the other side of the stairwell entrance. There he was—crouched in a far corner of the roof, in a shadow made by the chest-high ledge, his arms hugging his knees, his back against the cement. She saw him look up at the sound of her feet, but he didn't react, kept staring ahead, blankly—or somewhere else entirely. She walked slowly, quietly closer, until she was in front of him, thought about crouching there, then shifted and sat down next to him, leaning her back against the cement. Somehow, she was not frightened—for the first time in hours, in weeks, in months.

What are you doing? What happened? I'm sorry.

But before she said anything, he spoke. Quietly. "I imagined you massaging my shoulders. I saw myself lying on our sofa with my head in your lap, looking up at you, and you stroking my hair, leaning over and kissing my forehead, pressing your hand to my beard. The food that you would cook for me—that's what I thought about the most, always food. But with all the time I had to think, and think, and think, I never stopped to think that the real you and my imagined you could be different."

She was silent. Was how Anna saw her more real?

"They called me an animal."

Who? But she didn't ask, and instead waited, the cold of the concrete seeping through the back of her jacket. She shifted a centimeter in his direction.

"They called me an animal. But they were the animals. Cruel beyond cruel. Brutal beyond purpose. They knew I had no information—knew I never had any. They were sick. And now I've become like them."

"Yaman ..." But what did he mean—*I've become like them?*

He leaned forward, pressed his fingers to the gray concrete rooftop, and slowly pushed himself up. She watched, frozen, as he stepped on the back of one heel of his leather shoes, slipped his socked foot out, and did the same with the other.

"What are you doing?"

He brought his shaking fingers to the front of his shirt and undid the top button. He kept fumbling with his shirt, undoing more buttons. She stared. He slid his shirt off his arms. He took off his undershirt. She'd never seen his bare torso. He turned. There were burn marks up and down his back. She thought about the screwdriver.

"Yaman."

He unbuckled his belt. He pushed his pants down, the ones she'd ironed for him yesterday. He stepped out of one leg, then the other, folded the pants, and lay them down on top of his shirt. Now he stood in front of her wearing only his boxers.

"What are you doing? Yaman."

"I need you to see this."

She'd never seen him naked. She'd never touched him. He pushed down his underwear. She turned her head. "Look." She did. A tuft of black pubic hair. His penis—swollen, mangled, splotchy. "They tied a string round and round, and from the other end, they hung a two-liter bottle of Fanta."

She was not disgusted. She was not even shocked. After reading the report, she'd understood in the back of her mind that it was impossible for him to be unscarred. Cruel beyond cruel. This is what one person did to another.

"Put your clothes back on."

He turned and bent, and slid his boxers back up his legs, stepped into his pants, put on his undershirt, buttoned his shirt, tucked it into his pants, buckled his belt, slipped into his shoes. Then he put his hands on top of the concrete ledge and looked out.

She rose and stood next to him, also placing her hands on the ledge. The sides of their hands touched. After a moment, she withdrew her hand, wrapped her arm around his back, and squeezed.

"I love you," he said. "I need you."

She leaned her head against his shoulder. She stared at the three perforated aluminum figures in the river, felt the early spring sun on her back, smelled her husband's sweat, and touched the muscles of his back.

"Anna said you're programmed a certain way."

One silhouette appeared bright, one dark, and one nearly invisible. She let her gaze rise. A plus sign reflected off the sphere of the television tower at Alexanderplatz. She breathed out. "It's not that simple."

"I need to apologize to Anna."

She swallowed, her grip on him loosened. "For what? What did you say?" At this, he crumpled.

FORTY-FIVE

Still lying on the carpeted conference room floor, she looked up at the two paramedics in their red-orange uniforms. In the few minutes it had taken them to get here, she'd stopped shaking.

They crouched and examined her. Reassured her. "Let's get you back into your chair."

Had they not been listening to Sofia? "I need you to keep me immobilized—I could have broken my back and I wouldn't know it. I'm not taking any chances. I need to be checked out at the hospital." Déjà vu; this time she projected authority.

They wheeled her on their stretcher and loaded her into the ambulance. As it pulled away from the curb, she began to mentally probe her body. A dull pain in the back of her head, likely where she had banged it on her chair. She shouldn't have nodded at him. Nothing felt broken. She shouldn't have told him. She *wanted* him to know. If something serious had happened, would she be able to tell, would her body be convulsing? Had he known when he entered the room? If not, she'd betrayed Batul. There was the teacher she'd met in the hospital, the one whose leg had needed to be amputated below the knee because of complications from a fracture she'd been unaware of until too late—

"Frau Werner, how are you doing?" asked the paramedic riding in the back with her. The way her head was facing, fixed in place by a collar, she couldn't see him, or Sofia, who was on the other side.

"I'm fine, I think." She listened to her voice. It was strong. "How much longer?" They'd wanted to take her to the closest ER but she'd asked—insisted on—BKM.

A pause, presumably as he looked out the window. "Fifteen minutes with this traffic, I would say."

Despite everything—possible serious injury, that she might need to be hospitalized again for who knew how long, that they would fall further behind—there was a germ of possibility. Something had happened between Batul and Yaman. The ground had shifted.

"Sofia?"

"Yes, sunshine. I'm here."

"Do you still have Batul's number in your phone? Can you text her and make sure she's okay? Tell her Yaman knows."

FORTY-SIX

"My blood boiled. I'm not sure what I said."

"What?" She removed her arm from his back and pivoted toward the vestibule. "I need to go talk to her."

They took the stairs back to Anna's floor and swiped in. "The one at the end," Yaman said. She followed him into the conference room. Her wheelchair! "Where is she?" Batul looked around, out the door. In her manual chair? But what was the electric one doing here? How could she—her stomach dropped. Yaman looked down. "I was holding her arm, and she pulled on the joystick, and she slid out, onto the carpeting."

What! Her slack body would have slammed into the metal frame. If she'd sliced open her skin, if she was bleeding internally, if she'd fractured her right arm, if she'd injured her head. Anna. "Was she conscious? Did you—"

"Yes. She was conscious."

"Did you call for help? Where was her aide? Why'd you leave her here?" Everything snapped into focus. They must have called an ambulance. Anna would have made sure nobody tried to put her back in her chair. Which hospital? If in critical condition they would have taken her to the closest ER. Otherwise, she'd go to where they knew her. She pulled her phone out of her pocket—

A text from Sofia from four minutes ago. She was with Anna. Thank God. Batul texted back.

How is she?

Vitals are normal. Speaking is clear. Lucid. Arriving now. Need xrays.

On my way.

She bent over and disengaged the motors from the wheels. Yaman insisted on pushing it.

"How do we get up?" he asked at the S-Bahn station.

"The elevator's on the other side."

On the train, Yaman stood next to the parked wheelchair. She sat on the bench across the aisle. This small separation of physical space, the rumble of the moving train, knowing there were many stops before they had to get off—she could think. They would get to the hospital. They would find Anna. And then what?

She closed her eyes. A breeze had rustled the grass. She took over pushing. Anna joked with the woman behind the counter. She watched Anna cut into her lemon cake with the side of her fork. She felt Anna's hand to see whether she was cold.

She loved her. Orange blossoms and dancing fountains and seven thousand years; blood cells and air and twisted strands of sugar. She loved the sound of her voice, the precision of her mind, the way she poked fun at her, her weird observations, how her glasses slid down her little nose, her laughter, her strength, the shape of her ears, the smell of her skin, the taste of her mouth, how it felt staring into each other's eyes. She loved her because she loved her. If she could heal her by trading places, she would not hesitate. If she needed her, she would do anything, including giving up on medicine, telling Baba, divorcing Yaman, ostracization, forsaking her principles, rejection by Allah.

But Anna did not need her. Anna was Anna.

FORTY-SEVEN

"I have good news." Anna, on her back, looked up at the doctor. "Nothing is broken. No lacerations. No internal bleeding. No bruise on your arm. The swelling on the back of your head is minor and the bump should disappear in a week. You were fortunate. Dr. Eckert will come down to see you and then you can go home."

She took a deep breath. So she wasn't so fragile after all. "Thank you, Doctor."

She asked Sofia to turn her onto her left side, and then to pass her her phone. She texted Batul.

Got checked out. I'm fine. We need to talk. Be careful.

On way to BKM. Almost there. Bringing your chair.

"Did you tell Batul we left my chair at the office?" she asked Sofia.

"No."

The first time they'd talked, one floor up and in the other wing, she called her Frau Werner. She'd scratched an itch beneath her eye. A little more than a year and a half ago. There'd been the janitor. The friend. The caregiver. The partner. Now this explosion. Life worked in mysterious ways. *Auf Regen folgt Sonnenschein*—sunshine follows rain. Or maybe sunshine followed thunder.

"Frau Werner, you have a visitor, Frau al-Jaberi. Shall I show her in?"

Batul came close. She could smell her shampoo, her soap, her skin. Batul stroked the side of her head, tucked her hair behind her ear. Like a bath for her frayed neurons. She pulled over a chair. Anna held Batul's hand and looked at her lips and then into her eyes. "I love you," she whispered.

Batul leaned in. Kissed her cheek. Gently squeezed her hand. Thinking back to this moment, which she would do over and over in the coming decades, each time with more and more life experience, she would be sure that, despite what Batul was about to tell her, Batul still felt for her what she felt for Batul.

"I'm so sorry," Batul said. "What he did—"

"It's okay. I'm going to be okay. Maybe this needed to happen."

Batul let go of her hand. "What do you mean?"

"For him to learn about us. Bring it into the open. You can get divorced—"

"Anna." Her voice shook. "Stop. Nothing's changed."

Or it had; but not how she thought. This was what Yaman said about black becoming white. Did Batul not understand—that he knew, that he'd screamed at her, gripped her arm, caused the fall—or did she not care? He was a maniac. He would be reported. Fired? How could someone so smart be so blind? "You don't owe him anything, Batul. Getting married was a mistake. You see that, right?"

"Anna, please, please stop. Listen to me: he is ashamed. He wants to apologize—he's not a bad person. And he is my husband." Anna bit her lip, looked hard at Batul, said nothing.

"He came with me."

He was here? She'd brought him with her?

"I don't want his apology. I don't want him anywhere near me."

She saw tears trickling down Batul's delicate cheeks, a tremor in her hand, but also resolve in her eyes. Suddenly the conviction she'd had before Batul walked into the room seemed obviously wrong, an invention of her desire for things to be a way that they would never be.

Re-evaluate. Her desperate mind and starved body had spun a unilateral fantasy. They had never been soulmates. They were two people who became entangled due to proximity and loneliness. Nobody was the soulmate of a tetraplegic woman who required twenty-four-seven care. Well, she did not need a soulmate. She was tough. How many times did she need to be told before she got the message? She was clear. She would stop the bleeding.

"I understand." She clenched her hand, locked her jaw, stared into Batul's eyes, unblinking. "I don't want to have anything to do with you or *your husband* ever again. Don't text me. Don't call me. Don't visit me. Don't ask me for help. Ever."

Batul's upper lip quivered. She opened her mouth, about to say something—

"Please leave."

She slowly stood. Her face was wet.

As angry as Anna was, as much as she didn't want him anywhere near her, there was one last thing she could do for Batul. "Actually, get him."

Yaman's head was down, his shoulders were hunched, he kept his distance. She shook inside.

"Anna," he said in English, "I am so, so sorry. I—"

She cut him off. "I don't want to hear it. I want you to make me a promise."

Batul looked at her. Yaman nodded. "Anything. I will promise you anything."

"I want your commitment that Batul will come first. You will support her in every way. You will put her academics and her career above your own. Always."

He nodded, slowly, as if carefully considering what she was saying.

"Do I have your word?"
"Yes."
"Please leave now. You live your lives and I will live mine."

PART 5
EPILOGUE

FORTY-EIGHT

"Can you help me with this proof?" Nivo asked.

"Is it your homework or my homework?"

"Please, Mom. I can't figure it out."

She had a big day at work tomorrow. And with Erika in Munich, she'd need to make sure Dale got up early enough for breakfast before practice. She wanted to relax, read, fall asleep. The opposite of wrapping her mind around a math proof.

"Nivo—come on. Why'd you wait to the last minute? Ask a friend. When I was your age, I wouldn't have dreamed of asking Grandma or Grandpa for help."

"Yeah, because they suck at math. Please."

She whispered: *transfer to chair*. The soft arms of the robot aide gently inserted themselves under her body, raised her to a seated position, and moved her into her manual chair. She pushed herself to the kitchen. Nivo followed.

Mint tea, hot. The aide placed a steaming mug of the herbal tea on the table. "Okay, show me."

Starting was always painful. But once they got into it, it would be fun, and good bonding, unless he ended up screaming at her, saying the teacher never taught this, her telling him that was the point of homework, Erika's voice in her head: *That's what you get for encouraging him to do accelerated math.*

She sipped her tea. "What'd you try so far?"

Later, proof complete, she and Nivo still on speaking terms—"I knew you could do it, Mom!"—"How about thank you?"—"Thank you!"—she wheeled into Dale's room, looked at the swim medals hanging on the wall, watched her sleep, saw her powerful body butterflying through the water. She looked different—more mature—with the new hairstyle she'd switched to today, bangs curling onto her forehead. She wheeled back to her room. *Transfer to bed.*

Next. The extension of the extension of the deadline to turn in paper euros.

Next. A new exhibit at Topographie des Terrors.

Next. A Swedish-Syrian gastropub opening in their neighborhood.

Next. A clinical trial from an American biotech. A therapy to regenerate nerve growth in the spinal cord. Approved today for first-in-human trials by the US Food and Drug Administration. She read the whole article. Read it again. When Dale was in kindergarten she'd asked if spinal cords could heal. "Not yet," Anna had said.

A sleepless night; dreams of standing. In the morning she called Dr. Dahlmann, BKM's new—as of two years ago—and overly rigid chair of the treatment center for spinal cord injuries.

"What do you think?"

"You know, Frau Werner, there are many, many hurdles before a therapy makes it to human trials. So it's a big deal. I'm cautiously optimistic."

She asked, almost in spite of herself, the question that had left her open-eyed at three a.m. "Should I volunteer?"

"For the trial? Absolutely not. I won't let you be a guinea pig. And, at any rate, you don't qualify. Patients must have complete paralysis and be between six months and one year post-injury."

"I saw. But how strict is that?"

"Very. You have to understand that it's an investigational therapy. Much will depend on the early results. The developer, this American biotech, needs to maximize the chances of demonstrating efficacy. The more time that has passed since injury, the less likely that regrowth of nerves can be stimulated in the correct way, which is why enrollment is limited to recently paralyzed volunteers."

She wasn't surprised. She wanted his thoughts, but common sense told her not to be first. She hadn't considered, though, that this or a future therapy might work, but it would be too late for her.

"You may ask why only complete paralysis. It's the risk. I looked at the data. In primate trials there were complications and side effects that were not understood. The regulatory authorities in the US only granted approval to test in patients with the worst physical quality of life. That is certainly not you. All that aside, Frau Werner, this trial is excellent news, and should be taken as a sign of progress. In a few years, more will be understood."

"How are the shoulders? How about the left arm?"

"Fine," she told Dr. Dahlmann. Now five years in, he was settled into his role, slightly looser—with her, at least. "No change really. The pain is always there. I can handle it. As long as I'm busy, I barely notice."

"I don't understand why you refuse painkillers. These new ones aren't addictive. What are you proving?"

She'd kept her medicine to a minimum for over two decades: cardiovascular drugs to prevent another stroke, and a muscle relaxant for her bladder. She was used to the pain. Save the strong stuff for if things ever got really bad. There was, though, something else, and today she wasn't going to be talked out of it.

"I'd like to get ReNeura."

He looked down. He looked out the window. Finally, he looked back at her. "Frau Werner. I understand. Believe me I do. The recoveries we've seen reported in the media are miracles. I follow the literature. I compare notes with my colleagues at other institutions. I attend, religiously, the annual meetings of the DGP and ISCoS. You have to understand—for every miracle, there is someone else now dealing with debilitating pain and increased spasticity, without any restoration of function, or so little as to have no impact on quality of life.

"You have Frau Schur, your children, a big career—you have too much to lose. You should wait. The science is advancing. My prediction—and mind you it's only a prediction—is that in five to ten years, ReNeura or similar next-generation therapies will be so well understood that it will be possible to know with high confidence whether you can be helped, and if so, to proceed without the risk of these adverse effects. You're still young. You have time."

She wasn't young. Dale was in university. Nivo would be there soon enough. Almost a quarter century. She'd stayed healthy, gotten married, had kids, done well—exceptionally well—professionally. She'd found exercises she loved. Technology had increased her independence. Still, at night, sometimes, she would wake in the middle of a dream in which she was running along the canal—her arms pumping, her calves flexing, her feet leaping from the gravel path. She wanted to hug with force. She wanted to be touched everywhere and feel it. She wanted to enjoy her body in old ways before old age broke it down. Enough with ever-vigilant.

"Dr. Dahlmann. You've devoted your career to caring for people like me and I'm grateful. When you look at me, it's me you're seeing, not my body, and that's rare, even among doctors. When you leave this building, though, you do so on your own two legs, and when you get home, you don't need your wife to crouch down so you can give her a kiss.

"I've lived like this for twenty-four years. I know. If I looked at it objectively, you're right, I should wait. What's another decade? The last thing I want is for our kids or Erika to see me even more debilitated. But in my mind I still run. And now that there is proof that paralysis can be cured, including for people who've been paralyzed for longer than me, I can't stop thinking about it. I want to get ReNeura. If I insist, can you administer it, or will I need to go elsewhere?"

He pressed his thumb and index finger to his eyes, then looked at her again. "I can. It will be off-label. You'll need to pay the full cost. Insurance will not cover it. The protocol calls for ..."

This she already knew. The protocol was three injections into the spinal cord, each a month apart, and aggressive, daily physical therapy during those three months and the twelve months following. She'd already worked out with her boss, the CEO, the best time to take an extended leave of absence from DDB. And she'd already fought with Erika, who'd only ever known her like this and couldn't understand why she'd want to take the risk.

"I want to do it."

"Frau Werner, I advise against it in the strongest possible terms. Have you discussed this with Frau Schur? With your children? I'll contact my colleagues. I'll arrange for you to speak with a patient for whom the treatment has been a failure, who now experiences phantom pain and increased spasticity, or a patient for whom restoration of function was accompanied by increased neuropathic pain. I want you to understand what could happen."

"Doctor, I understand the risks. It's my decision and I've made it. I'd like to schedule the first injection for July."

FORTY-NINE

For the twentieth time she played the recording. The first time was two months ago, a few minutes after it was streamed live, when Dale, on parental leave from her cardiology practice, sent her a message: *Mom—watch this. What an incredible story. Did you come across her when you were researching ReNeura?*

The overlay indicated this was the Karolinska Institute in Sweden. Five people, dressed formally, entered the lecture hall and sat at a long table. The short man at the far right then stood, stepped over to the lectern, and began speaking in English.

"I wish you all good morning, and a very warm welcome to the Nobel Forum for the announcement of this year's Nobel Prize in Physiology or Medicine. So I will first read the announcement in Swedish followed by English. And we will then present some background to the prize.

"The Nobel Assembly at Karolinska Institutet has today decided to award the 2051 Nobel Prize in Physiology or Medicine to Batul al-Jaberi for her discovery of the key mechanism governing restoration of neurological function from regenerated neuron cells.

"Professor al-Jaberi was born in Aleppo, in Syria, in 1992. She received a bachelor's degree in biochemistry from Heidelberg University in Germany, and completed her doctoral studies at Baylor College of Medicine in Houston in the United States. She performed her prize-winning research at Baylor and at Harvard University, where she is still active.

"I will now leave the word to Professor Karlsmo, member of the Nobel committee, who will describe the discovery."

The woman in the navy suit rose, traded places with the man at the lectern, and scanned the room. "Esteemed colleagues and guests, let us start by stating the clinical impact of this work. Fifty years ago, at the turn of the century, one in a hundred people lived with some degree of paralysis, and every year, half a million people suffered a spinal cord injury. The most severe injuries resulted in the loss of motor control and sensory functions in arms, legs, and body; an inability to self-regulate the body's core systems; and chronic pain. Today, many spinal cord injuries can be cured, with therapies that are possible because of Professor al-Jaberi's discovery of the mechanisms that control ..."

She hadn't known. After she and Erika got married, a beautifully wrapped box of baklava—three different kinds—had arrived from Heidelberg. She texted Batul to thank her, and the brief exchange, their last, messed with her equilibrium for months. Later Batul had moved to Texas and started her PhD, and her name was buried in the long list of authors of a scientific article. Then, around the time Erika became pregnant, she'd stopped googling.

"I won't be over on Saturday," she'd told Dale. "I'm going to Stockholm. I'm planning to spend the weekend." Dale assumed it was for business.

Yesterday, from her hotel, she'd watched the livestream of the ceremony and saw Batul—beaming, her head covered—walk up and receive her medal from the king.

Now, on this dark, early Sunday morning, she put on her winter running gear and slipped her feet into her sneakers. She bent over, used her right hand to pull the laces tight, crossed one end over the other and formed a knot, used the friction between her left wrist and the side of the sneaker to keep one end of the lace taut, and tightened the knot with her right hand.

She exited the hotel, stepped off the curb, carefully crossed the trolley tracks, stepped up the curb on the other side, turned right, and started jogging. Right foot. Left foot, dragging. Right foot. Left foot, dragging. She found her rhythm.

Half a year after the first injection she could shuffle from bed to kitchen leaning on her walker. Six months later she could walk without support—slowly, clumsily, for short distances. After another year she was able to go for multiple kilometers without resting.

Erika was thrilled. And then less so. Theirs had been a partnership—she earned more, she was more optimistic, Erika had more opinions, Erika took care of everyone. "I don't feel I have a role anymore," Erika had said. Or it was because Dale and Nivo were out of the house. Or Erika had never quite forgiven her for risking the therapy. Erika left her during Nivo's last year of university. By then she was running again and had figured out that vigorous exercise was the best way to soothe the new, excruciating pain in her dead left hand. Her speed was half of what it used to be, but she made up for it with distance. Two years ago, at fifty-nine, she'd run her first marathon.

Now she passed the outdoor skating rink in Kungsan. She'd run a similar route yesterday. The short loop, which she'd been repeating, took her through this park, then to Berzelii Park, then to Museiparken, then back here, passing the ferry terminal and the Grand Hotel.

The Grand Hotel. For the past hundred and fifty years it was where the laureates stayed. Later, at a respectable hour, in jeans, she would come back, step through that revolving door, and ask for Batul. Batul would come down the elevator and walk into the lobby with some mixture of disbelief and warmth in her smile. Her posture and gait would be unchanged, like she'd seen at the medal ceremony—

upright, floating, calm. Anna, not calm at all, would rush over, throw her arm around her.

Her pulse was elevated from running. When she imagined approaching that reception desk—*Can you let Batul al-Jaberi know I'm here?—My pleasure, madam. What is your name?—Anna Werner* —it got even faster. Hard to believe at her age.

Of course Batul might not be alone. Yaman could come down to the lobby with her. Or their son, who'd inherited his father's height and looks. Wouldn't he have taken time away from his own research to make the trip?

Step. Step. Not many people out at this hour. She nodded at a man running toward her. From the light in his eyes she could tell he was watching something. She never did that. Running was for thinking.

She'd read everything. From before the announcement, there was little outside of Batul's publications in scientific journals. From after, there were hundreds of articles and interviews. There was one interview that she'd watched a dozen times—conducted by a young woman at Harvard, a graduate student. They sat on armchairs on a stage in a packed auditorium. Batul looked serene, interested, beautiful.

"Professor al-Jaberi, how do you cope with failure?"

Batul took a sip of water and put her glass back down. "That's an important question." She sounded American. "You have a hypothesis. You design an experiment, you have good controls, you collect data, and the data doesn't match your hypothesis." She raised an open, horizontal palm, as if weighing the air. "Is that a failure? Maybe. But it's the good type."

The grad student nodded.

"In science, our objective is to uncover new knowledge. So, naturally, you can't expect that your predictions will be correct most of the time. The insights come when you think deeply about why your results don't match your predictions, or, to use your term, why the experiment failed."

"In other words, you can learn more when things don't work out than when they do?"

"Yes, that's been my experience. I have a technique. I used it as a grad student three decades ago, and I still use it today."

The young woman nodded, expectantly.

Batul gestured at herself, exactly like she used to. "I talk things through with a rubber duck." There were a few chuckles in the audience. The grad student looked puzzled, unclear if Batul was setting up a joke—obviously she didn't know her. "I go through everything and explain it to her, step by step, as if—"

"Professor, sorry to interrupt. I want to make sure I'm following. You're talking about an AI?"

"No," Batul smiled. "This is all in my head. I explain everything to this imaginary duck step by step as if she had no a priori knowledge. This forces me to see things fresh and to question assumptions. A quarter of the time, I would say, this leads to an ah-ha moment—noticing a flaw in my experiment, or something interesting in the data, sometimes a new hypothesis."

She was passing the Grand again. Ahead she spotted two old men walking slowly. The one on the left was a prize-winner. She recognized him from the ceremony. She asked her AI—*Yes, that's Xin Liu, former head of the World Bank, winner of this year's Nobel Prize in economics.*

Batul might also be out, getting fresh air. At first she would register another early riser, running, moving toward her. Then, as she got close, she might recognize her. She'd see her on her feet in her form-fitting running gear. She'd spent decades losing muscle tone, she'd given birth to Nivo while paralyzed, but now at sixty-one she was fit, looked like someone ten, fifteen years younger.

Batul would be surprised, obviously, unsure if it was her. And in that moment, Anna would close the distance, put her right arm around her, squeeze, feel her back under whatever warm coat she was wearing. She would bring her head close, kiss her on the cheek, breathe in the scent of her skin, and tell her, "Herzlichen Glückwunsch zu deinem Nobelpreis!"

Batul would take a second to recover, to decipher the German. Then she would ask, in her American English, "Anna? What are you doing here?"

"I came to find you. I was planning to come to your hotel later."

"You'll never guess what I was just thinking about."

"If they'll have pickled herring for breakfast? The king's nose? That we're the same height?"

Batul would laugh. It would be the same deep and full-throated laugh she remembered, and the laughter would erase thirty-six years. "Not herring." Then Batul would take her hand, turn serious, look into her eyes. "Changing my return flight. Sending you a message. Seeing if I could visit you in Berlin."

Anna would look down at her sneakers, her legs on which she stood, at her torso, at her two arms. She'd remember what she'd wanted to say. "I'm sure you've heard it from so many other formerly paralyzed people. I had no idea. I'm sorry ... I didn't ... all these years ..."

She'd have trouble staying coherent. Her thoughts would get jumbled. She'd keep going. "I'm so grateful. You know ... the technology got better, things got easier, I became more independent ... but once I could walk again, feel again ... thank you. Thank you. I'm flattered and shocked and humbled and nervous that now, when you're getting the biggest recognition, you would think about me."

Batul would stare at her. "Anna, I think about you every single day. Your voice is always in my head. The months we were together were the best of my life."

A tall woman in a glowing jacket nodded, half waved, ran past her. The night she got her scores. *No matter where I am, you're there with me. I love you.* Temper expectations. Later in the interview, "Professor, what qualities do you need to be a successful scientist?"

"It's a good question and I'm sure everyone has their own opinion." Batul brought her open hand to her chest. "Whenever I'm interviewing someone for my lab, the quality I look for is where you might be frustrated, you might feel like you need to give up, except you don't. You get discouraged, but then you dust yourself off, you get back up, you go back out the next day and try again. Science is trial and error and you need to keep going."

The grad student motioned toward the audience and herself. "I bet a lot of us are pros at getting discouraged." The room laughed. "Was it having to flee your home and start over that taught you how to persist?"

"Yes." Batul paused. "But there's something else. I've always been surprised that more people didn't ask, but then again, until last week, people weren't all that interested in me. It's strange that we've filled Sanders Theatre."

A few chuckles from the audience.

"When I arrived in Germany from Türkiye—this was nearly forty years ago—I got a job on the housekeeping staff of a hospital." The grad student leaned in. "I was around patients with tetraplegia. For them, not a single thing was easy. Brushing teeth, eating, tapping the screen of a handheld phone—that's how we got online back then—all these daily activities we take for granted were a hundred times more difficult. Some of these patients—they didn't let it stop them; they kept moving, lived their lives, got married, had kids, built big careers.

"In the early days, nothing panned out. I spent years collecting data from thousands of axolotls using then-state-of-the-art spatial transcriptomics techniques. When our primitive machine learning algorithms could make no sense of the gene expression data, when I was years delayed in completing my doctorate, when even my advisor lost faith in me, every time I thought about giving up, I thought—if those patients could keep going, how could I not?"

She was into her third loop. No—fourth. She was circling Berzelii Park, the water to her left, turning the corner—

That could be her. In the distance. Her stomach twisted. Walking with someone tall. Their backs to her. No question—the gait, the covered head, the posture. Not how she'd imagined it.

Now she was closer and could see them in the illumination from the streetlights. Batul and Yaman. Both in winter jackets. No gap between them. Their legs moved at the same cadence. She slowed her pace and got even closer. In the quiet dark she could hear them speaking in Arabic. Yaman said something. Batul said something back. Yaman laughed. Now steps away, her eyes traced Batul's arm. Her hand was in the crook of his elbow.

Anna picked up her pace again and accelerated past them. Half a kilometer. Around the corner. Out of view. She slowed and jogged across the bridge, stayed right, traversed another bridge, and then stopped on the wooden dock at the edge of the tiny island.

Her pulse dropped. She scanned the waters of this archipelago of the Baltic Sea. She heard a train passing on a track far behind her. She massaged her left arm with her right hand. In the distance she watched a ferry crossing from one island to another. She stayed, listening, gazing out, bouncing slowly on her toes to keep warm, until the dawn light appeared and she became chilly. Then she turned and started back. She felt the cool air on her face and smelled the winter sea air. There was beauty around her—morning in the city, her legs and feet moving over the cobblestone sidewalk. Right foot. Left foot, dragging. Right foot. Left foot, dragging. Right. Left. Right.

NOTE ON ARABIC ROMANIZATION

The (German-owned) U.S. supermarket chain Trader Joe's used to sell a "ZA'ATAR Seasoning Blend." Every time my spice jar runs out, I refill it from a big plastic bag of Salloum Bros-brand "ZAATAR." In Arabic, this wild-thyme seasoning is spelled زعتر, or with vowels زَعْتَر. Arabic is written right to left and letters change their form based on position. The four letters here are ز = "zayn," ع = "ayn," ت = "taa," and ر = "raa." So why is there an apostrophe in the Trader Joe's version? In one of many conventions for romanizing Arabic, the apostrophe represents "ayn." However, to be slightly stricter about it, a left-facing apostrophe ('), as in the Trader Joe's label, represents the letter/vowel "hamza" and a right-facing apostrophe (') should be used for "ayn." Other standards forgo this distinction altogether and use a straight apostrophe (') for both "ayn" and "hamzah." Still others represent "ayn" with a backwards question mark or the number three (which itself looks like a backwards ع).

Speaking of standards, if we carefully follow one of the many, many romanization systems (say, ISO 233), we end up with "zaʿtar." Notice that there is no "a" before the "t" and that that apostrophe-looking thing is actually not an apostrophe, but a character known as the "modifier letter left half ring." So why do Trader Joe's and Salloum Bros and nearly everyone else include a second "a"? My guess is that, a long time ago, someone (a spice merchant?) transliterating the name into the Latin alphabet figured "zaatar" would guide the average non-Arabic speaker into pronouncing the word approximately correctly, and that the double "a" stuck.

Now that's just one word. Let's talk about "manaqish za'atar," flatbread topped with za'atar. You'll find "manaqish" online, but "manakeesh" and "manakish" are perhaps more common. The popular Lebanese fast-casual restaurant chain Zaatar w Zeit, with outlets all over the Middle East, uses "manakeesh." In Arabic, it's مناقيش. In the middle there, you'll see the letter ق = "qaaf," which is why even though it's often romanized with a "k," a "q" comes closer to following a standard.

To make life even more complicated, someone from Aleppo is likely to think and say the colloquial مناﺋيش. You could say, "I'll have a hamburger and fries," but you're more likely to say, "I'll have a burger and fries." In this urban pronunciation, instead of "qaaf" (ق) we have a "hamza" (ﺋ), which is why in the novel it's romanized as "mana'eesh za'atar."

And on and on. I had to make judgement calls for every Arabic word, phrase, and proper noun in the novel, informed by advice from experts since I don't speak Arabic. Here's what I aimed for: A reader with no background in Arabic should be able to pronounce the Arabic approximately correctly and not get knocked out of the story by the unfamiliar symbols used in the more academic romanization systems. Meanwhile, an Arabic speaker should recognize which Arabic words are intended and not get thrown by "spellings" that range too far from any standard. I apologize if I have not achieved this in all cases.

ACKNOWLEDGMENTS

There are three things I love about writing: the writing, the research, and the feedback. The first is solo—you sit down, start typing, and discover what your characters do. The other two, though, are social. Writing is the catalyst; friendships that open your eyes are the result.

For sharing their experiences and expertise I thank: Eyas Adi, Majid Albunni, Shahed Alghrsi, Ali Aljasem, Waleed Farahat, Stacey Furtado, Yaman Halawi, Tonia Khalil, Angela Kijewski, Anthea Krings, Kerstin Rehahn, Stanley Sagov, Yaman Saudi, and Elly Tanaka. Contributions ranged from single conversations on specific topics (e.g. how school transcripts transfer from Syria to Germany) to chatting dozens of times over three years and reviewing every sentence in the novel.

Thank you, too, to my beta readers: David Abrams, Ali Aljasem, Cindy Alvarez, Joel Bard, Ahmad Barghash, Angela Beninga, Zac Bentley, Tim Brown, Gabriel Chesman, Dario Ciriello, Thomas Close, Karen Combe, Erika Dixon, Lynne Doctor, Maritza Ebling, Hend ElShemy, Nina Ephremidze, Geanna Flavetta, Ezra Freedman, Kathleen Gough, Janna Hansen, Anthony Horne, Hui Huang, Zeba Hyder, Runa Islam, Philip Kaufman, Tonia Khalil, Heather Krill, Anthea Krings, Naomi Lee Baumol, Samantha Levien, Elizabeth Levy, Emmy Linder, Frances Liu, Hae-Won Min, Sayuri Miyamoto, Janet Mozes, John Nakazawa, Elizabeth Navisky, Ashley Lyn Olson, Lucy Perez, Debra Poli, Natalka Roshak, Stanley Sagov, Ann Schiff, Silvia Schubert, Nathan Sekiguchi Scales, Rashu Seth, Jessica Shattuck, Rosemary Shirey, Alan Silberstein, Meredith

Silberstein, Casey Silver, Andrea Wan, Linda Whitaker, Karen Wiswall, Arron Zaretsky, Gregory Zaretsky, and The International Camberville Book Club (Leah Ellis, Stephen Filippone, Raul Longhini, Susan Sharpe, Akshay Singh). When you really care about a project, honest feedback is a gift. I'm grateful for the responses I received: loved it, hated it, you have no business writing it, Anna would never do *that,* this doesn't make sense, I cried here, I cringed there. I'm so fortunate to have people in my life who care enough to be brutal.

Thank you to my editor Rose Jacobs. No conflict means no opinion or no passion. We had many wonderful fights about what was in and what was out, from characters to commas.

In Berlin is dedicated to Anthea Krings. Thank you, Anthea, for your friendship.

ABOUT THE AUTHOR

Eric Silberstein is the bestselling author of *The Insecure Mind of Sergei Kraev*. He was the co-founder of TrialNetworks, a clinical research software company, and a winner of the MIT TR35 prize. *In Berlin* is his second novel.

EricSilberstein.com